THE LAST SUMMER

A Novel

JOHN HOUGH, JR.

Simon & Schuster

New York London Toronto

Sydney Singapore

SIMON & SCHUSTER
Rockefeller Center
1230 Avenue of the Americas
New York, NY 10020

For information regarding special discounts for bulk purchases,
please contact Simon & Schuster Special Sales at
1-800-456-6798 or business@simonandschuster.com

Designed by Jeanette Olender
Manufactured in the United States of America

1   3   5   7   9   10   8   6   4   2

Library of Congress Cataloging-in-Publication Data
Hough, John, date.
The last summer : a novel / John Hough, Jr.
p.   cm.
1. Young men—Fiction.   2. Middle aged women—Fiction.   I Title.
PS3558.O84 L37 2002
813'.54—dc21   2002025158
ISBN 0-7432-2705-0

Acknowledgments

I'd like to thank my agent, B. J. Robbins, for her advocacy, for her friendship. Thanks also to Chuck Adams, Michael Korda, Ellen Edwards, and Carolyn Nichols.

For my father, Jack Hough.

Best newspaperman I've ever known.

Chapter One

THEY LEFT Virginia in the soft blush of the summer dawn, the Camaro crammed to the roof with suitcases, string-tied cartons, TV, stereo, a two-foot stack of LPs, and Claire's IBM Selectric in its vinyl shroud. April rode beside her tucked down sullen and silent in the bucket seat with her arms folded, uninterested in the sights along I-95.

They crossed the empty four-lane bridge into Washington, where the Lincoln Memorial glowed lambent in the wash of the rising sun. The city hadn't wakened yet, not quite; the broad avenues were as free as superhighways, and Claire drove out Constitution with the needle dancing on the high side of fifty-five. They swung around the Capitol, Claire's last view of it, looming flagrant and serene and outsized even in this city of shrines, of monuments and temples. Power and secrets, Claire thought. Yes, that's what was hidden, locked, inside all that marble vastness, the only currency that mattered. Power and secrets—like the gold in Fort Knox. She pushed in the dashboard lighter and felt down between the seats for her cigarettes.

April wrinkled her nose. "Already?" she said.

"You bet," Claire said. She drew the gentle, savory smoke down through herself, felt it take hold in her bloodstream, restful as liquor.

"I hate it when you smoke in the car," April said.

"I know," Claire said.

She tried not to look at the marble fortress of the Old Senate Office Building as they passed it on their left where Constitution rode up past the Capitol and the park. A Capitol policeman in dark blue stood at the top of the corner steps with his hands behind him, staring out into the new light. He didn't notice how fast the Camaro was moving, or didn't care. Not at 5 A.M. Claire thought of the lofty cave-dim corridors with their lustrous wood doors, their muted echoes and whispered voices, and everywhere the heady sensation, the quiet thrill, of history being made all around you, day to day, moment to moment.

"The smoke gets in my clothes," April said.

"Grandma's got a washer," Claire said.

"It doesn't get the smoke out."

"April, don't be a pain," Claire said.

"It isn't fair."

"Don't expect life to be fair," Claire said.

April sighed. "What are you going to tell Grandma?" she said.

"About what?" Claire said.

"You know what. Leaving like this."

"I'll tell her what I told her over the phone."

"That won't cut it. Not in person."

"It'll have to," Claire said.

The park and Capitol were behind them now, the giant dome bathed in the clean, sweet light above the trees, dropping out of sight off the rearview mirror, gone. Pretty soon the colored neighborhoods began, dingy brick houses with rickety-looking front porches. Black, you were supposed to say now. Black power, black pride. Black is beautiful.

"She'll bug you till you tell her," April said.

"Can we talk about something else?" Claire said.

"Ezra says I have a right to know."

"Ezra ought to mind his own business."

"I asked his opinion," April said.

"You do know," Claire said. "I'm sick of Washington. The politics. How many times do I have to say it?"

"You don't leave in three days because you're sick of a place. Ezra agrees."

"Ezra's a nice boy," Claire said, "but he ought to mind his own business."

"I am his business."

"I'm sorry about Ezra. You know that."

"I'll never see him again," April said.

"Sure you will."

"Bull."

"Don't use that expression," Claire said. She crushed out her cigarette in the pullout ashtray on the dash and thought immediately of lighting up another. In three days she hadn't slept much, existing on coffee and cigarettes and the savage desire to leave this place forever, to be back north where she belonged, if it could be said that she belonged anywhere.

"You swear all the time," April said.

"I'm the grown-up," Claire said.

"So?"

"Are we going to fight all the way to Boston?" Claire said.

"We're not fighting," April said, "we're discussing."

They were on I-95 again, wide and empty and white in the hardening morning light. On either side the land lay low and rolling under the gin-clear air, the building heat.

"How do you like the car?" Claire said.

April shrugged. "It's okay."

"Better than the VW, huh?"

"I hated the VW," April said.

Claire had bought the Camaro two days ago through an ad in the *Post*. It was a '65, yellow with a black-vinyl roof, 42,000 miles on the dash. A rash expenditure: $1,500, but Claire had the money and didn't know when she would again. Then she'd unloaded the Volkswagen at a used-car lot in Silver Spring, taking what the man had offered, $500, not bothering to try to dicker him up.

"You'll be driving it soon," Claire said. "Less than a year."

April didn't answer. She wasn't interested yet in a truce. She had no interest, either, in cars or learning to drive. Cars were a boys' thing, though Claire had learned to drive when she was fourteen, receiving private lessons from her boyfriend at the time, Tommy Riordan, in his father's snub-nosed Chevrolet. Tommy's father was over in Germany helping the good guys finish the war Hitler had started when she, Claire, was still a little

4

girl. A war that had a logic in it that anyone could see, not like Vietnam.

"That's another thing," April said.

"What is?"

"The car. Why'd we get a new one?"

"Did you want to drive eleven hours squeezed inside a VW bug?"

April shrugged her shrug. "We could have."

"April, I want to remind you of something. You hated Fairlington. You told me that a million times."

"I didn't hate Ezra."

"There'll be other boys."

"I don't want other boys."

Claire turned on the radio, found Feliciano's "Light My Fire." It was all over the airwaves that summer. "You will," she said, "believe me."

"Maybe I will, maybe I won't," April said.

The sun climbed higher up the blue dome of the sky and the highways came alive with their heavy summer traffic—families on the move, trucks, and Greyhound buses. The roads now gave back a dull, persistent glare while car chrome flashed and glinted till Claire's eyes hurt, even under dark glasses. Have I ever been this tired? she wondered. And later: What happens next? And where? She smoked cigarette after cigarette and brought out a large coffee each time they stopped for food or gas or to use the ladies'.

In New Jersey, in the noise and hurry and swelter of the Turnpike, April looked up from the book she was reading. "Mom? What did Senator Mallory say when you told him you were quitting?"

Claire kept her gaze pinned to the road. "I didn't tell Senator Mallory."

"You didn't say good-bye?"

"I didn't see him."

"Why not?"

"I never went back to the office. The AA came over to the apartment. Mark Fairchild. You were at school."

"Why didn't you go back?"

"I didn't want to see the senator again."

"Why?"

"He did something, April. I didn't want to work for him anymore. I didn't want to see him."

April thought a moment. "Did he want to see you?"

"I don't know. I doubt it."

"What did he do that was so awful?"

"I can't tell you, sweetheart. I can't tell Grandma, either."

"You can tell your own daughter."

"Not now. Maybe sometime."

"'Sometime' means never."

"No, 'sometime' means 'sometime.' Hand me a Kleenex, will you?"

"You aren't going to cry, are you?"

"I don't think so."

April doubled down and found Claire's purse on the floor. She rummaged around in the purse and dug out the Kleenex and passed a wad of tissues to Claire. Claire placed them in her lap.

"Want to pull over?" April said.

"I'm all right," Claire said.

"Because I don't want to have an accident."

"I don't either," Claire said.

. . .

SHE KNEW it wouldn't be easy holding off her mother. What was ever easy with Violet O'Brien?

"I just quit, Ma," Claire said. "I had some trouble I don't want to talk about."

"Trouble."

"Correct."

They'd washed and stacked the dishes. April was upstairs lying on the double bed in the guest room reading a book. Daylight lingered at the windows, golden where it struck the high trees and slanted rooftops.

"What kind of trouble?" her mother said.

"Did you hear me say I didn't want to talk about it?"

"Give me a hint," her mother said. "What'd you do, get caught screwing somebody in the office?"

Claire blushed hard and didn't look at her. "Ma," she said. "Jesus."

"Well, it must be something like that, they throw you out on your ass without giving you notice."

"I told you, Ma. I'm the one that quit."

Her mother got up, put the kettle on to boil, and sat down again at the little drop-leaf table. She lit a cigarette and crossed her legs, sitting sideways to the table. She still had good legs. She still had boyfriends, Claire knew, till she drove them away with her nagging.

"What about April?" she said.

"What about her?"

"You took her out of school?"

"There's two weeks left, Ma. She's getting all A's."

"It's illegal to take a kid out of school."

"What are they going to do, put me in jail?"

"Why not let your daughter finish school?"

"I'm done talking about it, Ma."

"Well, you must have screwed up royally, is all I can say. Best job you ever had. A frigging senator, Clairie. Bigger than Teddy Kennedy. Big as Jack was when he was a senator, God rest his soul."

"It isn't so hot when you get to know it," Claire said.

"You didn't seem to mind it. I mean, how bad can it be, you spend ten years down there?"

"Eight," Claire said.

"You look thin," her mother said. "You been sick?"

"I haven't slept in three nights."

The kettle began to whistle. Violet unfolded herself from the spindle-backed chair. She went to the counter and spooned instant coffee into a mug, standing small and willowy with a hip swayed out. Claire watched her. She seemed to have shrunk over the years, to have withered, but she had a fineness of neck and waist and ankle, a sexy slouch, that won and held men's interest until the poor bastards got fed up with taking orders. But another would always appear.

Violet lifted the steaming kettle and poured. "You want some of this?" she said.

"I drink any more coffee, I'll be up peeing all night," Claire said.

Violet sat down with her coffee. She recrossed her legs.

"Tell me this," she said. "They give you decent severance?"

"No," Claire said.

"What's 'no' mean?"

"It means I didn't get any."

Her mother looked at her. She reached for her smoking ciga-rette and shook her head. "This gets worse and worse," she said.

"I didn't want any," Claire said.

"Just like you didn't want any child support from Scott."

"Something like that," Claire said.

"They screw you up the old wazoo and you let 'em off free."

"I don't want their money," Claire said.

"Just a little saint, aren't you?"

"No," Claire said. "I'm not a saint."

"I got every penny I could out of your father."

"I'm not saying you shouldn't have."

"You take what they owe you. Think of April before you act so proud."

"I support April just fine."

"She looks like hell, by the way."

"April?"

"She ever brush her hair?"

"What kind of question is that?"

"Does she?"

"Sure she does. She's got a boyfriend now. She's paying more attention to herself."

"She isn't paying enough."

"In three, four years April's going to be beautiful. It's all going to come together for her."

"Who's the boyfriend?"

Claire shrugged. "Just some scrawny kid. Name's Ezra. He plays the violin."

"Ezra. Must be Jewish."

"I don't know. Ezra Teller. Maybe."

"I dated a Jewish guy one time. It wasn't so bad, actually."

"Ma, for Christ sake."

"Well, it wasn't."

"I'm going to bed," Claire said. "I got about three hours last night."

"What are you going to do, Clairie? Where you going to go? You're almost forty years old, do you realize that?"

"I realize it."

"Be a secretary again, I guess. Right back where you were eight years ago."

"I was a secretary in Washington," Claire said.

"You weren't a *secretary*."

"Yeah, I was."

"You weren't a *secretary* secretary."

"I know what I was," Claire said.

"There was a difference," her mother said. "Don't tell me there wasn't."

There was a difference, all right. Claire watched her mother shoot out a cloud of blue smoke and drop forward to rub out her cigarette. In the pale, rouged face Claire couldn't see any trace of what a mother was supposed to be feeling at a time like this, only censure, a moody impatience. She wondered if Violet really wanted her to succeed or if maybe this was better, the punishment Claire deserved for a lifetime of sassing and disregarding her mother.

"I'll be okay," Claire said. "There's always somebody can use a secretary."

"When you going to start looking?"

"Soon, Ma. Don't worry."

"I'm not worrying. I was just wondering how long you'll be staying."

"Ma, I've been driving all day. I can't think straight."

"I go out sometimes, you know."

"I expect you to," Claire said.

"Just so you know," Violet said.

. . .

HER MOTHER'S house was a frame two-story in a quiet crime-free neighborhood an easy walk from the last stop on the T, which Violet rode into the city two or three times a week to shop or have lunch with a couple of friends left over from the days when they were all married. Violet had bought the house out of her alimony. Claire's father had paid through the nose for his sins and had gone on paying. The nice car, the color TV, the clothes. Fortunately, Richie O'Brien knew how to make money, if nothing else. He'd begun as a derrick operator, had become a partner in the business and then full owner when the other man went to prison for giving kickbacks to elected officials. Richie had done very well as sole proprietor. He'd sold the business a few years ago and headed for Florida.

"Does he ever come up here?" Claire said.

"If he does, I don't know about it," Violet said.

"Are Joey and Kevin in touch with him?"

"You'd have to ask them."

"How're they doing?"

"You ought to go see 'em."

"I will."

"Their wives give me a pain in the ass," Violet said.

"Me, too," Claire said.

"That Angela. Little wop princess. I'd like to shoot her sometimes."

Claire smiled. "I wonder how Daddy likes Angela."

"He probably does, knowing him."

"He still sends me a present every Christmas," Claire said.

"Me, too," Violet said. "Every month I get a present from him."

"You shouldn't gloat, Ma."

"He asked for it," her mother said.

"I know that," Claire said.

.   .   .

THE TWO kids she'd hired turned up in the U-Haul with her furniture as promised and lugged it uncomplaining down the narrow, treacherous stairs to the cellar, knocking the leg off an end table and a knob off the frame of Claire's double bed. She paid and tipped them for carrying the furniture down the stairs, then followed them to the U-Haul return. She waited while they dropped the truck off, then drove them to Logan for a 10 P.M. flight back to Washington. They'd left at daybreak this morning, hadn't even brought toothbrushes.

"You guys are amazing," Claire said.

They apologized for the breakage and Claire told them not to worry about it.

"Where'd you find those kids?" Violet said.

"American University. I put an ad on the bulletin board."

"They looked like hippies."

"So what?" Claire said.

"They looked like drug addicts."

"Ma. Please."

It was exhausting living with Violet. Like being in a place where the wind never stopped blowing, never stopped worrying at you. Claire wondered if her father had made Violet that way, had aroused the sleeping mistral with his neglect and infidelities.

She bought the *Globe* and studied the want ads. Every day she saw five or six jobs she could get even without a reference from Bob Mallory's office. She could get them just by showing up for the interview and crossing her legs where they could be seen, provided the employer was a man. *You can always screw your way up the ladder, Mark said. You'll always have that, won't you, Claire?*

She held off.

On the fourth night she sat again with her mother at the drop-leaf table while the dishes dried in the rack and the sun went down behind the trees and utility poles and peaked rooftops. Upstairs, April talked long-distance with Ezra Teller, her voice a smoke-thin murmur through the flooring.

"What's the point if she's never going to see him again?" Violet said.

"I'll pay for the call if that's what you're worried about," Claire said.

"You better save your money," her mother said.

"Ma, listen to me. I'm going to drive down to the Cape tomorrow."

"What for?"

"Look for a job."

"On the Cape?"

"What's wrong with that? I want to try someplace new."

"Not some hick town on the Cape," her mother said.

"I need a change, Ma."

"You think what happened to you in Washington won't happen on the Cape?"

"I know it won't."

"You going to tell me what it was?"

"Someday, Ma. Not now."

"Someday I'll be dead."

"I'll tell you before that."

"I'm your mother, Clairie. I'm your goddamn mother."

"Someday I'll tell you," Claire said.

.   .   .

THEN GOD, luck, fate—whatever you wished to call it—took a hand. In the morning her car wouldn't start. Her new Camaro. She cursed it. The man had said the battery was brand-new. She cursed him, too.

There wasn't any good reason not to call the garage and get a late start or even go tomorrow, and Claire almost did. She got out of the car and stood in the blue-gray early-morning shadows listening to the traffic sough by over on the highway, thinking. Dew glistened on the dark green grass; Claire thought she could smell it, like sweet white wine. She filled her lungs with the summer morning air. She looked to the south, toward the Cape, and above the still treetops saw a sky that was as soft and bright as blue silk. She relocked the Camaro.

April and Violet were still asleep. Claire went quietly into the house and left them a note on the kitchen table. She walked to the subway, rode a train into the city, and got on a bus.

And stepped down two hours later at a little bus station of white-painted brick in a cul-de-sac, an open expanse of warped and bleaching asphalt with woods running uphill beyond, the new leaves pale green in the clean light of June. There were, she saw, rusted railroad tracks passing between the depot and the woods. Weeds and baby pitch pines wriggled up through the cinders between the rotting splintered ties.

Beside the tracks on the same side as the bus station, sharing with it this quiet sunny space in a kind of partnership, crouched a low white-shingle building with Irish-green shutters and an elm tree towering over it like an umbrella. Above the door a sign in Gothic letters: THE COVENANT. A newspaper office. Claire studied it, crouched there in its elm shade across the uneven, often-patched blacktop where the buses maneuvered in their comings and goings, then went into the depot, to the ladies' room, thinking about what she might do in a newspaper office.

The bus was gone when she got back outside. The arriving passengers had all disappeared. She wondered where Main Street was, with its law and insurance offices, its town hall. A taxi waited by the platform where the trains had once dropped riders from Boston and New York. The fat cabdriver leaned back against his car with his arms folded. He looked at Claire, squinting against the sun.

"Take you someplace, ma'am?"

She glanced at him and again regarded the newspaper office. She thought of the Camaro refusing to start this morning and her now standing where she never would have otherwise, face-to-face with this unpretentious little building beside the abandoned railroad tracks where you couldn't miss it getting off the bus, couldn't ignore it.

"I guess not," she told the cabdriver and went across the

blacktop cul-de-sac, watched by him, high heels clicking in the stillness.

A receptionist was clipping stories out of a newspaper with a pair of long scissors. She put the scissors down and looked pleasantly up at Claire. She was plump and very short. Round. Her hair was snow-white, close-cut, and frizzy.

"Can I help you?" she said.

"I was wondering if you had any job openings," Claire said.

"Could be," the woman said. "Would you like to talk to John?"

"John would be . . . ?"

"John Hillman. The editor, dear."

"If it isn't any trouble."

"No trouble," the woman said.

She got up and went into another room, swaying as she walked. Claire waited, standing with her purse hung on her shoulder. There were three desks besides the receptionist's, packed in tight. A second woman, plump also but younger, was tallying figures on an adding machine. Two men talked on the telephone. One of them sat hunched over, thin in his white shirt and loosened necktie, scribbling notes with a pencil. The other tilted back leisurely in his chair. He wore an ink-smudged canvas apron. Neither of the men paid any attention to Claire. She could hear a rattle of typewriters in the adjoining room where the receptionist had disappeared, and from a back room a whir and clatter of machinery. Her heart beat fast now, and she wondered if she'd made a mistake coming in here.

The receptionist waddled back in from the side room. Behind her came a dark-haired, balding, thickset man, not tall but big-boned, solid. He moved with deliberate grace. His white shirt looked unironed and his sleeves were rolled and his tie loosened.

"John Hillman," he said, and put out his thick hand.

"Claire Malek."

His grip was strong, brief, impersonal. He took in her face with a glance, then turned and moved in a smooth and weightless-seeming trudge toward the back room. Claire understood she was to follow him and did, walking well behind.

The back room was easily larger than the two front rooms combined. Daylight seemed to stop at the open windows, as if the inside air were too thick, too clamorous and pungent, to admit it through the glass panes and window screens. The pungency was a sour-sweet perfume of oil, solvents, black grease, printer's ink, newsprint, and wood. The noise came from a pair of tall loomlike machines operated by a man each, sitting at a keyboard. Along high workbenches under pallid fluorescent tubes, men were setting type, ramming the blocks of shiny lead in snug with the heels of their hands. The press, idle at the moment, was long and jet-black and primitive-looking, with square-toothed cogwheels and a drive shaft like a locomotive's. A sheet of newsprint ran through it, doubling back on itself.

Claire followed John Hillman into a modern carpeted little room, anomalous in its newness and knotty pine decor, attached to the rear of the building. He closed the door, shutting out the noise, and sat down behind the desk, on which sat a covered typewriter, a telephone, a clean ashtray, and a photograph in a leather frame of a woman kneeling with her arm wrapped affectionately around a collie dog. Claire sat down in the wooden armchair in front of the desk. She unstrapped her purse and placed it in her lap.

"You're looking for a job," Mr. Hillman said.

Claire nodded.

"What sort of job?"

"Maybe you should look at my résumé before this goes any further," Claire said.

She brought it out of her purse and handed it to him across the desk. He studied it awhile. His broad ruddy face was shadowed in melancholy, as if he were wistful for something long gone or for some promise, perhaps, unkept and forever unattainable. Claire looked out the window across the rusted red-brown tracks to the leaf mosaic of the woods. Mr. Hillman passed the résumé back to her. He folded his arms. He looked out the window.

"I lost a reporter day before yesterday," he said. "A young boy."

Claire said nothing.

"Can you spell?" Mr. Hillman said.

"Spell," Claire said. "I think so. Yeah. Sure, I can spell."

"Because that boy couldn't spell. He'd been to the Sorbonne, but he couldn't spell."

"I guess it's hard for some people," Claire said.

"I need a reporter."

"Look, I'm not . . ."

"For the summer, at least. Longer, if I can get a good one."

"You read my résumé, right?"

"My son's coming home from college tomorrow. He'll work for me till September, but I need someone else. Summer's a busy time."

"I don't have any experience."

"I have to teach all my reporters. I've never had one I didn't have to teach."

"Yeah, but they were reporters to begin with. I'm a secretary."

"Reporters who couldn't spell. Reporters who didn't have any curiosity." He unfolded his beefy arms and pawed a pack of Lucky Strikes from his shirt pocket. He shook a cigarette halfway out and offered it to Claire.

"I have my own, thanks."

He lit it for her, lit his Lucky. He pushed the ashtray halfway across to Claire.

"I need someone right now," he said.

"I just don't know," Claire said.

"I don't need a secretary. I couldn't use one."

"I mean, I'd like to, but like I've been saying, I'm just not . . ."

"*As* I've been saying."

"What?"

"*As* I've been saying. 'Like' is a preposition."

Claire blushed, then smiled slowly out toward the woods.

"My son's a good reporter," Mr. Hillman said. "Not as good as he thinks he is, but he's good. I never have to tell him anything twice. I tell him once and he remembers."

"Like '*as* I've been saying.'"

"If I were you, I'd take the job."

"And you really think I can do it?"

"I'd start you at a hundred dollars a week. We've got a good health plan."

"I'll need a few days."

"The fewer the better."

"Give me three," Claire said recklessly.

"All right."

"You sure you want to do this?" she said.

"Why not?" he said.

.　.　.

THAT NIGHT they ate Chinese takeout at the kitchen table. Claire and Violet drank Bud out of the bottle.

"A hundred dollars a week," Violet said. "Why'd you say yes?"

"What was I supposed to say?"

"Tell 'em Lincoln freed the slaves after the Civil War."

"During it," April said.

Violet looked at her. "What?"

"The Emancipation Proclamation was during the Civil War."

"What did I say?" Violet said.

"You said 'after the Civil War.'"

"You read too much, you know that, April?"

"It's what they pay, Ma," Claire said. "Anyway, I've never been a newspaper reporter. I can't expect to start high."

"Higher than that."

"I don't have any experience. I've never written anything that someone didn't dictate to me."

"You tell him that?"

"Of course I told him. I gave him my résumé."

"And he still hired you."

"Yup."

"Well, you better not screw it up, Clairie."

"I don't need to hear that, Ma."

"When are we moving?" April said.

"I told him I could start in three days."

April looked at her. "Three days?"

"Sit up straight, April," Claire said.

"Where you going to live on a hundred dollars a week?" Violet asked.

"I'll find something. I'm going to drive down tomorrow, look around."

"I thought you were going to see Joey and Angela."

"I'll see them another time."

"When?"

"I don't know, Ma. Sometime."

"Will I have to go back to school?" April said.

"No," Claire said.

"The whole thing's nuts," her mother said. "You'll go crazy in a small town. How you going to meet any men?"

"Maybe I won't. Maybe I'll be lucky."

"May I ask what that means?"

"It isn't at the top of my list right now, that's all."

"Why not?"

"It just isn't."

Her mother pushed her plate back. "It just isn't," she said.

"I'm not thinking about men right now, that's all I mean. Let's not make a big deal out of this."

"It won't last," April said.

Claire glanced at her, wondering what she suspected, but April's face was sullen and inscrutable, her head propped on her hand, her eyes lowered.

"You have man trouble down there?" Violet said.

"No, I did not."

"Did she, April?"

April shrugged. "Not that I know of."

"Can we please change the subject?" Claire said.

"Guess we'll have to," Violet said, "if you won't talk about it."

April seemed not to be listening. She played sullenly with her food.

"I'm going to be a newspaper reporter," Claire said. "Will somebody please look happy around here?"

"We're happy, aren't we, April?" Violet said.

"No comment," April said.

Chapter Two

THE OLD door latch woke Lane, releasing with a hard, sharp sound that seemed to come from inside him, the furious echo out of an already forgotten dream. Then his father's voice: abrupt, bitter with the news he brought.

"You'd better get up. Bob Kennedy's been shot."

Lane came instantly full awake, but instead of rising sank back down, as if a bullet had hit him too, pinning him to the bed. Already his father was gone, turning as he spoke and letting the door swing open. The bedroom was downstairs, at the front of the house; in the kitchen, two large rooms away, Lane could hear his mother sobbing. He could hear the taut, rapid voice of a radio newsman.

For a while he lay there staring at the plaster ceiling, which was whorled and ridged like a white relief map. The room

23

swam in purplish shadow. It smelled sadly of mildew. A car muttered by out front, beyond the lilac hedge. Shot, Lane thought.
Not dead. Shot. He rolled his head, looked out above the lilacs.
The sky was pure blue. *Bob Kennedy's been shot.* His father never
said "Bobby Kennedy," always "Bob," as if the diminutive were
inexact or misleading. Lane threw back the covers.

His father and his sister Meg were at the dark oval of the dining table when he came to breakfast. His father was reading the
Boston Herald. KENNEDY WINS CALIFORNIA said the headline.
John Hillman didn't look at Lane or speak to him. Nor did Meg.
Her eyes were tear-swollen and unseeing, and she was spooning
hot cereal into her mouth without tasting it. Meg was fifteen
and brittle.

The kitchen was sunlit, cluttered, and smelled of coffee and
sweet spices and overripe fruit. On the counter the radio blared
its newscast. Lane's mother stood at the stove with a spatula in
her hand. She was weeping silently now, her cheeks wet and
palely luminous. She smiled wanly at Lane.

"I'm making you an egg-in-the-hole," she said.

Lane patted her shoulder. "He isn't dead," he said. He'd been
listening to the radio while he shaved. "He's breathing on his
own."

He took his coffee and plate of food into the dining room. His
father didn't look up from his newspaper. "I want you to spend
the day out of the office," he said. "Move around. Make a record
of what people are doing today. What they're saying."

"He might not die," Lane said.

His father looked up from the paper. "He might not," he said.

"It'd be a waste then, wouldn't it?"

"You write it well, it won't be a waste."

"All right," Lane said. He ate his fried bread and egg.

"The new girl starts today," his father said. "I'm going to give her the Julius Littleton obit."

"I was going to do that," Lane said.

"You're going to be busy."

"It's an important obit," Lane said.

"I hired the girl, I might as well use her," his father said.

Lane shrugged.

Meg got up from the table. She picked up her cereal bowl. "Martin Luther King," she said, "and now Robert Kennedy."

"He's got a chance, Meggie," Lane said.

"All the good people get killed in this country," she said.

"He's got a chance," Lane said again.

"They always say that," Meg said.

"Why don't you two argue somewhere else?" their father said.

· · · ·

THE NEWSROOM was spacious and sunny and smelled of pipe and cigarette smoke, of newsprint and liquid paste, a soothing sweetish odor that reminded Claire of the insides of old books or an attic on a rainy summer day. Maple desks butted up against each other along three walls, two desks to a wall. Along the fourth wall, by the door to the business office, was a waist-high counter with wide drawers containing the precinct maps and voter lists. The dictionary lay on top of it, a huge time-stained butterscotch *Webster's* unabridged.

In the corner farthest from the door, behind Mr. Hillman, stood the graveyard file, three file cabinets of battleship-gray as tall as Claire in heels. Anyone who ever made news in the town, if it was only by being born, had his or her own brown envelope that opened at the top like a shirt pocket with a flap. Everything went into the graveyard file, from items of no more than an inch or two to long writeups folded over double or triple, the older ones fraying along the folds, beginning to come apart. Some had turned brown as flypaper with age. Some were so old they crumbled when you handled them.

A file could be copious or pathetically meager. Some people had built files so thick the envelopes were stretched taut and stiff. Some people had two envelopes. Other envelopes felt empty; you shook them, and out fluttered two or three yellowed items of a paragraph or two, the entire written record of a life after sixty, seventy, eighty years.

This was where Claire began, the graveyard. John Hillman gave her the names—hastily typed, caps floating off the line—of three prominent dead men whose obituaries she was to study for style and content. She pulled as well the file of Julius Littleton the artist, dead of a heart attack at seventy-eight. She placed them on her new desk, then turned and sat down on the maple chair beside Mr. Hillman's. A deeper melancholy than before, a look of strain and weariness, shadowed his face. Claire wondered if the Hillmans were Democrats, supporters of RFK. Probably. She wondered if the son who was working here this summer was in danger of being drafted for Vietnam.

"Call the funeral home," he said. "You might need to make some other calls. Family, if he had any. Museum curators. Gallery owners. See what's in the file."

Claire nodded. How am I going to do this? she thought.

"When you're ready to write, slug it 'Littleton Obit' in the top left corner with your initials in lower case underneath. Start your copy about a third of the way down."

How am I going to do this? She'd had dreams in which she was expected to play the guitar or piano, had pretended she knew how. People were gathered around, waiting, and there was no way to explain it had been a joke, a lie, a misunderstanding.

"I guess you'd better meet everybody before you start," Mr. Hillman said.

He walked her around, wordless except to introduce her. Jean and Ellie, Everett and Manny in the business office. Walter, Frank, Red, Sterling, Jimmy Wheeler in the back shop. Jimmy was the boss out there, the foreman, tall and muscular and florid, his black hair oiled and parted in the middle so that he looked like the big baritone in a barbershop quartet. The men were ink-begrimed already. They greeted Claire politely, shy in their stained T-shirts, their gray chino trousers (she in spike heels and a flowered summer dress, like a gaudy butterfly in their midst), oppressed perhaps by the shooting of RFK. Only Jimmy Wheeler smiled at her: a broad face-splitting grin of bonhomie and welcome, as if to say life goes on here at the *Covenant* even on days of national tragedy.

In the newsroom were Fred Purdy, the associate editor; Henry Braden, photographer and features writer; and Ruth Engle, a longtime reporter who, Claire soon learned, never left her desk, having somehow over the years earned the privilege of covering only what could be done by telephone. Mrs. Engle's hair was wood-ash–gray, but her face was finely sculpted if not young, and she still had her figure.

"Anyone think to offer you coffee?" she said.

"No, but that's—"

"Come on." Mrs. Engle pushed back her chair. "I'll show

you how to work that urn. It's always the women who have to refill it."

"I know how that is," Claire said.

The coffee was just inside the doorway to the back shop. Ruth Engle found a mug at the back of the ink-smudged, teal-painted wall cupboard and wiped the dust out of it with a paper towel. There were ink marks on every touchable surface in the room: walls, windowsills, steam radiators, light switches, bathroom door and doorknob. The hardwood floor was stained to an oily almost-black. This is real, Claire thought. This is *honest*.

"Have you met Lane yet?" Mrs. Engle said.

Claire shook her head. "No milk for me," she said.

"He went to school with my son, you know."

"Did he," Claire said.

"Every now and then give a dollar to Jean toward the coffee."

"All right."

"Well. If you need any help with that Littleton obit, let me know."

"I appreciate that," Claire said.

. . .

LANE HAD the privilege of driving the office car while he was working at the paper. After work he drove it home, kept it; it became his car for the summer, for business and pleasure both, with the unspoken permission of his father. He charged the gas to the *Covenant* at Dimmock's Gulf down Depot Avenue at the corner.

He loved that car. It was a finned '56 Chevrolet of limeade-green with automatic transmission. The paint job looked brand-new and the body had been oddly immune to rust. THE COVENANT was stenciled on both doors in small white Gothic

letters, giving him, Lane thought, an air of importance and professionalism as he drove around town.

The engine was sluggish, but powerful once you roused it.
You floored it and there was a pause, as if the car were a big cat
gathering itself to spring, until with a muffled velvety snarl the
Chevy took off, the needle swinging, rapid and steady, to forty,
fifty, and on up. The lack of a radio was the car's only draw-
back. Lane's father considered a car radio the height of needless
luxury.

He drove on that June morning, heartbreaking in its loveli-
ness and clarity, to the police station, always the place to begin
when you're looking for a story. Lane had been coming here to
gather news almost every day for two summers. Housebreak-
ings, traffic accidents, vandalism, drunk-and-disorderlies. He
parked out front where the little fleet of cruisers, painted white
on black like spats, stood side by side in the sunshine. He went
up the cement steps with his notebook.

A TV was on, soft, on a shelf high on the wall. An enormous
slope-shouldered man in plainclothes stood watching it with his
hands stuffed down in his trouser pockets. A woman in uniform, navy skirt instead of pants, was at the desk. She watched
the TV, sitting sideways to the desk.

"Morning," Lane said.

The big man glanced at him and nodded. The female desk
cop ignored him. On the television a reporter was interviewing
a doctor.

"Anything new?" Lane said.

"It don't look good," the big man said.

"I heard there was no brain damage," Lane said.

"What's he doin' in a coma if there's no brain damage?"

"He's being operated on," Lane said.

"You get shot and don't wake up, that's a coma."

"Shot in the head," the desk cop said. "In the brain."

Lane put his notebook down on the counter and made some notes. The TV on the wall. Captain Murcer standing massive and gloomy in front of the desk. Ginny Woodling behind the desk. He returned the pencil to his hip pocket.

"Is the chief in, Mrs. Woodling?"

"He's busy," she said, watching the TV screen.

"For how long, do you think?"

"I couldn't tell you."

Lane reached down behind the counter and picked up the stack of pink cards recording last night's auto accidents. He went through the cards, taking his time, letting a couple of minutes go by.

"Maybe you could let him know I'm here," he said.

Mrs. Woodling gave no indication she'd heard him. Lane continued to look through the cards. Mrs. Woodling watched the newscast. A revolver was strapped to her skinny hip; Lane had always wondered what she expected to do with a gun, sitting as she did behind the desk from eight to four in the daytime. He came to the last card in the stack and began again. There wasn't anything worth reporting, just fender benders. He continued shuffling through the cards, listening to the TV, and finally Mrs. Woodling picked up the phone. Lane heard a faint muffled ring down the hall.

"Lane Hillman's here, sir." She hung up and gestured with her chin. "He'll see you."

Lane thanked her as if he were truly grateful and went down the narrow lightless hallway to the chief's office. He knocked.

The chief, Paul Williams, told him to come in. Williams was behind his desk, sitting back with his hands clasped over his gut.

"Hey, buddy," he said.

"'Lo, Paul."

A squat, dark, tough-faced man sat in one of the captain's chairs in front of Williams's desk. He watched Lane come in and close the door behind him. He wore a short-sleeve white shirt open at the neck, no jacket.

"This is Ed O'Neill," Williams said. "Ed's with the state police."

"Nice to meet you," Lane said.

O'Neill nodded. He didn't offer to shake hands. Lane sat down with his notebook on his lap.

"Lane just finished up at Harvard," Williams said.

"That right?" O'Neill said.

"A football player," Williams said. "The all-American boy."

O'Neill looked at Lane. His eyes were small, black, penetrating. He didn't say anything. Lane wondered what he was doing here.

"Sad day, huh?" Williams said.

"Yes," Lane said, "it is."

"An idealist like you, you're going to take it especially hard."

Lane shrugged. "I believe in him," he said.

"Sure you do," Williams said.

"I guess you either do or you don't," Lane said. "You either see it or you don't."

O'Neill watched him.

"Lane's going into the Peace Corps in the fall," Williams said.

"Not the Peace Corps. VISTA."

"All right. VISTA." Williams looked at O'Neill. "They put

you in some fucking slum on about forty bucks a week and expect you to wipe out poverty."

"Not wipe it out," Lane said.

"Ameliorate it," Williams said.

"Try to," Lane said.

"Can't hurt," O'Neill said.

"Fuckin'-A right," Williams said. "It can't hurt."

He'd been in town just two years. The man he'd replaced had been police chief for almost thirty-five years, since before this obsolete and too-small Georgian-style building had been erected with money from the WPA. Williams had been brought in to bring the department into the modern era. He'd accomplished this task once previously, rapidly and efficiently and without making enemies, in a town up in New Hampshire. Before that he'd been a beat cop who'd made captain in a tough city south of Boston.

"I was wondering," Lane said, "if you had any thoughts about the shooting."

"You doing a story?" Williams said.

"Yeah," Lane said.

"Give him a quote, Eddie," Williams said.

"I don't think so," O'Neill said.

"He's a good kid, Eddie. Give him a quote."

"Think Bobby's going to make it?" Lane said.

"No," Williams said, "I don't."

"It was a .22, Paul," O'Neill said.

"Might make a difference," Williams said.

"A .38, he'd bleed to death. A .22, you got a chance."

"Slim," Williams said.

"Slim," O'Neill agreed.

Lane made some notes. "Any news I should know about?"

"Can't think of any."

"Bar fights? Break-ins?"

"It's June. Things are quiet yet."

"Why is Mr. O'Neill here?"

Williams smiled. "Why are you here, Mr. O'Neill?"

"Just passing through," O'Neill said.

Lane looked at Williams.

"It isn't anything," Williams said. "A parole jumper. Eddie heard he had some friends took a room at the Ebb Tide. There wasn't anything in it."

Lane nodded. He shut his notebook. "Well," he said. "Thanks."

"Any time, old buddy."

Lane stood up. He could feel O'Neill's sharp eyes on him. He looked past Williams out into the brightening morning. Behind the police station the land fell gently to the dark blue bowl of a kettlehole pond where swans drifted and kids fished for perch and bluegills through the long summer afternoons.

"Eddie's right about the .22," Williams said. "Your boy might make it yet."

"I think he will," Lane said.

. . .

THE DESK abutting hers belonged to Fred Purdy, the associate editor. He was about Mr. Hillman's age, she figured, mid or late forties. He smoked a cob pipe. He was lank and rawboned with a backswept mane of rust-red hair above a face that was long and hollow-cheeked and sleepy. His manner was relaxed, almost languid, and he seemed to Claire to typify the place in a way that Mr. Hillman did not.

By nine o'clock the newsroom was busy, alive with the ring-ing of phones and rattle of typewriters and traffic of people coming and going, and yet there was a measuredness in all its constant activity, something casual and plain and unselfconscious, reflected in the placidity of Mr. Purdy. It wasn't in the least like Washington, like the Hill, where everyone believed in the high importance, the sweeping relevance, the *necessity,* of every little thing they did. As if they had a direct line to God and were pulling the strings for Him. Not just the senators and congressmen but aides at all levels, down to the pretty girls who answered the phones. *And you were just as bad,* Claire thought. *You had your head turned like everybody else.*

Mr. Purdy never looked at her, though he sat so close they could have reached across the two desks and shaken hands. Everyone, in fact, minded their own business. No one eyed her when they thought she wasn't looking. No one seemed curious about what she was working on, as if that were strictly between her and Mr. Hillman. Jean or Ellie coming in to hand Mr. Hillman a note or leave a phone message under the bail of Lane Hillman's typewriter didn't look at her as they went by. Nor did Mr. Hillman, silently crossing the room to deliver copy to the linotypists. He would pass within a few feet of her and not look down. Until Claire wondered if this fastidiousness was an unwritten rule of the newsroom applicable to everybody or if they sensed her unease, knew of her inexperience, and were kindly looking the other way.

She called the funeral home and took down the undertaker's information on Julius Talbot Littleton. She called Littleton's sister in New York City, and got through to an assistant to the director of the Museum of Modern Art. She read everything in Littleton's thick file, then spread the clippings in chronological order on her desk. She studied the obituaries of a bank president, a superintendent of schools, and a longtime selectman.

She rolled copy paper into her typewriter. She slugged it LITTLETON OBIT and typed her initials underneath. She was used to the light touch and sensitivity of electric typewriters, had forgotten how simple and rugged a manual was. You had to *make* it do your bidding: attack, strike, bully it.

She rolled the page a third of the way down and lit her first cigarette of the day. She took a deep breath and put her hands to the keys. She took them off again. She reached for her notebook and read her notes once more from beginning to end. Again she examined Littleton's clippings. She reread the leads of the obits of the bank president and school superintendent. She swiveled back to the typewriter, put her hands to the keys, withdrew them. She folded her arms and stared at the blank ecru-white sheet of paper. *Julius Littleton* . . . No. *Julius T. Littleton, who was a well known artist in this area* . . . No. *The well-known artist, Julius T. Littleton, had a heart attack and* . . . No. *Julius T. Littleton died on Tuesday evening.* . . . No. *Julius T. sonofabitch why can't I do this?* She smoked her cigarette down and lit another, and still hadn't written anything.

· · ·

HE PARKED in front of Martin's Photo Supply and walked down Main Street toward the village green. Store doors were propped open and from within came the taut portentous voices of radio newsmen, reminding Lane of the World Series when he was a kid, of clear fall afternoons with the shadows creeping out and the play-by-play, the cheering, behind and ahead of him as he dawdled along Main on his slow walk home from school.

He went into Donnelly's Barbershop and sat awhile listening

to the radio and talking to Phil LeBrach and George Blair, whose silver hair Phil was trimming. Mr. Blair was a lawyer who'd turned most of the practice over to a younger partner. Lane had heard somewhere that he'd become slightly senile. Phil LeBrach had been a couple of years ahead of Lane in school, too old to nod or say hello or learn his name, though they might pass one another in the hallway two or three times a day. But you catch up when school is behind you; one day in the barbershop Phil spoke to him, called him Lane, as if it had always been like that between them. Maybe he thought it had.

"What I want to know," Phil said, "is what that guy was doing in the kitchen. Waiting for him. How'd he know Kennedy was going out through the kitchen?"

"Somebody told him," Mr. Blair said.

"Exactly," Phil said.

"Who?" Lane said.

The radio reporter said there'd been no change in Senator Kennedy's condition. *His condition is extremely critical, although his heartbeat at this time is good.*

"I bet it was Johnson," Mr. Blair said.

Phil paused, holding his scissors in midair. "President Johnson?"

"Sure."

Phil resumed cutting, stroking with the comb, snipping here, snipping there. "I don't think so, Mr. Blair."

"Why not?"

Phil paused again and looked over at Lane. "You believe in these conspiracies, Lane?"

"I don't know," Lane said.

"I don't either," Phil said.

He went across the street to Kasselman's Pharmacy and bought a pack of Dentyne.

"What a terrible thing," Mr. Kasselman said.

He had a bald head and a pink baby-soft face, and Lane couldn't remember him ever looking any different, any younger. The magazines were at the front of the store out of sight of the counter, and while Mr. Kasselman had put up prescriptions—Lane's mother sending him on his bike for cough syrup or nose drops or penicillin—he would pass the time browsing through *Playboy* and *Penthouse* and *Escapade,* marveling at the existence of such women and wondering if someday a girl as incredibly endowed would stand alone and naked before him, smiling the same amenable smile.

"Your family well, Lane?" Mr. Kasselman said.

"Except for this," Lane said.

"We'll all say our prayers," Mr. Kasselman said.

The other Main Street drugstore was Chamberlain's, just up the street. It was older and larger than Kasselman's and had a lunch counter. Beth Weeks was behind the counter, as Lane had hoped.

"Hey," she said.

"Hey, Beth."

"When'd you get back?"

"A few days ago." He sat down and laid his notebook on the counter. A radio played mutedly in the background.

"You're looking good," Beth said.

"So are you."

"Terrible about Bobby, huh?"

He ordered coffee and watched her go down the counter to the stainless-steel urn. She'd been his classmate since grade

school. She'd been overweight all through high school, an un-
happy girl burdened with too much flesh, her quiet, dark eyes
smoldering with resentment. Then a couple or three summers
ago Lane had come into Chamberlain's and beheld a zaftig sexpot with a pinched-in waist and slender ankles, and he had
stopped, had frozen, and stared at her. Beth had looked at him
and smiled; she'd seen identical surprise on other male faces,
had become used to it.

After that he'd wondered if you could go to bed with a woman in friendship and not love. No strings attached. It seemed
reasonable enough, ideal in some ways, but there'd always been
another girl in his life, or too little left of the summer, one or another reason to postpone trying his luck with Beth Weeks.

"So how's Harvard?" she said.

"Well, I graduated."

"I know. I read it in your dad's paper." She glanced down the
counter where a man slouched glumly over a mug of coffee. She
looked at Lane's notebook. "You working for your dad?"

"For the summer."

"Then what?"

Lane told her about VISTA.

"Just stay out of Vietnam," she said.

A woman came in with a little boy. She lifted him under both
arms onto a stool. " 'Scuse me," Beth said. Lane watched her go.
He drank his coffee and listened to the radio. The suspect, as
they called him, had not yet been identified. Some lost soul,
delusional and messianic, like Lee Harvey Oswald. Like John
Wilkes Booth, Lane thought. No grasp, no idea, of the evil they
were doing. A sudden despair gusted through him, there would
be no good news on the radio, and he imagined himself being

comforted by Beth Weeks. Touched by his grief, loving him for it, she would strip, hold, mother him.

He watched as she put a Coke in front of the little boy and gave his cheek a pinch, bending sassily forward with her other hand on her hip. He'd never asked her how she lost all the weight: diet, exercise, or what. She came back and stood in front of him again.

"Guess what?" she said. "I'm engaged."

"Really," Lane said.

Beth was watching him. Smiling. "Look," she said and extended her pale soft hand, showing him the ring. "Nice, huh?"

"Who's the lucky guy?" Lane said.

"Brad Wormel. Remember him?"

"Sure."

She glanced down the counter, checking on everyone. Lane opened his notebook.

"You going to put me in a story?" Beth said.

"Say something about Bobby Kennedy and I will."

"I don't know what there is to say."

"That'll do, right there."

"Really?"

He made a note then swung away from the counter on the high round stool and slid down. He reached for his wallet.

"Coffee's on the house," Beth said.

. . . .

SLOWLY, a word at a time, she began to write. *Julius Talbot Littleton, the well-known artist, died on Tuesday of a heart attack. He was 78 years old. He died at home.* She lit another cigarette and studied what she'd written. Mr. Purdy and Mr. Hillman were writing. They wrote in bursts, spraying words and whole paragraphs onto paper as fast as a person could speak. Then they'd fold their arms and sit back and think awhile. Then they'd move their hands to the typewriter, lightly, hoveringly, and after a moment the furious rattle would begin again.

She dropped to a new paragraph, then turned and scanned her notes and the newspaper clippings. *Mr. Littleton was born in New York City on March 17, 1890.* She took a sip of cold black coffee. She put down the mug and x-ed out the date and wrote *St. Patrick's Day, 1890.* She took a drag on her cigarette. *His father taught philosophy at Columbia University.* She x-ed it out. *His father, William C. Littleton, was a professor of philosophy at Columbia University. Mr. Littleton went to Choate Academy and Harvard University. He left Harvard after two years of study and went to Europe to become a painter.*

A few minutes after twelve the machines ceased their racket in the back shop. Mrs. Engle stood up and shouldered her purse.

"Buy you lunch," she said.

Claire threw her a grateful smile. "I'd better not. This is coming kind of slow."

"Sometimes it's good to take a break from it," Mrs. Engle said.

"I'd better not," Claire said.

Mr. Braden, the elderly photographer and features writer, got up from his desk and slouched out, gaunt and leatherskinned, with crew-cut iron-gray hair. Mr. Purdy dropped forward in his chair and hung up the phone. He tapped the ashes out of his pipe and placed it upside down in his ashtray. He stood up, stretched, and sauntered out of the building with his hands in his pockets.

Mr. Hillman rose finally. He picked up a newspaper and

folded it to take with him. "You'd better get some lunch," he said.

"I'm all right," Claire said.

He stood a moment, looking down not at her but at the beige linoleum floor. Then he nodded and went out. She watched him cross the street to the depot platform, where evidently the newspaper employees had permission to park. There was a dirt lot as well, smothered in elm shade. Mr. Hillman folded himself down into a little Ford Falcon and drove away.

Now she could hear a couple of the men conversing quietly in the back shop. In the business office Manny Dutra, the circulation manager, talked on the phone. A bus arrived with a groan and grinding of gears. The engine revved and died. Claire pulled the sheet from her typewriter, rolled in another and rewrote her first page, improving it, she thought, here and there. She rolled in page 2 and lit another Salem.

.   .   .

HE WOULD remember how slowly the day passed, the sun wheeling as if reluctant to cross the fierce blue sky while the world waited for Bobby Kennedy to live or die. He drove to the outlying villages, sleepy places with one-room weathered-shingle post offices and Indian names bequeathed by the Wampanoags who once held this land of low hills and scrub plain and ocean. He sat at lunch counters and visited boatyards and filling stations where men sat in the shade on tilted chairs and talked of Robert Kennedy and the times they lived in. The war, the assassinations. Hippies and black militants. The SDS. A world being remade, Lane thought, and so did they all, for better or for worse.

At four he was back on Main Street. He drove out past St.

Patrick's Church and the old-age home and the town rec building to the new shopping plaza. There'd been fields out here
when Lane was a boy—all stores and blacktop now. He parked
and went into Friendly's, where a teenage waitress, red-eyed
from weeping, told him that if she were old enough to vote
she'd write in Kennedy's name in November, living or dead. He
drank a cup of coffee, and when he came out again into the
warm gray shade of the overhang, he saw his old teammate Ron
Viera coming out of Marshall's carrying a white shopping bag
with handles.

"Ronnie," he said.

Ron squinted at him for a moment as if he didn't know him.
His older brother Tommy had been killed in Vietnam two
months ago, the third boy from town to die over there, and the
grief lay deep and eloquent in Ron's chiseled olive face. They
shook hands, but Ron still didn't smile.

"I'm sorry about Tommy," Lane said.

Ron looked out over the sunlit parking lot and nodded.

"Buy you a coffee?" Lane said.

"I got to get home," Ron said.

"Talk a few minutes," Lane said. "It's been too long."

They sat down on a bench in the shade. Ron hunched down
with his wrists on his knees. He wore Bermuda shorts and his
legs were copper-colored and leanly muscled. He and Lane had
been the backfield: a two-pronged slashing attack that tore holes
in a defense, broke it like eggshell. Ron had gone to Springfield
College, and the first two summers he and Lane and three or
four teammates from high school played touch football every
evening on a mown field near Lane's house—fast pauseless
games that built their wind and legs and polished their moves.

Afterward they would sit in the uncut grass beside the playing field and unlace their cleats and talk about football and girls and the old days of high school. The sun would be down, the air cool and sweet-smelling with bayberry and honeysuckle. It was the best part, the talk and laughter afterward, night descending, the muffled wash of the ocean in the distance, the pleasant sourish smell of your own sweat, a good tiredness down your thighs and calves.

"You upset about Bobby Kennedy?" Lane said.

Ron blew air through his lips and shook his head sadly. "It's just one more thing, isn't it?"

"One more," Lane agreed.

"It's a bitch, isn't it?" Ron said.

"They aren't going to draft you, are they?" Lane said.

"Not now. Last surviving brother."

"I'm not going," Lane said. "I've filed as a conscientious objector."

Ron didn't say anything.

"Does that bother you?" Lane said.

"Why should it?"

"On account of Tommy."

"You know what he told me last time he was home on leave? He said, 'You're not going. No way. Go to Canada if you have to.'"

"I feel a little guilty," Lane said. "Guys like Tommy getting killed and I refuse to go."

"Don't worry about it," Ron said. He sat quiet for a while still slumped down with his hands clasped between his knees.

"Did you know my parents broke up?" he said.

"Broke *up?*"

"I'm leaving in a couple days. Driving out to Seattle. Going to get my master's at the university."

"Seattle," Lane said. "That's a long way, Ronnie."

"I can't stay here anymore."

"I'm leaving myself, in September."

"I saw it in the paper. Chicago, right?"

"Detroit."

"I guess one's about as bad as the other where you're going."

"I guess," Lane said.

"I better get home," Ron said.

"I'm sorry, Ronnie."

"It happens so fast," Ron said. "You can't believe how fast it happens."

"I'm sorry," Lane said again.

Later he thought that that was the moment in which he understood that the touch football and talk afterward in the summer twilight were not just gone but irretrievable, and that there was a difference. And how it had never occurred to him to treasure those vivid evenings as entities finite and soon to pass, as if there were no endings in life, just beginnings.

· · ·

AT FIVE o'clock Lane Hillman finally showed up in the newsroom. He came in frowning and preoccupied, and when he looked up and saw Claire he stopped, hesitated, as if she'd startled or disoriented him. She noticed him, certainly, but didn't make the connection right away, thought he was just some good-looking boy who'd come in off the street for one reason or another, as people had been doing all day. He looked at her in a surprised and almost disconcerted way, then lowered his sea-blue gaze and came on across the room to his father's desk.

And then she knew. He had his father's frown and black hair, but the son was taller, more loosely assembled, with an angular fluidity of movement. He fell dejectedly into the chair beside Mr. Hillman's desk.

She'd written five pages by now and smoked a pack of cigarettes and still hadn't finished. She hadn't left her desk except for coffee and to use the bathroom. She had eaten nothing since breakfast.

"Claire," Mr. Hillman said.

Impatient of the interruption she swiveled around in her chair to meet the boss's son. Lane got up like a gentleman and gave her his suntanned hand. Again he looked at her face, his gaze catching on hers, searchingly this time, as if he'd misplaced something and wondered if he might find it there. She smiled politely and lowered her eyes.

"Nice to meet you," she said.

"Same," Lane said.

"Why don't you knock off?" Mr. Hillman said.

Lane watched her.

"I'm almost done," she said.

"If I get it by noon tomorrow, that's soon enough."

Tomorrow was Thursday. The paper came out on Friday. Tuesdays and Fridays.

"I want to finish," Claire said.

"There's no hurry," Lane said. "Really."

She looked across the room, out the window, and now there were tears in her eyes. Lane and his father looked at each other.

"It's five o'clock," Mr. Hillman said. "Better knock off."

"No," she said and spun away from them in the swivel chair and rolled to her desk, her unfinished story. Mrs. Engle looked

45

up briefly but didn't say anything. Mr. Purdy, poring over an evening newspaper, went on reading as if he were alone in the room.

"Well," Lane said behind her, "I guess I'll write my story."

"You get out to the villages?"

"The villages, the Plaza, Main Street. I even went to the DPW shed."

"Go write your story, then," his father said.

. . .

THE OFFICE emptied one or two or three people at a time. They drifted out through the flat-roofed shadow of the building into the intense blond sunlight that lay on the blacktop apron of the bus station. Mrs. Engle and Mr. Purdy said good night to her as they left. Mr. Braden had disappeared several hours ago, taking his camera. At five-twenty Mr. Hillman got up in his slow way, shoved some mail into a leather briefcase and zippered it.

"What can I do to get you to go home?" he said.

"Fire me," Claire said.

Perhaps he smiled; she didn't look up to see. "I'm not going to fire you," he said.

. . .

LANE HILLMAN didn't write as fast as Mr. Purdy or his father but almost, attacking the keys with similar confidence and aggression. He was still writing when Claire finished the obituary. Seven pages. She rolled the final page out of her typewriter and read the obit through. It read awkwardly and reminded her of something hammered together by a child, or a simple structure, a doghouse, say, built by someone not a carpenter. She thought of beginning again but knew she was too tired and would only stray deeper into error.

She gathered the graveyard clippings and pocketed them in their envelopes. She returned them to their alphabetical places in the file cabinets, her legs stiff when she got up from sitting so long. Lane now had stopped writing and was studying his notes.

"Excuse me," Claire said.

He looked up.

"Do I leave my obituary on your father's desk or give it to him tomorrow?"

"Leave it under the bail of his typewriter. Are your initials on it?"

She nodded.

"Did you write 'thirty' at the end?"

"'Thirty'?"

"Didn't he tell you about that? At the end of a story you write the number thirty. It means there's no more."

"Thirty," Claire said.

"I don't know why. It doesn't make sense, but that's what it means in a newspaper office. Dash, thirty, dash."

She sat down one more time and rolled the last page back into her typewriter. She centered the page, spaced down and wrote what he'd told her. She pulled the sheet and stacked her seven pages and got up slowly and wearily and placed them under the bail of Mr. Hillman's typewriter. She slung her purse on her shoulder. The thrashing of keys began again, and again ceased.

"Hey," he said, "you really stuck with it."

She looked at him. He couldn't have been more than twenty-one. "What I don't need is to be patted on the head," she said.

"I wasn't," he said.

She stood in the doorway watching him. He eyed her a moment, then shrugged and leaned forward to read what was in his typewriter. He passed the back of his hand over his mouth. He had big-veined athlete's hands.

"What are you writing?" she said.

He told her.

"How's he doing?" she said.

"The same, I guess. Still unconscious." He folded his arms, turned and gazed out the window. "You were in Washington, right?" he said.

"Yes."

"Did you ever meet him?"

"I never actually met him. I saw him sometimes."

Lane nodded, staring out the window. "I never saw him in person," he said.

"Well, maybe you will."

"Maybe."

"Well. Don't work too late."

"I'm almost done," he said.

Crossing the street to her car she could hear the steady muffled tapping of Lane's typewriter through the open window. Her car was in the dirt lot, in the shade. She tossed her purse on the passenger seat and got in. She sat for a moment and thought about getting on the highway and pushing all the way to her mother's house and April, but she remembered that she hadn't eaten since morning and was due back here in not much more than twelve hours. She wished she'd brought April, but that would have been one more thing to worry about. She put the car in gear and drove out of the shaded parking lot and down the tree-lined street toward Main.

Chapter Three

SHE'D TAKEN a room at a moderately priced motel at the east end of Main Street called the General Swift. Tonight she continued past it to the shopping plaza just beyond, where Main Street ended, branching in two directions. She parked and went into Friendly's and sat at the counter and ate a BLT and a dish of peppermint ice cream, watching the customers drift in and out. They were all either elderly or kids still too young to get into bars. She bought cigarettes out of the machine, then walked to the liquor store several doors down and bought a fifth of Johnny Walker Red. It was getting dark. She drove to the motel.

There was a message for her: April had called. Claire got ice from the machine in the hallway and poured herself a stiff scotch in the motel bathroom tumbler. She took a shower, put on her bathrobe, and sat on the bed with her drink and dialed her mother's house.

"Where've you *been?*" April said.

"I worked late, then went to get something to eat, if that's okay with you. You wouldn't believe the day I've had."

"Grandma's not here. I think she's on a date."

"A date."

"I think so."

"Who with?"

"How would I know?"

"She upset about Robert Kennedy?"

"I don't know. I guess so."

"You guess so?"

"Well, she had the TV on all day. God, it's depressing."

"Sure it's depressing. It's awful." Claire sipped her scotch. She'd killed half the glass and felt pleasantly light-headed and floaty, above the reach of things.

"Mom, I want to come down. She's driving me crazy."

"Aren't you going to ask me how my day went?"

"You already told me."

"I've never been so tired."

"How can it be tiring? You're just sitting there."

"Just sitting there," Claire said.

"Sitting there writing, I mean."

"Writing wears you out, I've discovered. It drains you."

"You did okay, though."

"I don't know. Maybe not. Did Grandma tell you where she was going on this date of hers?"

"She said she was meeting a friend for dinner and a movie."

"Did she leave you a number?"

"No."

"Jesus."

"Mom, I'm fifteen years old."

"How about supper. She leave you anything to eat?"

"Mom, please, can I come down there?"

"You're coming in three days," Claire said. She drank some scotch.

"Why can't I come now?"

"I don't want to worry about you cooped up alone in a motel room."

"I wouldn't be cooped up. I could go to the beach."

"I'm too tired to argue, April."

"Why don't we just move into the house? Sleep on the floor."

"We can't get into the house till Saturday. Did Ezra call today?"

"Don't change the subject," April said.

"I love you, sweetheart. Remember that, okay?"

"Yeah," April said, "okay."

.   .   .

ROBERT KENNEDY died sometime during the night. The news was on the clock radio that woke her in the soft light of the new summer day. Claire had expected him to die and that made it easier. It was true also that RFK's death failed to touch her in the deep place his brother John's had, though she knew it ought to and even wished it might, if only for a while. The few quiet tears she shed that morning were for something larger and more un-defined than Robert Kennedy—life's stubborn refusal, perhaps, to work out for the best. The constant betrayal.

She was at the office at eight. Mr. Hillman was waiting for her with her edited obituary. "Sit down," he said. He'd drawn slant vertical lines through the first paragraph, written *kill* in the margin, and composed a new lead on a fresh sheet of copy paper. He handed it to her wordlessly.

Julius Talbot Littleton, the self-taught abstract artist whose work hangs in the Museum of Modern Art in New York and the Boston Museum of Fine Arts, died at his home on Walker Street Tuesday evening of a heart attack. He was 78.

"Someone dies," Mr. Hillman said. "How do you summarize his life, capture it in a sentence or two?"

"You're telling me, right? Not asking."

"Both, I guess."

"I didn't do very well, did I?"

"You didn't do badly," he said.

The newsroom was waking up. Mr. Purdy and Mrs. Engle were writing. Mr. Braden was muttering into the phone. At the desk abutting his, catercorner across the room from his father, sat Lane. His back was turned and he was sitting still, looking out the window.

"There's no point," Mr. Hillman continued, "in saying someone died at home unless you tell the reader where home is."

"All right," Claire said.

"We never say 'seventy-eight years old' in a newspaper. It's a waste of space. He was seventy-eight." He looked past her at Lane. "Lane, you'd better get started."

"All right," Lane said without moving.

"Look this over," Mr. Hillman said, handing Claire the obituary, "then give it to one of the linotypists."

She glanced at the second page, the third. Hardly a line hadn't been mutilated. Deletions, inserts, whole paragraphs x-ed out and rewritten.

"I didn't write one good sentence," Claire said.

"When you've looked it over, come see me and I'll have something else for you to do," he said, turning, already moving on to the next thing before she'd risen from the chair.

·   ·   ·

THE PRESS was a Goss Model A Duplex flatbed built in 1946, the year Lane was born. It ran with a rhythmic pounding din that shook the building. A press run began around one and continued deep into the afternoon, the deafening grease-fragrant machine dropping newspaper sections onto a waist-high tray where the men waited in a straggling little line. The papers fell at the rate of not quite one per second; as fast, say, as a blackjack dealer flipping cards. When the tray was full, the next man would scoop up the papers and carry them to a makeup table, all of which were now covered with sheets of cardboard, and, working with two piles, slip one section into another, assembling today's newspaper.

The press run ended sometime after four. The drivers had loaded up and gone by then, and the delivery boys with their canvas shoulder bags. The Duplex stopped gradually, the drive shaft pumping slower and slower, with more seeming effort, the thumping, grinding din ebbing from the room like a vapor. There would be a final gnash of cog teeth and a sullen snarl or groan like a donkey's bray cut short as one last paper dropped listlessly onto the tray, then silence.

Silence. Pure, sweet, as if newly minted by God. In its awesome clarity you could hear the flutey twitter of birds, the mutter of a car, the musical trill of a phone in the business office or newsroom. Up and down the makeup tables the men began to talk, cheerfully, because the workday was almost over.

On Friday they talked about the new reporter.

Lane had come out to slip papers and help wrap them for the mail. It wasn't part of his job and in fact no one had ever asked or suggested that he help out in the back shop on publication days, but he liked to work with his hands, get them dirty, and to listen to the men kid each other and talk about sports and local events and the trials of married life.

"How's that new reporter doing?" Frank asked Lane on Friday.

"Good," Lane said, slipping papers.

"Where's she from?"

"Up near Boston somewhere."

"She's got Washington, D.C., plates on her car," Red said.

"She was working down there," Lane said.

"Lane knows all about her, I guess," Walter said.

Only Jimmy Wheeler took no part in their banter, listening to them with an air of benevolent detachment, as if they were high school boys and couldn't help being this way. Jimmy was too happily married and too old-fashioned to take any but a professional interest in a woman in the office, new or otherwise. He'd been at the *Covenant* since 1934, when Lane's grandfather was running things. He'd seen everything: hurricanes that knocked out the power, the forest fire of 1944 that swept down the hill and nearly jumped the railroad tracks to the building. The men had fought the wind-blown sparks, taking turns on the roof with a garden hose.

"Lane, you ought to get her phone number," Sterling said.

"She married, Lane?"

"I think divorced."

"Well, hell, get her phone number."

"She's too old for Lane. He wouldn't know what to do with it."

"I'd know what to do with it," said Walter.

"Shit," Frank said. "You wouldn't know what to do with it if it sat on you."

Then Claire came in to get coffee, materializing suddenly and without warning in a summer dress and high heels, her bare legs smooth and brown as varnish, and everyone stopped talking. She looked at Lane, surprised to find him out here, and then at the rest of them. She nodded and dropped them all a friendly unshy smile, then turned and stood at the coffee urn with her back to them. No one spoke. She filled her mug and went out, and when talk finally began again, it was of other things and markedly decorous, as if a priest had walked in and caught them blaspheming.

·   ·   ·

THE HOUSE she'd rented was on the corner of a quiet dead-end street that stopped at the edge of a field beginning to grow in with bittersweet and pitch pine and wild cherry. It was a narrow, intimate street with no sidewalks. The houses sat close to it behind pale dusty hedges. Most of the houses had roofed porches where on warm evenings people sat in rocking chairs talking lazily of this and that and listening to the occasional sound of a car passing on the adjoining street, the voices of kids going by in the dappled lamplit darkness, a dog barking in the distance.

Claire and April were lucky; their house was the largest on the street. It had a yard and a garage. It was an ugly thing, mustard-yellow trim on brown shingles, but it had a comforting sturdiness: a plain building of uncertain age that wouldn't let you down. The worn hardwood floors rang solidly underfoot. The papered walls were faded but without water stains. It cost half what Claire had paid for the tiny apartment in Fairlington, Virginia.

In the evening she liked to sit on the little brick porch off the kitchen with her coffee or a glass of wine and watch the kids play in the street. They came out almost every night, boys and girls, to play red rover or kickball or capture-the-flag until their mothers called them in, their high-pitched voices carrying up and down the darkening street.

On the third night they'd been in the house April came out and sat with her on the porch. The fireflies had begun to flicker above the yard between the house and the garage, and the kids still played, flitting like pale smears in the thickening dusk.

"Wouldn't you like to play with them?" Claire said.

"I'm not into games. Anyway, they're all younger than me."

"I was thinking," Claire said, "we could sign you up for sailing lessons at that yacht club over by the harbor."

"Sailing lessons? I don't think so."

"It'd be a good way to meet people."

"I'm fine, Mom. Stop worrying about me."

"It's what mothers do, hon. They worry."

"Well, don't."

"How come you don't talk to Ezra anymore?"

"We broke up. I *told* you I'd never see him again."

"You know, April, maybe if you didn't always take a book to the beach you'd start meeting people."

"What about you? You don't have any more friends than I do."

"That's different," Claire said.

"Why? Why is it different?"

"Because I've had enough friends to last me a lifetime. More than enough."

"That's bull."

"Don't use that word."

"Bull? Don't say bullfighter? Don't say Ferdinand the Bull?"

"You know what I mean."

"How come you don't have any friends from work?"

"They're all older than I am. That, or they're married." Except for Lane Hillman, she thought.

"So what?" April said.

"Right now it's all work and no play for me. I have so much learning to do. It takes up all my energy."

"If I said that about school, you'd have a fit."

"It's different when you're young," Claire said.

"I don't see why."

"It just is."

"I hate it when you say that," April said.

. . . .

HE WAS patient with her, a good teacher. Use simple declarative sentences, he said. Avoid the passive voice whenever possible. Never say "whether or not," just "whether." Precision is everything. Inclement weather is imprecise—inclement how? "Virtually" is imprecise, a lazy word that qualifies without qualifying. She wrote it all down, memorized it, crammed her head with new knowledge.

He sent her to the dictionary to look up *leisurely, gibe, jive, convince,* and *persuade.* She would cross the room like a tractable schoolgirl, avoiding the looks, the speculative glances she imagined from the others. If Lane was at his desk, she might look at him because youth is open, youth is accepting. Lane would meet her eye and a look would pass between them, an unspoken understanding, the two of them set apart by their youthful outlook and the lives they'd been leading elsewhere.

The heavy *Webster's* had to be heaved open with two hands. Its thin pages were cool to the touch and brittle with age. She would find the word, note its root, commit it to memory.

Often Mr. Hillman communicated with her in writing though she sat not ten feet away, handing her a typed note as he passed her desk, wordlessly and without making eye contact, or leaving it under the bail of her typewriter when she was away from her desk. The notes were terse, unadorned. *He was given a prize. She was awarded a medal. This is called the false passive and is acceptable to some grammarians. We don't use it here.* He never raised his voice, never reproached, but neither did he praise her, as if praise were a luxury neither of them had time for.

She wrote nothing but obituaries and weddings for a week and a half, deskbound from eight to five, and then without warning he sent her to the fire station to get the news of the previous two days. The station house stood halfway up Main Street, a two-story red-brick building shrouded in ivy. Claire stood in the bay, where a fire truck stood ready to roll, and talked across a counter to one of the fire captains. He was a courteous man not much older than she, and he read the log to her while she took his every word down in shorthand as he spoke. There'd been several brush fires, a fire in a restaurant kitchen, a fire under the hood of a car. She went back to the office and wrote them up together in one story, and Mr. Hillman rewrote it.

A fire engine doesn't rush to a fire. Rush indicates intent, purpose, or motive.

He sent her to the police station one morning in Lane's place. The police chief looked her up and down from behind his desk and smiled at what he saw. He was older than she but youthful, with a fearless twinkle in his pale blue eyes, a knobby sunburned face, and cherry-blond hair. He answered all her questions, gave her everything she wanted, smiling amiably and never taking his eyes off her.

"Mr. Smooth," she said back in the office.

"Oh, he likes the ladies all right," Ruth Engle said.

"He's married," Lane said, "so don't get any ideas."

"He isn't my type," she said.

Mr. Hillman looked up from his typewriter. "What have you got?" he said.

She opened her notebook. Lane watched her. She knew he looked at her often and didn't mind. "A break-in last night at the Gifford Insurance Agency," she said. "Some kids drinking and driving."

"Go ahead and write it," he said.

And afterward a note, a single line on a clean sheet of copy paper that seemed impatient, irritable in its abruptness. *The cops say driving under the influence. We say drunken driving.* When he'd finished with the copy itself, six pages eked out word by word over a couple of hours, it was barely recognizable as her own. She wanted to scream at him then, to stamp her foot and tell him she was doing her best and if it wasn't good enough he ought to fire her and not put her through this. But she didn't. She kept her pride hidden from him and the others, including Lane, and went on to the next thing.

She read. She bought paperback books off the rack at Kasselman's; she bought *Time,* the *Boston Globe,* even the *New York Times.* She read while dinner cooked, sipping white wine or scotch or a Miller's High Life. She took a book to bed with her and read till midnight. She began to make out the rhythms of the language, its lilt and flow. As if she'd been tone deaf all her life and had now, with John Hillman's help and her own will and resolve, wakened to the music of the printed page.

.   .   .

TWO WEEKS after the assassination Lane waited till she went out to get her morning coffee and followed her with his own empty mug.

"I want to ask you something," he said. "About Bobby Kennedy."

She turned to face him with her coffee in her hand. He wasn't ruddy like his father but a gentler, more earth-warm shade. The sun browned rather than reddened him. The Linotypes whirred and slammed, and out at the edge of their metal clamor Claire and Lane could speak privately.

"Do you think I'm naïve about him?" Lane asked.

She didn't answer right away, and he stepped past her to get his coffee, passing close enough for her to smell his laundered shirt and the strong, clean breadlike breath of his skin. He filled his mug, looked for the little carton of milk.

"No," she said, "I don't think you're naïve."

"Then why do you hesitate?" he said.

"Look," she said, "I'd have voted for him if he'd gotten the nomination."

"You see," he said, "I had this feeling about him. It was more the promise in him than what he'd actually done."

"You might be right."

"I *might* be."

"You work in Washington a while, you can get a little cynical. You see these guys up close, you see they're human."

"You do think I'm naïve."

"You're twenty-one years old. A little naïveté is a good thing at your age."

"I'm twenty-two," Lane said.

"It's good at any age, you want to know the truth." And turned as she said it, leaving him standing there watching her, her legs and the way she moved. She knew it, without looking back over her shoulder.

Chapter Four

A ND THEN on the Thursday before the Fourth of July weekend, she walked in at eight in the morning and found Lane seated in the maple chair beside his father's desk looking thoughtfully out toward the woods while Mr. Hillman spoke quietly on the phone. Mr. Hillman hung up and gestured Claire over with his head. She unshouldered her purse and laid it on her desk. She rolled her chair over and sat down next to Lane.

"Have you heard the news?" Mr. Hillman said.

She shook her head. News. Something had happened in Vietnam, or to one of the presidential candidates. *Please not another shooting.*

"We had a murder and a drowning last night."

"Here?"

"Here," Lane said.

"A murder and a drowning?"

"That's right."

"The murder was a girl from Oregon, a waitress at the Cozy Nook," Mr. Hillman said. "The body was found this morning in the woods off Route 110. Strangled. The cops have no idea who did it."

Strangled. In its guttural stops you could hear, feel, constriction, the violent blockage of oxygen.

"The drowning's also a mystery," Mr. Hillman said. "A local boy. David Kasselman. Bernie Kasselman's boy."

Bernie Kasselman. That sweet man in the drugstore.

"The girl was about twenty, they think. They don't know much about her yet. The Kasselman boy was fifteen. He was found this morning on Pine Neck Beach."

"Out of the water," Lane said. "Someone had dragged him up the beach."

Claire looked out across the railroad tracks and thought of Mr. Kasselman. His rosy face and the kind way he smiled at you across the pharmacy counter. He'd taken to saving her newspapers for her because sometimes they sold out before she got there after work. He'd done this without her asking him.

"We don't have a lot of time," Mr. Hillman said. "I want obits and two good stories by the end of the day. I don't want to have to scramble tomorrow morning."

"Excuse me," Claire said, "but am I covering any of this?"

"You and Lane."

"Let's go," Lane said.

. . .

HE WAITED for her across the street, sitting on the stone wall in the shade, while she got her coffee. He watched her come out of the building and cross the street with her mug in her hand, the sun bright in her face. She sat down beside him with her legs dangling.

"David Kasselman was naked when they found him," Lane said. "His clothes were lying around nearby."

"Poor Mr. Kasselman," Claire said.

She put down her coffee, unsnapped her purse, and dug out a cigarette, her first of the day. Lane took the matches out of her hand and scratched a flame on the second try. He lit her cigarette and blew out the match and tossed it into the street. Claire nodded thank you. She blew smoke away from him and tapped ash onto the sidewalk.

"A couple of kids found the girl's body," Lane said. "They were cutting through the woods to go fishing. She'd been dead since last night. Chief Williams and one or two other cops recognized her from the Cozy Nook."

"I wouldn't have thought this kind of thing happened around here," Claire said.

"It doesn't."

"It does now."

"The last murder was twenty years ago and it wasn't anything like this. A doctor poisoned his wife. A genteel crime. Like an Agatha Christie novel. Before that, you have to go back to the 1920s."

Claire smoked and sipped hot coffee and looked across the street at the newspaper office with the sun lighting its white-shingle façade.

"Who did it, do you think?"

"Some guy passing through. Picked her up at a bar, talked her into his car. We get some pretty rough characters down here in the summertime."

They sat awhile. Claire smoked her cigarette down. She wondered why Lane wasn't in more of a hurry to get started. His deliberation, his quiet aplomb, irritated her slightly.

"You know where the funeral home is?" he said.

"Sort of."

"You go out the King's Highway. Past the old fire station. The state pathologist'll be there around nine. Why don't you go hang around, see what you can find out. I'll meet you out there later."

"All right." She rubbed her cigarette out on the wall. "Lane?" It was the first time she'd called him by name. He looked at her, aware that it was. "I don't write very fast, in case you haven't noticed."

"You'll do fine," he said.

"It takes me two hours to write a story sometimes."

"We've got all night," he said, and popped down off the wall, landing weightless and catlike and setting their long day irrevocably in motion.

· · · ·

THE KING'S Highway was the old road out of town, before the dual highway was built a few miles over. It wasn't a highway in any modern sense but a winding, hilly, shaded country road with an occasional view of the bay, the body of water that had claimed the life of David Kasselman. The houses stood close to the road, weathered-shingle and clapboard antiques painted lively shades of red and yellow as well as white, with picket fences smothered in Dorothy Perkins roses.

The funeral home was a turn-of-the-century mansion that stood in the open against a luminous backdrop of bay and sky. A police cruiser and a Karmann Ghia were parked in the circular driveway. Three men stood on the roofed porch eating dough-nuts and drinking coffee out of Styrofoam cups. One of them was the police chief, Paul Williams. They watched Claire get out of her car with her notebook.

"Here comes Lois Lane," Williams said with a grin. He was shorter than she'd thought when he was lolling behind his desk. Compact, a little heavy in the gut.

"Boys," he said, "this is Miss Malek of the *Covenant*."

The two other men nodded.

"Les Jacobson and Ed O'Neill," Williams said. "Les is the medical examiner. Eddie's with the State Police."

"Hi," Claire said. She stood below them, squinting up with the sun in her eyes. The state cop, O'Neill, sipped his coffee and watched her.

"So what's happening?" she said.

"Nothing," said O'Neill.

"Nothing," she said. "That's why you're all here, right?"

It got a smile from Williams and the doctor, nothing from O'Neill.

"The pathologist is working on the girl," Williams said. "White Caucasian, twenty-three years of age. Name of Jane Clifford of Eugene, Oregon. Cause of death strangulation with a synthetic rope. No suspects as of this moment."

She took it down in her shorthand.

"There's preliminary evidence of sexual penetration," Williams said. "We think it was consensual."

"What about David Kasselman?" she said, scribbling.

"It looks like an accident. The question is whether he had any foreign substances in his body."

"Drugs, you mean."

"Or alcohol."

"And he was found on the beach."

"About thirty feet up."

"You don't know how he got there."

"Correct."

"Do you know where he was last night?"

"He was supposed to meet somebody at the county fair. That somebody got there late and couldn't find him. His mother dropped him at the fairgrounds, but we don't know what happened after that."

"Who was that somebody?"

"Boy named Donald Simkins." Williams spelled it for her. "A school pal."

O'Neill drained his coffee. He set the cup down on the porch railing. "Shall we go in, gentlemen?" he said.

"Okay if I wait?" Claire said.

"We'd all be thrilled," O'Neill said.

. . .

SHE SAT in the warm shade at the top of the wide porch steps. The day was turning hot, humid. A car hummed past in the stillness. She opened her purse and found her cigarettes. There were woods across the street and an old stone wall wandering alongside the road, rocks piled a century ago and loosened and tumbled by time until what remained was more the idea of a wall than the actual thing.

She smoked four Salems while the light crept toward her up the deck-gray wooden steps. At eleven she drove down the road till she came to a general store at a fourcorners and bought an egg salad sandwich and a coffee. She sat on the porch again and ate the sandwich. She took what was left of the coffee to her car and sat listening to the radio and trying not to think about another cigarette. The news came on. The war, the upcoming conventions. Nixon, Humphrey. Then music by Dylan, the Lovin' Spoonful, the Beatles, the Supremes with their Motown sound. From the Motor City, said the DJ. Lane was going there in September, he'd told her at the coffee urn one morning. Detroit. Some hellish black ghetto. So this is my last summer, he'd said, and she'd known what he meant.

Finally, Paul Williams came out onto the porch, stretching as if he'd just gotten out of bed. Claire turned off the radio. Williams watched her legs swing over out of the car. He came down the steps into the muggy glare.

"She'd had sex, all right. The time of death was early morning, one or two in the A.M."

"Did she have parents?"

"We all have parents, Miss Malek."

"It's Mrs. Malek, by the way."

"My apologies. I didn't see a ring."

"I was asking you about her parents," Claire said.

"Norman and Lucille Clifford of Eugene. The girl was adopted. An only child."

"An only child," Claire said. "Those poor people."

"We'll be getting some photographs of the girl," Williams said. "I'll see that you get one if you like."

"I'd appreciate that," Claire said.

Then Lane drove in.

"I was wondering where he was," Williams said.

He got out of the car, the green office Chevrolet, and shoved his notebook down into his hip pocket. He was frowning like his father, a man with things on his mind, a job to do, the face incongruously youthful, smooth-skinned, and caramel-brown.

"You're too late," Williams said with his easy smile. "I've told her everything."

"Hi," Claire said. She was glad to see him. It surprised her how glad.

"You doing okay?" he said.

"She's doing great," Williams said. "She's doing better than you would have."

"I can believe it," Lane said.

"They've done the autopsy on the girl," Claire said. "They're working on the boy now."

"I wouldn't expect anything surprising," Williams said, "unless he was high on something."

"I don't think he was the type," Lane said.

"Oh? And how would you know?"

"One of my sisters was in school with him."

"That may be, but it was a clear night last night. Calm. Nice moon."

"Could he swim?"

"He wasn't Johnny Weissmuller, but he could swim."

"I wonder," Lane said, "if there was a connection with the murder."

"I doubt it," Williams said.

"Seems like an amazing coincidence."

"Funny thing about coincidences: they happen."

"I suppose," Lane said.

"You suppose?"

"Can we go get some lunch?" Claire said.

"How long do you think it'll be, Paul?" Lane said.

"I don't know. Another hour."

"Can I call you later?"

"Sure, Lane. You can call me anytime."

.   .   .

THE BUSTY waitress behind the lunch counter in Chamberlain's Drugstore eyed her coolly, but with a certain interest.

"Claire Malek, this is Beth Weeks," Lane said. "Beth and I went to school together."

"Really," Claire said.

Beth Weeks smiled vaguely and turned her attention to Lane. "You hear about David Kasselman?" she said.

"Claire and I are working on it," he said.

Beth glanced at Claire.

"Claire's our new reporter," Lane said.

"He teaching you?" Beth said.

"He's trying."

"I bet he is."

"Be good, Beth," Lane said.

He ordered two cheeseburgers and a milkshake.

"Just coffee," Claire said.

"I thought you were hungry," Lane said.

"I changed my mind."

"You're either hungry or you aren't."

"I wanted to leave. Williams was getting on my nerves."

"Flirting with you?"

"A little bit. I don't like the way he talks to you, either."

"He talks, that's the important thing. He'll give you a story. Most cops, it's like pulling teeth."

"He's a talker, all right."

"If he bothers you, I could say something to him."

She eyed him, smiling the ghost of a smile. "I think I can handle him."

"You get plenty of practice, I bet."

"A little."

"You dating anybody?"

She smiled again and turned and opened her purse. He took the matches from her as before and struck one and lifted it to her cigarette. She turned and blew the smoke down away from him, and again regarded him with a slow half-smile.

"Not at the moment," she said.

The waitress came back with her coffee and Lane's milkshake. She smirked at Lane and didn't look at Claire.

"Why not?" Lane said when Beth Weeks had left them.

"Why not what?"

"Why aren't you dating anyone?"

"I'm taking a vacation from it."

"Why?"

"What about you? You have some sweet young thing stashed away somewhere?"

"I'm taking a vacation from it."

Claire smiled. "You're too young to do that."

"So are you."

"That's what you think."

"What are you, thirty-one, thirty-two?"

She didn't answer right away but studied him a moment, wondering if in fact he knew her age and this was a bit of youthful gallantry, or if he truly believed she was that young. She decided it didn't matter; either was good.

"Thirty-seven," she said.

"You're kidding."

She laughed and shook her head. "You're full of it, you know that?"

"I mean it," he said.

"I've got a fifteen-year-old daughter," she said, and watched to see if the news would surprise or discourage him, but it didn't seem to.

"What's her name?"

"April."

"April. I like that."

The waitress brought the cheeseburgers, which came with a hill of french fries.

"How can you eat like that and not get fat?" Beth Weeks asked.

"Lucky, I guess," Lane said, and watched her move away down the counter.

"Maybe you ought to give that one a shot," Claire said. "She looks pretty receptive."

"She's engaged."

"She doesn't act engaged."

"I used to think about asking her out. I just never got around to it."

"And now you're kicking yourself."

He looked down the counter at Beth Weeks, then turned and

shook his head. "No," he said quietly. "I'm not kicking myself."

He ate the cheeseburgers and every last french fry, then scraped the milkshake residue out with a spoon. "On the house?" he asked the waitress.

"Don't press your luck," she said, and tore the check and handed it to him. He paid and tipped her a dollar, then he and Claire sauntered out into the gray shade that fell on the sidewalk on that side of the street.

"Which obit do you want?" Lane said.

"You're the boss," Claire said.

"No I'm not."

"Come on," she said. "You know it and I know it."

"Maybe you'd rather not write about a strangulation."

"Why don't you just tell me what to do and we'll get going, all right?"

Lane shrugged. "All right. Go see the Kasselmans. Work up an obit on David."

"Go see them?"

"Of course."

"Shouldn't I at least call them first?"

"If you call them, they can tell you not to come."

"If they don't want to see me . . ."

"You have to," Lane said.

"Shit," she said.

"They live on Pleasant Street," he said. "Right around the corner from the drugstore. The first house on the left."

She nodded and turned, and he watched her walk to her car, the skirt of her pale-blue summer dress swinging, reversing back and forth with a sinuous flick.

"Good luck," he said, and she stopped and turned and acknowledged it with a wry smile that made her look, for a moment only, young and very vulnerable.

.   .   .

A TALL hedge hid the house, shielding the Kasselmans in their grief. Several cars were parked out front. Two more sat in the driveway. Claire went in through the narrow opening in the hedge and up the paved front walk. She rang the bell. A girl of perhaps eighteen opened the door. She was pale-skinned and sweet-faced and pretty.

"I'm sorry to bother you," Claire said, "but is Mr. Kasselman here, or Mrs. Kasselman?"

The girl nodded. She looked back and spoke over her shoulder. "Uncle Bernie?"

Claire could hear voices, hushed and murmurous, like the softened conversation in a church. Footsteps sounded, Claire and the girl waiting silently, neither looking at the other, and then Bernie Kasselman appeared in the doorway, dazed and tearful and wanly smiling. The pretty girl took a step backward and looked anxiously into the face of her uncle.

"Miss Malek," he said.

Claire didn't correct him. "Mr. Kasselman, I hate to be bothering you like this."

"You're writing about David," he said.

"I know it's not a good time," she said, "but the paper comes out tomorrow."

"It's all right," Mr. Kasselman said. "Come on in."

"If I could do this later, I would."

"No," he said, "it's all right."

She followed him and the niece down a hallway to a bright daylit living room full of people. Adults, teenagers, children. They crammed the sofa, spilled across the white shag rug where they sat close together, hugging their drawn-up knees. They ceased talking when Claire entered. Everyone looked at her.

"Who's this?" demanded a small, thin woman, dark-eyed like the niece but with an asperity in her look, a sharpness. She was ghost-pale, luminous with grief.

"She writes for the *Covenant*," Bernie said. "She's doing the obituary."

"We're too busy," the woman said. "We're planning a funeral here."

"The paper comes out tomorrow," Bernie Kasselman said gently.

"That's their problem."

"Esther," said a petite woman with tinted red hair, "you want a nice obituary in the paper. You really do."

"Do I care?" Esther Kasselman said. "Do I care what's in the goddamn paper?"

"Yes you do, sweetie," said the redhead.

"I'm sorry, Mrs. Kasselman," Claire said. "I don't like doing this, believe me."

"Why don't we go into the den?" Mr. Kasselman said.

"Would you like me to come with you, Uncle Bernie?" asked the niece.

He threw her a grateful smile. "I'll be fine, Judy," he said.

"Esther," said the redhead, "you go, too. You help Bernie out."

"Bernie doesn't need help. Anyway, I can't think straight."

"Can I offer you something to drink?" Bernie said. "Coffee? We've got lots of food."

"No thank you," Claire said.

"Esther," said a big man, gut-heavy in a rumpled white shirt and loosened tie, "you go the hell in there and help Bernie."

Esther still didn't move. Bernie looked at her, mildly and forgivingly, and led Claire to the den, the two of them picking their way among the kids and teenagers strewing the living-room floor. Claire could smell the food now—baked dishes and fragrant cakes and pies. They reentered the hallway and crossed to the den, which was paneled in knotty varnished pine that drank the sunlight, casting the room in a warm, autumnal, whiskey-brown light. Framed photographs climbed the walls. Many were of David: as a baby, a little boy, an adolescent. He was small, bony, jug-eared. Claire looked at the pictures and felt her heart fill up with something she couldn't give a name to. Sadness, yes, but more than that; the knowledge, perhaps, that life is a series of blows, a steady toting up of losses that must in the end break everybody, until your own turn comes. Bernie unhooked a picture of the teenage David. He was smiling an impish smile. You could see the mischief in him, the sweetness.

"This one I like," Bernie said. "Maybe you could use it in the paper." He smiled at his son and Claire thought he might break down, but he clenched his jaw and closed his eyes and after a moment was all right again. "Can they shoot it through the glass?" he said.

"I don't know," Claire said.

"I think they can," he said and gave her the picture.

Then Mrs. Kasselman came in. She glanced, annoyed, at the

picture in Claire's hand and sat down on the sofa. Bernie lowered himself beside her. She felt for his hand, pulled it into her lap and sat ramrod-straight, watching Claire with eyes as dark as char.

"Sit down, Miss Malek," Bernie said.

"Claire," she said and sat down in the leather armchair facing the TV.

"I told her she could borrow the picture," Bernie said. "To put with the story."

Esther didn't say anything. Bernie took off his glasses with his free hand and set them down beside them. He rubbed his eyes. "What was he doing at the beach?" he said.

"Better we don't know," Esther said.

"No. I want to know, Esther. I want to know what happened."

He bowed his head and closed his eyes. Esther held his hand in her lap with both of hers. Bernie opened his wet eyes and smiled.

"You'll do a nice obituary, won't you, Miss Malek?"

"I promise," she said.

. . .

LANE HADN'T come back yet. She pulled Esther and Bernard and David Kasselman's files and lit a cigarette and rolled paper into her typewriter. The sunlight struck oblique and golden across the floor; without her noticing, the day had gotten on, was nearly gone. She wrote a couple of pages and knew they weren't good. A little after four, Lane came in. He stopped by Claire's desk.

"I hate to tell you this, but David Kasselman was drunk."

"Drunk?"

"It was in the autopsy report."

"I don't believe that," she said.

"How drunk?" his father said.

Lane opened his notebook. "Alcohol level of point-one-eight. That's pretty high for someone his size."

"He wasn't the type," Claire said. "He was a child."

"Paul Williams was wondering about drugs or alcohol, if you'll remember," Lane said.

"It's the fair," said Mrs. Engle. "That's what kids do at the fair, they drink."

"Suppose he did have a couple of drinks," Claire said, "so what?"

"He had more than a couple," Lane said.

"What'd you get on the murder?" Lane's father asked him.

"Wait a minute," Claire said. "We aren't going to print that, are we?"

"We're going to have to," Mr. Hillman said. "What'd you get, Lane?"

"Why?" Claire said. "It's nobody's business."

"Because it happened," Mr. Hillman said. "It's part of the story."

"The news story," Lane said, "not the obituary."

"It'll kill the Kasselmans to have that in the paper," Claire said.

"It's the reason he drowned," Lane said gently.

"We can't," she said. "Please."

"I'll take the heat, if there is any," Mr. Hillman said.

"It isn't that," Claire said.

"Lane?" Mr. Hillman said.

"No suspects," Lane said. "She left work at eleven o'clock and disappeared."

Claire rolled her chair back and stood up. "Hey," she said. "Is anyone listening to me?" They all looked at her: Ruth, Mr. Purdy, old Henry Braden. She could feel Lane's blue eyes, the worry in them. For a moment no one moved or spoke.

Then, very gently, Lane said, "We have to print it, Claire."

"All right," she said, and in an abrupt and furious half-shriek, *"print it."*

And as they watched in bland, mute surprise, she whirled, snatched up her purse, and fled.

· · · ·

LANE went quickly to his desk and sat down and watched her through the window. She crossed the street, rapid on her high heels. She did not go to her car but continued instead past the bus station toward the dirt road that came in the back way.

"Oh dear," Ruth said.

"Gee," murmured Henry Braden.

Lane's father dug in his shirt pocket for a cigarette. "If she doesn't come back you're going to have to write that obit," he said.

"She'll come back," Lane said.

"I don't intend to wait very long for her," his father said.

"I'll go get her," Lane said.

He went out into the warm, sticky late afternoon and took off across the street at a lope. People waited for a bus; they watched him jog by. He almost missed her, almost kept going down the seldom-used weed-grown road where it curled out of sight into the woods. She was sitting on a paint-faded bench near the end of the depot platform. She looked solitary, and very stubborn and proud. Her legs were crossed. Her back was straight. Lane stepped up onto the sun-whitened asphalt platform. She glanced at him briefly, showing no surprise, as if she knew he'd be the one to come after her, if anyone did. He sat down beside her on the old green bench.

"The train'll be along in ten minutes, ma'am," he said.

She didn't speak, didn't move.

"We used to take the train to Pennsylvania to visit my grandmother," he said. "I remember looking down the tracks and watching the headlight come up out of the dark. Why'd you bolt?"

"Because I couldn't stand what was happening," she said.

"You'd better get used to it."

"Maybe I don't want to get used to it."

"Then you don't want to be a newspaper reporter," he said.

"I'm not cut out for it."

"Sure you are."

"I can't write and I can't stab people in the back."

"No one's stabbing anybody in the back," Lane said.

"That's what you think."

"A newspaper has to tell the truth. Our readers count on it."

"I wasn't talking about not telling the truth," she said.

"The whole truth," he said. "Once you start leaving things out, there's no end to it."

"How'd you get so fucking deep at your age?"

"There's nothing deep about it."

"Righteous, then."

"It isn't righteous, either. It's what a newspaper does. Print the news. The news means all the news."

"You didn't see the Kasselmans. You don't know what they're going through."

"You think my father doesn't understand that?"

"I guess he and I are different, then."

"Not as different as you think."

Claire didn't say anything.

"Look," Lane said, "I'm the one who found out he was drinking. I'll write it in the news story. It won't be in the obituary at all."

"It doesn't matter who writes it," Claire said.

"The Kasselmans'll get over that part of it," Lane said.

"How do you know?" She turned to face him. "Just how the hell do you know that at the age of twenty-two?"

He looked down between his knees. "I don't, I guess."

"Damn right you don't."

"I didn't say it was easy," he said.

"I know what you said."

She opened her purse, fished around for a cigarette, and held it a moment unlit, gazing across the tracks to the wall of young trees—white oak and swamp maple and wild cherry—crowding each other as they swarmed to the edge of the rail corridor where the ghost trains brushed them as they passed in the air.

"Come on back," Lane said. "Write your story."

"Did your father send you?"

"No one sent me."

"He's pissed off, I imagine."

"A little."

"Maybe he'll fire me."

"It's a lot harder than that to get fired from the *Covenant*," Lane said. He stood up and pushed his hands down into his pockets and gazed down the shaggy, ruined railbed. Then he looked at Claire. She met his gaze, tilting her head in a way that he loved, and her face softened, and she sighed. Lane shook his head and smiled.

"Come on," he said. "Put the cigarette away."

"I never should have been on this story in the first place," she said. "It's going to take me all night to write it."

"I'll help you."

"Hold my hand, you mean."

"No," he said.

"Because I don't need that," she said.

"I know you don't," he said.

.   .   .

FIRST, she apologized. She sat down beside Mr. Hillman's desk uninvited and bowed her head contritely. Mr. Hillman said nothing.

"I'm sorry," she said. "Will you accept my apology?"

"You'd better get back to that obit," he said.

"I know you're good at what you do."

"I've been in this racket a long time," he said.

"I know you have," she said.

"It takes a certain toughness, I guess."

"I'll try to get there," she said.

"You'll get there," he said.

.   .   .

IT WAS ten past six when Lane finished his story.

. . . was identified as Jane P. Clifford, 23, of Eugene, Oregon. She had been in town a little over a month, working as a night waitress at the Cozy Nook on Main Street and renting a room in a private residence on Queen Street.

Police and coworkers described her as petite and attractive. On the

*night of her murder she worked at the Cozy Nook until 11 and left
alone. Coworkers said she regularly walked to and from work.*

*"She was a loner," said Police Chief Paul L. Williams. "No one
knew much about her. We do think she had a boyfriend."*

*According to Miss Clifford's landlady, Mary C. Hurley, Miss Clif-
ford was often out of the house until two or three in the morning. She
would sleep until noon and often spent the afternoon on the beach.*

*"We'd like to talk to the boyfriend," Chief Williams said, "but he
seems to have left the area. My guess is he's in Oregon or California
about now."*

*Chief Williams said that Miss Clifford's parents had been notified
and that her father, Norman G. Clifford, was flying east to retrieve
his daughter's remains.*

"They want to bury her in Eugene," Chief Williams said.

Claire was still working on the obituary of David Kasselman.
She wrote slowly, a few words at a time, pausing to examine her
notes or a news clipping or to reach for a cigarette, groping for
it and lighting it abstractedly while she studied the page in her
typewriter.

Lane proofed his copy and carried it to his father's desk. The
big machines were asleep out back, where all was shadows and
silence. Again he and Claire were alone in the paste-fragrant
newsroom, the empty building, as they'd been the first day he'd
known her.

"How's it coming?" he said.

"Okay," she said, "except for the interruptions."

He smiled. "I'll knock off the drowning story," he said.

"Knock it off, huh? Nothing to it."

"It'll be short. Three, four paragraphs."

It took him fifteen minutes. He left it for his father and went and stood by the window with his back to Claire and watched the six-forty bus pull away.

"Why don't you go home?" she said.

"Did you call any of his teachers?" Lane said.

"Am I writing this or are you?"

"My sister said he was a good student. It might be a good idea to find out what his interests were. His best subjects."

"I know what his interests were."

"Call a teacher."

"He won the science prize last year," Claire said.

"Call his science teacher. Find out what he won the prize for. That'd be Jim Kalperis. Say hello to him for me."

"You know you're a pain in the ass, right?"

"Want me to get you something to eat?"

"No, I do not."

"You didn't eat any lunch."

"I'm not hungry."

"A coffee, then. A Coke."

"A Coke, if it would shut you up."

"I can get that at the bus station," he said.

The inside of the depot had a neglected look of dust and peeling paint. They'd let it go after the trains stopped running, as if a bus station were inevitably a dingy place and there was no point pretending otherwise. Lane remembered the dark winter mornings of their departures and his father buying their tickets while he and his sisters and their pretty mother waited in the sallow light of the overhead globes. He remembered the gentle thrilling lurch as the train began to move, the fluid forward motion building to a swaying rocketing glide past woods and back yards and intersections where cars waited, looking small as toys from the high train window.

He pushed a quarter into the slot. The can dropped with a resonant kerplunk. It was ice-cold and sweating in his hand.

"How much do I owe you?" she said.

"Nothing."

"How much? A quarter?"

"Nothing."

"Goddamn it," she said.

"Write your obit and then we can go home."

"No, then *I* can go home. You can go home now."

"I'm going to wait for you."

"I told you I don't need my goddamn hand held."

"I'll wait out front," he said.

He sat at the bare desk where Manny Dutra ate his lunch and made his phone calls and wrote in his ledger, keeping track of the drivers and delivery boys and their customers. He put his feet up and looked out into the purple twilight. Manny, Everett, Jean, Ellie. They'd all been here since Lane had first entered the building as a small boy to see the printing press in action, the jangling Linotype machines. They'd smiled at him and given him dark pencils and shiny lead slugs with inverted words raised on one narrow edge. His grandfather had hired them. Lane couldn't remember any of them looking any different than they did now, middle-aged and benevolent, as familiar and fixed in his life as the landmarks he'd grown up with, the vistas of wood and shore, the weathered New England buildings.

After a while he went outside and leaned against the black scabrous trunk of the old elm. He could hear, faintly, the clack of Claire's typewriter. He looked down the avenue at the traffic percolating through the intersection by Dimmock's Gulf. Just this side of Dimmock's was the Buick dealership whose owner's daughter Lane had dated one year. She had rosy cheeks and pouting lips and a grapefruitlike bust, but she was a good girl, as thoroughly virginal as Lane was, and in spite of all his vivid fantasies he never did anything but kiss her. She'd gone to Bennington or Sarah Lawrence, and Lane had often wondered when she'd surrendered that impregnable virginity, and who the lucky boy had been.

At seven-thirty he went back inside and found Claire proofing her story. She heard him come in but didn't look up. Her hair was awry. She looked exhausted.

"Want me to look at it?" he said.

"No," she said, the voice not sharp anymore but weary.

"Want another Coke?"

She put the pencil down. "Lane."

"What?"

"You go on home now, okay, hon? I mean it this time."

He nodded. "All right."

"I didn't mean to be so bitchy."

"I'm sorry if I irritated you."

"It wasn't you," she said.

"You sure you don't want me to look at your story?"

"I want to be able to say I wrote it myself," she said, "do you understand?"

"Sure."

"Does the door lock itself?"

"Just pull it shut," he said.

· · ·

THAT NIGHT she sat on the kitchen porch with a glass of chablis and watched the fireflies drift and flicker in the darkness. The neighborhood kids had melted away, and it was quiet now with the house windows glowing yellow under the porch roofs. After a while the screen door creaked open and April came out and sat down beside her.

"Hi, sweetheart," Claire said.

"I might as well tell you," April said, "I met a boy on the beach today."

"Why wouldn't you tell me?"

"He's seventeen, that's why."

"Seventeen," Claire said.

"His name is Kyle. He's really nice."

"Does Kyle have a last name?"

"Bagwell."

"Kyle *Bagwell?*"

"What's wrong with that?"

"Nothing, sweetheart. He drives a car, I suppose."

"He *owns* a car."

"Can I meet him sometime?"

"Mom. I just met him today myself."

"This isn't a boyfriend, then."

"I don't know. I'm going to the movies with him tomorrow night."

"In his car."

"Of course in his car."

"You're not going off in some kid's car unless I meet him, April."

"What's the big deal about a car?"

"How come you don't meet girls at the beach?"

"I can go tomorrow, can't I?"

"I don't know. We'll see."

"Great. I finally meet somebody I like and you won't let me see him."

"I didn't say you couldn't see him."

"I already told him I'd go with him."

"You bring him over here and we'll see."

Kyle Bagwell, she thought. Jesus.

.   .   .

SHE'D named April eight full months before she was born, knowing in some mysterious and absolute way that the baby inside her was a girl. A girl was overdue in a life lived always among hard, insensitive men, but that wasn't it, it wasn't wishful thinking. Claire simply knew.

She'd grown up in a male household odorous of gas heat and cigarettes and man sweat. Her father was a charmer, quick with a joke, a line; too smooth and handsome and possessed of too much ready money for his own good. He was nice to Claire, spoiled her in fact, but she knew better than to rely on him.

Her brothers saw through his warmth and good looks as well as Claire did, but it didn't seem to bother them. They were good boys, basically, just not very bright; football and hockey players who worked construction jobs in the summer and took minimal interest in girls except to tape centerfolds to their bedroom walls. They slouched over their food, fought each other with their fists, and gave off a rank, dark, unwashed smell no matter how often they showered.

Scott Malek was supposed to rescue her from all of this, and from all such dreariness forever. Scott had been a year ahead of her in school, an all-conference linebacker known and respected by her brothers. Claire had gone on to junior college but was still living at home when she started dating Scott. Scott had the brains for college, more or less, but he'd skipped it out of laziness and gotten a decent job at an insurance company in the city.

The engagement put Claire's mother on edge. Claire didn't know why, but there it was. Her mother began to pick at her. Don't wear tight sweaters, Clairie, you don't have the tits for it. Or: Poor kid, you got your father's chin but not his smile. Whatever that meant. In response, Claire dressed louder, cheaper.

You think Scott's going to appreciate you in *that?*

I know he is.

How about respect you?

How about minding your own business?

The squabbling took a hidden toll, like the damage of a slow-growing, unseen cancer. Then, when Claire and Scott had been married a little over a year, the two of them were in bed together, having just made love, Scott lying on his back with his hands clasped behind his neck staring at the ceiling.

You know, he said, your mother came on to me one time.

He said it casually, as if recalling some harmless idiosyncratic act of Violet's: a remark she'd made or a puzzling gift she'd given at Christmastime. Claire's heart turned instantly to ice. Maybe Scott had thought it would turn her on to hear that her mother wanted to fuck him. If so, he saw his mistake right away.

It wasn't any big deal, he said quickly. I let her know how things stood and everything was cool.

Claire didn't move a muscle. When did this happen? she asked quietly.

I don't know. Before we were married. It was nothing. I shouldn't have brought it up.

You're goddamn right you shouldn't have brought it up. But now that you did, where did this adorable little scene take place?

Don't get snotty.

Where?

In my car. Now let's drop it, okay?

Your car.

I went over one time, you weren't home. Your mother came sailing out of the house when I was halfway to the door. She'd just had a beauty of a fight with your father. She said she wanted to go for a drive to cool down, so we did. She gave it a shot, I said no. End of story.

Right, Claire said. End of story.

Don't say anything to your mother, Scott said.

Why not? Claire said.

What's the point? he said.

The point is I don't like my mother making passes at my husband.

I wasn't your husband. I don't even know if we were engaged yet.

Oh gee, Claire said, I guess that makes it all right then.

Just drop it, okay?

I'm not going to drop a goddamn thing.

Oh yes you are.

Claire didn't answer.

You hear me? he said.

She didn't answer.

I'm talking to you, Scott said.

She rolled off the bed and he lunged for her and missed. She grabbed her robe and was out the door before he was on his feet, thumping after her barefoot and naked. He followed her down the stairs and into the kitchen. Claire turned the light on. She put the kettle on to boil. Scott stood in the doorway big and white-skinned and growing a belly already. He had corn-silk hair, a sickle mustache like a Civil War officer or Dodge City lawman. Claire glanced at him and was surprised to feel nothing. She pulled a box of teabags off a shelf.

Scott said, You're not going to say anything to your mother, got it?

Claire ignored him.

Hey, he said.

She found a mug and hung a teabag in it.

I'll try it one more time, he said. You're not going to say anything to your mother, am I right?

Claire was at the stove now, waiting for the kettle to sing. She folded her arms and watched it.

Don't ignore me, Scott said. That's one thing I won't put up with.

She watched the kettle. Steam began to creep out.

Hey, he said and grabbed her chin and made her look at him.

She waited till he let go, then went back to watching the kettle. There was a long silence, the kettle beginning to snort clouds of steam while Scott mulled over his problem.

Look at me, he said.

She didn't.

Cunt, he said and hit her.

Claire never saw it coming. The punch exploded red inside

her skull and the world went black and the floor tilted, throwing her against the refrigerator, which tipped briefly back, then held as she slid down its cool surface to the floor, where she sat in a gray woolly doze that lasted seconds or minutes, she didn't know which, and woke to the scream of the teakettle. In front of her were Scott's white naked golden-haired legs. She drew herself in and huddled against the refrigerator in her bathrobe. The left side of her face was on fire.

Don't ever ignore me, she heard Scott say.

She didn't look up at him. He'd never hit her, had never been rough in any way. The kettle shrieked and rocked. Scott turned the burner off. He left the room. She heard him climb the stairs, heavy on his bare feet, and then the overhead thump of his footsteps. She heard the bed creak as he threw himself on it, then silence.

The kitchen light was still on. Claire wanted it off but wanted even more not to move. To move, rise, would be saying it was over. Scott would be listening to hear the kettle being lifted, a chair scrape. Claire didn't move. No man had ever hit her before. No one had, not her brothers, not anyone.

After a while she thought about the baby. She laid her hand on her stomach over the not-yet-swelling spot where life was growing inside her. It was the center of her body now, the center of herself. And in that instant she knew it was a girl. A girl, due in April. April, she thought, April, April, till it was April's name. A pretty name. Her daughter would be pretty.

Far into the night Claire stayed on the floor curled against the refrigerator. The pain in her face burned on, began to throb. Her cheek swelled, stretching the skin and closing her eye to a slit. She knew she should put ice on it, but she wasn't going to give the bastard upstairs the satisfaction of hearing her get up. Once he padded down and stood in the doorway, Claire didn't look at him. He stood there awhile without speaking. Then he turned off the light and went away.

I don't understand him, she thought. I don't know him. And realized she'd never known any of them, not in any deep, important way. She hadn't tried, hadn't bothered. The high school boys who had taken turns being her steady, the slightly smarter ones at Dean Junior: they wore her like a ribbon, a trophy, and in private couldn't keep their hands off her. It was her fault as much as theirs. Had she ever tried to be more than a looker, a fun date, a good lay? Being wanted, needed, had always been enough for her. What is wrong with me? she thought.

Above her Scott began to snore. She could hear him clearly through the ceiling. He snored like an animal. How to leave him was the problem. They'd been married in the Catholic Church. Well, she wasn't going to get the shit beaten out of her just to stay on the good side of the Catholic Church.

It was Scott who solved the problem months later when she'd begun to get big with April. This time he broke her jaw and she went next door and called the police. The cops brought her home, and the next day her father and brothers went and cleared her things out of what was now Scott's house, accompanied by a police officer in case Scott tried to make trouble. The divorce came through a couple of months later. By then Scott had made a serious pest of himself, calling her at all hours and following her in his car and trying to talk to her in front of stores and friends' houses, waylaying her on the sidewalk to beg for one more chance. Finally her brothers, who were stupider than

Scott and therefore feared by him, told him they'd kill him if he ever bothered her again.

The divorce was easy because Claire wouldn't take any money from him. Not one penny. Her parents pleaded, shouted, threatened. Her lawyer tried to reason with her and threatened finally to walk away from the case. Claire stood firm. How can you despise a man and take his money? It was a victory over her old pragmatic self, the good-time girl who had never asked, demanded, much more from a man than a superficial respect and his undivided attention. She was on higher ground now where money was beside the point. She despised Scott and all men like him and she despised their money.

After the divorce he washed his hands of her and of his own gestating baby and disappeared from their lives. He remarried less than a year later, Claire heard, and started a family. He never called or came back to see April; a high school friend of Claire's told her Scott had resorted to the old exonerating man's trick of denying that April was his child. April herself seldom mentioned him. Without Claire's saying much, she seemed to get the picture and to be content to leave Scott Malek in her mother's past.

You realize, Violet had said, you can't get married again.

Since when? Claire said.

Not in your own church you can't.

I wouldn't call it my church, Ma.

Maybe you ought to.

Ma, she said another time, I have to ask you something.

They were alone in the kitchen doing the supper dishes. Her father was in the front room watching basketball on TV.

Did you ever make a pass at Scott?

Who told you that?

Scott did.

And you believed him.

I didn't know, Ma.

Her mother slapped her face. Claire turned from the blow, raising her hands for protection and tucking her head. But Violet was gone, out of the room and in another moment pounding up the stairs. Claire went after her, heavy with her baby, through the front room, past the game on TV.

May I ask what the hell's going on? her father said.

Claire struggled up the stairs. Her mother had shut herself in the bathroom. Claire knocked on the door, timid at first then harder and harder.

Ma, she said through the door. I'm sorry.

No answer.

Ma. Please.

No answer.

Claire tried the knob, shook it. She sagged against the door and caught her breath. She'd broken a sweat.

Ma, she said, I'm sick. I'm going to throw up.

No answer.

I'm not kidding, Ma.

Her mother opened the door. Her eyes were reproachful and she didn't speak, but she stayed with Claire, closing the door and standing with a hand on her shoulder as Claire knelt, vomiting and vomiting into the toilet.

Chapter Five

ELLIE WHITING waddled into the newsroom leading a thin, bent, sad-faced man in a wrinkled seersucker jacket and crooked necktie.

"This is Mr. Clifford," she said.

Lane got up from his chair and offered Norman Clifford his hand. "Lane Hillman," he said. "Thanks for coming in."

Everyone in the newsroom turned to regard Jane Clifford's father, who hesitated before shaking hands, as if he were out of the habit and did not understand right away what Lane wanted. His grip was unfirm, tentative, though the hand itself was knotty and callused. Lane looked over at his father, who gestured with his head toward the rear of the building.

He led Mr. Clifford out through the back shop to the little office his grandfather had built not many years ago for his semi-retirement. Norman Clifford shuffled in and sat down slowly, as if it hurt to work his joints. Lane closed the door. He opened a window and sat down in his grandfather's swivel deskchair and set his notebook down in front of him.

"I appreciate your coming in," he said. "I know this isn't easy."

"No, sir, it isn't."

"The police gave us a picture of Jane. She was very pretty."

"She don't look like us because she was adopted, you see."

"We won't print that, in case you were wondering."

"You're welcome to use the picture."

"Thanks," Lane said.

"She always did take a good picture," Mr. Clifford said.

Norman G. Clifford, father of the 23-year-old woman found strangled to death last Thursday in the woods near Route 110, flew home to Oregon yesterday with his daughter's remains. Mr. Clifford, 62, owns an appliance repair business in the town of Eugene. He is the husband of Lucille Barker Clifford. Jane P. Clifford was their only child. Police have no suspects in the murder.

In an interview with the Covenant, *Mr. Clifford said that his daughter was graduated in 1966 from the University of California at Berkeley, where she majored in art history. She moved to San Francisco after graduation, where she held various waitressing positions in the Haight-Ashbury district. Last fall a friend or friends offered her a ride to New York City, and Miss Clifford accepted, apparently on the spur of the moment.*

She settled in the area known as Hell's Kitchen, according to Mr. Clifford, and took a job as a waitress at the Bitter End coffee house in Greenwich Village. The Bitter End is known as a mecca in

*the folk music scene. Mr. Clifford said his daughter became ac-
quainted with several famous performers but could not recall their
names.*

*Mr. Clifford does not know when his daughter left New York and
came to Cape Cod. She seems to have arrived here on June 5, the
date she rented a room on Queen Street. Two days later she was
hired as a night waitress at the Cozy Nook.*

*Mr. Clifford said his daughter's habit of trusting people, includ-
ing strangers, may have led to her death.*

*"She was a flower child," he said. "She didn't believe there was
any bad in the world."*

*Mr. Clifford was visibly upset. He spoke haltingly and twice suc-
cumbed to tears.*

"A hippie, you might say," said Sally Hillman.

"Yes, Mother, you might say," Meg said.

"Don't you be fresh," John Hillman said.

"I'm *kidding*," Meg said.

They always ate dinner as a family, their father presiding at
one end of the oval table, their mother dishing food at the other
end. Lane still ate ravenously of her starchy casseroles, her
bread pudding and apple crisp. He would sharpen his appetite
after work, when he would pull on shorts and sneakers and run
down the old rail line to where the tracks followed the shore,
and then along the beach, in shadow now below the wooded
ridges, the water dark blue and glittering. He would run three
or four miles and afterward feel the old hollow-bellied hunger
of playing out-of-doors until dark, of football practice lasting
into the cooling autumn dusk.

"She doesn't look like a hippie to me," Jessica said.

"The picture was from high school," Lane said.

"Why'd you use such an old one?" Jessie said.

"You use what you can get," Lane said.

"It's pretty scary," Elizabeth said. Lizzie was the oldest of the three girls but still two years younger than Lane. All four of them had come at two-year intervals.

"There's nothing to be scared of," Lane said. "She got mixed up with somebody she shouldn't have. You wouldn't have made that mistake."

"How do you know?" Meg said. Meg the dissenter, Meg the stickler.

"Because I know Lizzie," Lane said.

"I mean, how do you know so much about the murderer?"

"Deduction," Lane said.

"Then who killed David Kasselman if you're so smart?"

"No one killed him. It was an accident."

"Someone drowned him," Meg said.

Lane looked at their father. "Dad, will you help me out here?"

But John Hillman only shrugged. He was tired. Pretty soon he'd go back to the office and work till ten or eleven.

"Meg," Lane said, "that's what they have autopsies for. If someone had drowned him, there'd be signs of a struggle. He was drunk. That's why he drowned."

"David Kasselman would never drink alcohol."

"It was in his blood, Meg."

"Then someone made him."

"You can't make someone drink."

"You can entice them to drink," said their mother, "which can amount to the same thing."

"I wonder if there was a connection between David and the girl," Lizzie said.

"There wasn't," Lane said.

"Couldn't they have met somewhere?"

"I talk to the police almost every day," Lane said. "There was no connection."

"Doesn't it seem strange to you that they both died on the same night?"

"A little," Lane admitted.

.   .   .

AFTER DINNER he drove the office car to a dark little bar built on pilings above a harbor that was connected to the open water by a single narrow channel under a drawbridge. The landlocked harbor was very still, and on a summer night you could smell its rich mud through the open windows, mingled with the tang of beer and a soft fragrance of sawdust.

Lane bought a Budweiser from the bartender and looked around the dim noisy room. At one of the round tables sat Beth Weeks and another girl he knew, Cathy Corey, plus three boys from their school days, younger kids who'd been a couple of grades behind Lane and Beth and Cathy and who could not now have been old enough to buy a legal drink. They were all drinking beer out of the bottle, and there was a little forest of empties in the middle of the table. There was no sign of Beth's fiancé, Brad Wormel.

Lane leaned back against the bar and took a swig from the bottle and waited till Beth saw him and waved him over. She smiled at him as he sat down. He said hello to Cathy and shook the three boys' hands. Two of them had played jayvee Lane's senior year and still looked up to him in the same respectful and diffident way, as if the difference between them in size and ability were fixed forever, elevating him above them for eternity. He wondered why Beth and Cathy were sitting with Billy McGrath, Greg Pappas, and Skip Handy. To amuse themselves, he supposed, till something better came along. He saw that Beth was wearing her engagement ring.

"Long time, no see," Cathy said.

"Lane's a busy man," Beth said.

"You don't hang out anymore," Cathy said.

"Sure I do," Lane said. He looked at the boys. "How're you guys doing?"

"Good," they said.

"What have you got, two more years of college?"

"Two if we're lucky," Billy McGrath said.

"Then they'll send your little asses to Vietnam," Beth said.

"Not mine," Skip Handy said.

"You going to Vietnam, Lane?" Cathy said.

"Not if I can help it."

"Don't tell me you're one of those draft dodgers."

"Leave him alone," Beth said.

"I asked him a simple question," Cathy said.

"How's Brad?" Lane said.

"I don't know and I don't care," Beth said.

"She's pissed off at him," Cathy said. "Now's your chance, Lane."

"My brother's in Vietnam," Billy said.

"He wanted to go," said Greg Pappas.

"That's true," Billy said.

"There are a lot of ways to get out of it," Skip said. "I knew a guy at school took speed for three days before the physical. He flunked it cold."

"I know a guy had 'Fuck You' tattooed on his hand," Greg said, "right here along the edge where it'd be right in an officer's face when he saluted."

"They must have loved that," Cathy said.

"They didn't take him," Greg said.

"Cool," Beth said.

"I know a guy," Billy said, "stuffed a bunch of M&Ms up his ass just before he went to take the physical."

"I don't want to hear this," Cathy said.

"I do," Beth said.

"So right in the middle of the physical—" Billy said.

"I'll leave the table," Cathy said.

Billy grinned. "All right," he said. "I won't tell it."

Lane drank another beer and began to think about leaving. The three boys drank steadily, hunched down with their elbows on the table like veteran drinkers. Their remarks were irreverent and droll, and they watched the girls to see what effect they were having. A mild one, Lane judged.

"Well," he said, "good night, everybody."

"The big newspaper writer needs his sleep," Cathy said.

"Will you cut it out?" Beth said.

"You guys take care," Lane said to the boys.

"I'll walk out with you," Beth said. "I'm getting smashed. I need some fresh air."

"I told you here's your chance, Lane," Cathy said.

"Night, Cathy," Lane said.

A salt mist hung in the street, gauzy under the streetlamps.

Beth took his arm. They walked onto the drawbridge and stood at the rail looking out over the harbor with its pale motionless boat hulls and wavering trails of reflected light.

"What happened with you and Brad?" Lane asked.

"He's an asshole, that's what happened."

"Maybe you shouldn't have gotten engaged."

"It'll be all right," she said.

The water lapped gently against the pilings and channel walls under the bridge. The smell of mud and seaweed rose strong in the moist air.

"Can I ask you something?" Beth said.

"Sure."

"Were you a virgin in high school?"

Lane nodded. "Yeah."

"You never screwed Debbie Lawrence?"

"I never did."

"Why not?"

"I guess I didn't know I could," Lane said.

"Maybe you couldn't have. Maybe Debbie wouldn't have let you."

"Probably not."

"I was a virgin. Nobody wanted to screw me in high school."

"I liked you in high school. You used to wear pumps and nylon stockings."

"You like me now, don't you?"

"Yes, I do."

She turned and he kissed her, her lips pulpy and beer-tasting, her body surprisingly solid against him. She let him put his tongue in her mouth and after the kiss leaned back and smiled at him in the pale lamplight.

"Want to go somewhere?" she said.

Lane hesitated.

"You worried about Brad?" she said.

"I'm not *worried* about him. He's a nice guy, is all."

Beth released him and stepped back.

"It isn't that I wouldn't like to," Lane said.

"It's pretty obvious you'd *like* to," she said.

Lane felt himself blush. "Maybe if it doesn't work out with Brad," he said.

"It'll work out," Beth said.

He thought about her as he drove home, the beery taste of her mouth and the strength he'd felt in her hips and back, and wished he'd said yes. He considered turning around and driving back to the bar, but it was too late and he knew it; knew by instinct or surmise if not experience that you can't hesitate, demur, when a woman offers herself, or she'll withdraw the offer out of pride, and the moment, the chance, will be gone for a long time, if not forever.

. . .

HIS MOTHER was reading a book in front of the cold fireplace while the yellow Lab snoozed on the rug at her feet. The girls were upstairs or had gone out. Lane opened a beer and took it out onto the side porch and sat looking out to where the trees rose massed and shadowlike against the gray-black sky. He could smell honeysuckle, and as he drank the beer, he felt an ache in his heart that was part regret, part longing, and part foreknowledge of sweet times to come. He drained the bottle and went back inside.

"I'm going for a walk," he told his mother.

She looked up from her book. "At this hour?"

"I'm restless," he said.

It was too dark to walk the rail line, so he took the road, moving in and out of the shadows, past the lighted houses, the wild tracts of field and thicket. He passed the sandlot where he'd played baseball, the mown field where he and Ron Viera had played touch football in the summer twilight. He turned onto the Shore Road and walked toward Claire Malek's neighborhood. He knew the street she lived on but not the house. It was a couple of miles away in a newer section of town than his, but not brand-new—modest homes built in the 1920s and '30s when the town began to fill in between Main Street and the shore.

The water was black as ink in the moonless night. The waves soughed gentle as sighs. He imagined meeting her, she drawn out into the fragrant night as he had been, walking on impulse, a hunch, in his direction. They would be surprised to see each other, yet not surprised. They would walk together. She'd invite him in to meet her daughter, would offer him a drink. He looked for her up ahead, imagined her coming toward him through the thin light of a streetlamp in that purposeful skirt-flicking stride.

He turned inland on her street. His sense of smell and touch seemed heightened; he breathed the perfume of unseen honeysuckle and mown grass, and was aware of the breathless night air on his face and arms and the back of his neck. He looked for her on dark front porches, down side streets, in lighted windows where sometimes he could see people seated about, conversing or watching TV. When a car approached he slowed, made sure he was visible in its headlights, and looked as it passed to see if it was a yellow Camaro.

It never was. Nor was she out walking, or rocking on any front porch, or in the wine-yellow light of front rooms where he ached to glimpse her at least, dressed, as he imagined, in slacks or shorts and curled in a soft chair with a book held up before her face. Just to see her now would have been enough, but she was nowhere. He walked on and saw the diffuse whitish light of Main Street ahead and knew he wasn't going to see, much less speak to her. He felt a stab of irritation, as if she'd ignored or been willfully deaf to what had called him out here and had surely spoken to her as well.

"I was starting to worry about you," his mother said.

"I'm all right," he said.

"Is there something on your mind, child?"

"Just restless," he said.

"The summer'll be over soon," she said.

"I don't want the summer to be over," he said.

· · ·

IN SPITE of his name, Claire imagined Kyle Bagwell as an updated version of the smart-alecky, oversexed lifeguard-type seventeen-year-olds who had pursued her for dates when she was fifteen. He wasn't. He was mop-haired and stoop-shouldered and bookish, with a sudden nervous smile that vanished quickly without a trace, and deep dark eyes that were in constant, uneasy motion. Claire took one look at him and knew it would be all right to let April go out with him in his rusted little Triumph.

"Where'd he get the money to buy a Triumph?" she asked April the following evening at supper. They ate in the kitchen. The table stood against the wall where a window looked out over the yard and garage.

"It's old, Mom. He bought it secondhand."

"It couldn't have been cheap, even so."

"He works hard. He makes good money. What's your problem, Mom?"

"Where does he work?"

"Paul's Pizza, if you must know."

"Paul's Pizza," Claire said.

"Don't think he isn't intelligent," April said.

"I can see he's intelligent. Did you really meet him at the beach?"

April put her fork down. "What's that supposed to mean?"

Claire had cooked a pork roast with roasted potatoes, apple sauce, and cucumber salad. It was hard to put a decent meal together after the long workday, but the dinner table is the center of a family and she wanted badly to maintain that center, to make it pleasant and civilized. She wanted April to have a family, if it was only the two of them.

"It doesn't mean anything," Claire said. "He doesn't look like the beach type, is all."

"I suppose you want me to go out with some big dumb football player with a suntan."

"That's exactly what I don't want."

April picked up her fork. "You don't want me to go out with anybody."

"Don't be silly, April. I just don't want you to make the mistakes I made."

"What mistakes besides marrying my father?"

"Stupid ones that you're too smart to make. Why don't we invite Kyle to dinner?"

"Kyle's kind of shy."

"I'll be on my best behavior."

"Just relax, Mom, okay?"

"I'm perfectly relaxed," Claire said.

. . .

CHIEF WILLIAMS called the newspaper office and asked specifically for Claire. "I've got a story for you," he said. "Come on over."

"What kind of story?" she said.

"The Kasselman drowning. We know who was with him. We know how it went down."

"I'll tell Mr. Hillman," she said.

"You tell John I want to give *you* the story."

"I can't tell him who to send out on a story."

"Come on down," he said. "I'll tell you all about what happened." He hung up.

She spun her chair and repeated the conversation to Mr. Hillman. He folded his arms and thought awhile.

"I told him it wasn't up to me who covers a story," Claire said.

John Hillman rubbed the back of his neck. It was late in the afternoon. Lane wasn't in the office.

"All right," he said.

"All right what?" she said.

"Go get the story. Get it and write it."

The sour-faced lady cop at the desk told her to go on in. Williams's office door was open. He didn't get up when Claire entered, just smiled and looked her up and down.

"How are you, Claire?" he said. "You don't mind if I call you Claire, do you?"

"No," she said.

She sat down in one of the captain's chairs and crossed her legs and arranged her notebook on her lap. She looked at the American flag and the flag of the Commonwealth hanging in folds from their staffs on either side of Williams's desk. She looked past him, avoiding his pale blue gaze, to the pond, the swans. The swans were very white against the dark blue water.

"How are you coming down there at the *Covenant?*" Williams asked.

She looked at him and was surprised. The bad-boy smile had vanished. He was studying her in a close yet objective and even sympathetic way that instantly matured him, gave him for the first time some gravity, some depth.

"I'm afraid I'm a slow learner," she said.

"I doubt that," he said.

"The writing's hard for me."

"I don't always know who writes what, but what I've seen of your stuff looks pretty good."

"Thanks," she said.

"The thing about you guys is, you have to write fast and you have to write passably well. That can't be easy."

"It isn't," she said.

"Now, that young Lane Hillman, geez, he churns out the stories."

"He's very talented," Claire said.

Williams watched her. "Kid knows it, too."

She watched two swans drift, one behind the other. It's true, she thought. He does know it. Knowing it is part of who he is, that comfort he has with himself. No anger in him looking for a place to light.

"David Kasselman," Williams said. He sat back and folded his hands over his gut. "You stop me if I talk too fast."

. . .

THEIR FATHERS had brought Kenny Earle and Mike Sullivan in this morning. They filed into Williams's office and Mike's father Joe closed the door. Joe Sullivan was wiry like his son, beetle-browed and melancholy. He worked as a caretaker, was in poor health, and drank. Kenny Earle's father, Ken Senior, owned the Texaco station on East Main. The two fathers had never met each other until now.

The boys have something to tell you, Joe Sullivan said.

His son slumped down with his head bowed.

Tell him, Mikey, said his father.

The boy looked up at Williams. We were with Kasselman the night he drowned, he said.

Who's we? Williams said.

Me and Kenny.

Is that right, Kenneth?

Yes sir.

Ken Earle Senior cleared his throat. I want you to know it was their idea to turn theirselves in.

Your conscience got the better of you, did it? Williams said.

Yes sir, Kenny said.

So you were with him that night.

Yes sir.

On the beach at Pine Neck.

Yes sir.

Swimming.

We didn't know he was going swimming.

You went into the water and left him on the beach.

Yes sir.

Williams folded his hands and swiveled in his chair, then swung back the other way. You boys don't have to talk to me, he said. You have the right to remain silent.

We know that, Mikey said.

You have the right to have a lawyer present.

They don't want a lawyer, Joe Sullivan said.

I'm asking them, Williams said.

No sir. We don't want a lawyer.

Kenneth?

No sir.

Well, then, Williams said. He looked up, gazed a while at the ceiling. Boys, he said, David Kasselman had an alcohol level of point-one-eight in his blood. That's legally drunk. Any idea where he got all that liquor?

Yes sir, Kenny said. We gave it to him.

Gave it to him, Williams said.

He wanted it.

He'd never drunk alcohol in his life, according to his parents.

We didn't force it on him.

You offered it to him.

Yes sir.

You boys steal that alcohol?

No sir. We paid somebody to buy it for us.

And who was that?

We don't know his name, Mikey said.

That's the first lie you've told me, isn't it?

Yes sir, it is.

So you hooked up with David at the fair and got him drunk.

Not at the fair. He was down the road hitching.

What time was that?

About eight o'clock. It wasn't dark yet.

Where'd he want to go?

Home.

But you took him drinking instead.

He wanted to come.

You guys are how old?

Eighteen.

And he wanted to come with you. Little guy fifteen years old.

He said he did, Kenny said.

And then you ply him with alcohol.

He wanted it. He kept asking for more.

More what?

He was drinking vodka and orange juice.

The boy had never drunk before, and you were giving him vodka.

The boys hung their heads.

They're sorry, Chief, Joe Sullivan said.

I hope so, Williams said.

It's why they're here, Joe said. It's why they don't want a lawyer.

Williams looked at Kenny Junior. His head was lowered. There were tears in his eyes.

Whose idea was it to go swimming? he said.

Mine, Mikey said.

And why Pine Neck?

'Cause it's out of the way.

Why'd you want a beach that was out of the way?

We didn't have swimsuits.

So you went skinny-dipping, but David said no thanks.

That's what he said at the time. We swum downshore a ways and he must have changed his mind watching us. When we got back, he was gone.

You must have swum a long way.

Yes sir.

And you forgot all about David.

We didn't forget him, Kenny said.

He said he wasn't going in, Mikey said.

We came out and saw his clothes, Kenny said.

We tried to find him, Mikey said. Yelled for him, dived down. We kicked onto him finally in about four feet of water. Drownded. I gave him mouth-to-mouth, but it wasn't anything we could do.

So you panicked, Williams said.

Yes sir.

You went home.

Yes sir.

Which got you home at what time?

Kenny came in about quarter past one, his father said.

Mikey got home about one-thirty, Joe Sullivan said.

All right, Williams said. Now let me ask you one more question. Was it just the two of you and David?

Mikey nodded.

You agree with that, Kenneth?

I agree with it.

Again, Williams fell back in his chair, spun halfway around, spun back again. He looked at the two boys.

All right, he said, I'll tell you what's going to happen. You listen, and you be grateful. We're going to book you and release you on your own recognizance. That means no one has to post bail.

Thank you, Chief, Joe Sullivan said.

Day after tomorrow you'll go over to district court and be arraigned. The charge'll be contributing to the delinquency of a minor. It could go all the way up to manslaughter, so you boys pay attention to how lucky you are.

Both fathers breathed out and their shoulders untensed, settled.

God bless you, Chief, Joe said.

You'll want to thank Judge Boyle, too, Williams said. Your lawyer—you get a lawyer now—will ask for a continuance. It'll be granted. Neither of you has a record, that's the good news. You'll be looking at probation, maybe continued without a finding. Then you keep your noses clean. You act like boy scouts. Anyone sees you and alcohol in the same room and it won't be pretty what happens.

Right, Mikey said.

One other thing, Williams said. You might want to go see the Kasselmans. Or write to them, maybe. Something.

They ain't going to want to hear from us, Joe said.

It'd be nice to make the effort, wouldn't it? Williams said.

.   .   .

THE SUMMER'LL be over soon, his mother had said, but Lane didn't believe that, because six weeks is a long time when you're twenty-two. And yet time did concern him: the vivid present, these splendid summer days unfolding while he stood and watched, a passive spectator, a nonparticipant. Until he made a pact with himself and on the following day, the second Friday in July, he waited for Claire to leave work at the end of the day and followed her out of the building.

She was getting into her car over by the depot platform. She pulled the door shut and fitted on her dark glasses. Lane went straight toward her, with unmistakable purpose, conscious that he could be seen from inside the building but determined nonetheless. She watched him through her dark glasses.

"Did I forget something?" she said.

"I just wanted to say I hope you have a good weekend."

"I'll do my best."

"Any plans?" he said.

"I don't know. Go to a show, maybe. Go to the beach. Is there a reason you're asking?"

"What beach do you go to?" He pushed his hands down into his front pockets, turned and gazed down the elm-shaded avenue.

"This is leading somewhere, right?" she said.

He shrugged. "I just thought I might look for you if I'm down there."

"What do you suppose your father would think if he knew you were hanging out on the beach with me?"

"He wouldn't think anything," Lane said.

"What happened to that sexpot waitress at Chamberlain's? You ever call her?"

"She's engaged. I told you that."

"Too bad."

"What beach do you go to?"

"Well, I usually go down Queen Street and spread my towel somewhere along there. *If* I go."

"Maybe I'll see you."

"I'm not saying I'm definitely going to be there."

"I know."

"Just don't expect me, okay?"

"Okay," he said.

. . .

ON SATURDAY she arrived with April a little after one o'clock and they lay side by side under the burning sun, Claire penny-brown in her black two-piece, April even darker, angular, and long-limbed in a two-piece like Claire's, only white. She lay there with the sun beating down on her bare back and legs and wondered what he'd think of her figure, how it would look to a man his age and if he'd be disappointed. It was true that she could stand to lose a few pounds, but most men liked that little extra. The secret was to stay firm in the right places, and then the extra came as a not unpleasant surprise, a piquant bonus of flesh, of added value.

She read *Newsweek*. She put her head down and closed her eyes and listened to the muffled faraway crash of the waves, the wind-tattered cries of children. She could hear the crunch of sand when April shifted around beside her, the faint rustle when she turned a page of her book. She left April and went into the water, swimming hard for the exercise, then treading water and looking landward in case he should come along without noticing her out here. He wouldn't know April, of course.

She thought about how it would look, she with a boy young enough to be her son but clearly not her son, and how she would put him in his place without hurting him if he was crazy enough to make a pass at her. Some men's feelings you didn't worry about, either because they had none or they were way out of line, but Lane was different, he would require some kindness. She thought it all the way through and was ready for him, and then he didn't come. Which annoyed her. Then she got annoyed with herself for being annoyed, and annoyed again at Lane for putting her through this.

On Sunday she arrived with April at the same hour as the day before, and soon she saw him coming, sockless in low-cut sneakers with a rolled towel in one hand and a paperback book in the other. He led with his shoulders when he walked, rolled them the way her ex-husband did, and her brothers, and male athletes everywhere. As if they didn't know the difference between real life and the playing field.

"Why, here comes Lane Hillman," she said.

April looked up from her book and guardedly watched him come up the beach, angling toward them from the water's edge.

"He works at the paper," she said. "The boss's son."

"I know," April said.

"I wonder what he's doing here."

"It's the beach, Mom. What do you think he's doing here?"

Claire rolled over and sat up. She put on her dark glasses. Lane didn't wear them, even here, so you knew where his eyes were looking. Claire liked that about him.

"Well," she said, "look what the cat dragged up."

He stood over them, black-haired and caramel-smooth against the blue-dyed sky. His gaze slid down into the small of her back and over to the naked hip and on down her legs and then up quickly, as he caught himself.

"Am I intruding?" he said.

"We don't own the beach," Claire said.

"This little piece of it, you do."

She wished he'd sit down where he'd be less conspicuous.

"This must be April," he said.

"April, this is Lane Hillman."

"Hi, April."

"Hi," she said.

"What are you reading?"

She showed him *Great Expectations* in dog-eared paperback.

"I love Dickens," he said. "Have you read *Bleak House?*"

April shook her head.

"It's one of my all-time favorites," he said.

"Are you going to stand there all day or sit down?" Claire said.

"I'll sit down if I'm invited."

"Is he invited, April?"

"Mom, don't act dumb."

"Life with a fifteen-year-old daughter," Claire said.

"I have a sister who's fifteen," Lane said as he spread his towel. He sat down and stripped his T-shirt. He was stronger than Claire had thought. Bigger. He pulled off his sneakers and sat hugging his knees, eyes narrowed against the white light.

"I've got some Coppertone," Claire said.

"No thanks."

"You like dried-out skin?"

"Mom, will you stop?" April said.

"Stop what?" Claire said.

"You've got to read *Bleak House,*" Lane said.

"I might," April said carefully.

"Lane went to Harvard, in case you couldn't tell," Claire said.

"I could loan it to you," Lane said.

"If you want to," April said.

"Say thank you, hon," Claire said.

"Thank you, hon," April said.

"April, don't be a pain."

April sighed and picked herself up and moved slowly toward the water.

"It's a difficult age," Claire said.

"I know."

Claire looked at him. "You were a football player, right?"

"How'd you know?"

"Your build. The way you walk. I'll try not to hold it against you."

"Why would you do that?"

"My ex-husband played football. My brothers. There was an attitude that went with it. A pushiness. They were a little short in the subtlety department."

"I've known some great guys who were football players."

"I haven't. Did you play at Harvard?"

"When I wasn't hurt, which was a lot of the time."

"You were good, then."

"Yes and no."

"What does 'yes and no' mean?"

He looked out at April swimming parallel to the shore perhaps twenty feet out. She labored along at a half-crawl, half-sidestroke, cutting steadily through the water without disturbing it.

"I was inconsistent," he said. "Some days I had everything going. Other days a kind of panic would come over me. A paralysis. I'd be slow off the ball. I'd flinch when someone was about to hit me."

I was a headhunter, Scott said. Ask your brothers. They remember.

120

I'd hit 'em high. Chest, neck, head. Their legs are going one way, their head's going another. Why did I listen to that? she thought. Why was I the least bit impressed?

"I used to think it was like a guy freezing up on the battle-field," he said. "Stark, physical fear. But later I saw it wasn't the physical fear of getting hit, getting hurt, but fear of failing. I was afraid I'd lose my nerve when the moment came, and sometimes I did lose it. I suppose you could say I was afraid of being afraid. Does that make sense?"

"Sure."

She watched April, who had turned around and was swimming back toward them in the same steady, dogged way.

"In *Julius Caesar*," Lane said, "Caesar says, 'Cowards die many times before their deaths; the valiant only taste of death but once.'"

"Meaning you're a coward."

"I don't know," he said. "I don't know if bravery is the absence of fear, or being afraid and overcoming it." He thought a moment. "Or being afraid and *not* overcoming it, but still trying."

"You have to be a moron not to feel fear," Claire said. "No brain, no pain, as we used to say."

"Maybe," he said.

"Tell me about the good days. The days you were a hero."

"Your mind shuts down and your body takes over, your instincts. It's like a dream where you're watching yourself do these incredible things. You almost see it before it happens, as if you made it happen by imagining it. I made an eighty-yard touchdown run against Princeton my junior year. This year I caught a couple of touchdown passes against Dartmouth. I scored five touchdowns one time in a high school game."

"And you tell me you're a coward."

"I don't know what I am."

April stood up out of the water and smoothed her hair back.

"Lane," Claire said.

He looked at her.

"Take a swim with me," she said.

April stopped as they passed her, then turned and watched them go down to the water. Lane dove in first and waited for her, and they swam straight out, side by side, stopping perhaps sixty yards from the shore where they faced each other, treading water.

"Where'd you learn to swim so well?" he said.

"The ocean," she said.

The beach looked far away, the people tiny and out of hearing, and it felt very private out here, disconnected from land, people, everything. They could see April in the distance, lying on her stomach while the sun dried her.

"I think of you as a city girl," Lane said.

"Look at a map sometime and you'll notice Boston's on the water."

"You're pretty good with the sarcasm, aren't you?"

"I try," she said.

"Little wiseass," he said.

They treaded water and looked at each other. There was no sound but their own breathing and the slosh and tinkle of the water.

"I may be a wiseass," Claire said, "but you're a prude."

"What do I do that's prudish?"

"I'll race you in," she said.

"Wait," he said, "I want to hear this."

But she'd begun to swim, hard, and he went after her, smoother than she and stronger, passing her and moving out ahead. Halfway in she gave up and swam on leisurely, sliding herself through the warm buoyant water. Lane was waiting for her, crouched in waist-deep water.

"I'll show you who the prude is," he said.

She'd found her footing and now began to rise, and as she came up, he launched himself at her, catching her by the shoulders, his weight pulling her down and then all the way under. He rolled away grinning, and she came up spitting and blinking, and without hesitating lunged at him, knocking him backward. He sat down hard and she pushed his head under with both hands. Then she fell lazily back, smiling, and watched him flounder up with the water streaming off him.

"When you have two brothers, you learn how to play rough," she said.

"I'll show you rough," he said.

"You started it," she said.

"You did. You called me a prude."

"You *are* a prude," she said, and the game went on. She rolled over and tried to swim away, but he threw himself on her, tackled her, the two of them submerging, Claire wrapped in his arms with her back against his chest, Lane rolling under her and releasing her in the same fluid motion, impelling her up and out into the dazzling sound-filled world where she stood waist-deep like a gymnast who had just finished a turn and landed smoothly and effortlessly on her feet. She stood a moment and wondered what had just happened and why she'd permitted it. Lane breast-stroked toward her. He found his footing and stood up.

"Are you okay?" he said.

"Fine," she said, and turned abruptly and started in.

He followed her. "I didn't hurt you, did I?"

"I'm fine," she said. "Let's drop it, okay?"

April was gone. Claire looked around and saw her moving slowly away along the edge of the water. A man about Claire's age was staring at her and Lane, and so were two heavy women on beach chairs. Claire felt suddenly light-headed, disoriented.

"Where's April going?" Lane said behind her.

"Just walking. I think we embarrassed her."

They sat down side by side and looked silently out at the water. Claire put on her dark glasses.

"Maybe one of us ought to go get April," Lane said.

"She'll come back."

"She's getting pretty far down."

"Lane," Claire said.

"What." He didn't look at her.

"Maybe this isn't such a good idea, getting together like this."

"If I want to see you, I'll see you."

"Wait a minute. Do I get a vote in this?"

"I'm going to go get April."

"No," Claire said. "I want to talk to you."

"I don't want to have this discussion," he said.

. . .

HE LOPED down to the water's edge to get the firm footing and ran after her steadily at three-quarter speed. People stared at him as he cruised by. He was well out of sight of Claire when he caught up with April. She didn't hear him, and when he came up behind her and spoke to her, she jumped.

"*God*," she said.

"Sorry," he said.

She glanced at him sullenly and kept walking. He fell in beside her. The waves ran up foaming over April's skinny feet.

"We embarrassed you," Lane said.

April didn't answer.

"It was me," Lane said. "I was the one who was out of line."

"She was just as bad," April said.

"No," Lane said. "I was the one."

"She didn't have to wrestle with you."

"She was just trying to defend herself."

"Defend herself," April said. "Act ridiculous, you mean."

"Be mad at me, not her."

"I'm mad at both of you."

"I could shoot myself, would that help?"

"It isn't funny," April said.

"Who said it was funny?"

They walked awhile in silence.

"You're pretty lucky to have her for a mother," Lane said.

"Yeah, right. She drives me crazy."

"Well, she's your mother."

"That isn't why."

"Yes it is. You don't see that now, but you will."

"You sound just like her, you know that?"

"I don't mind sounding like her."

"You ought to. I sure would."

"Who else do you like to read besides Dickens?" Lane said.

"Don't change the subject."

"I thought it was time for a new one."

"God, you do sound just like her."

"You ever read *A Tale of Two Cities?*"

"Yes."

"What did you think?"

"How old are you?" April said.

"Twenty-two."

"Mom's thirty-seven."

"I know."

"Do you have a girlfriend?"

"I'm not sure," he said.

"How can you not be sure? You either do or you don't." She had dark eyes and good bones and Lane knew she'd be beautiful one day.

"Let's go back," he said, and stopped walking.

April went on a few more paces and stopped and turned and breathed a deep lugubrious sigh. "Might as well," she said. "Mom's probably calling the police by now."

"I doubt it," he said.

"You don't know her."

"She isn't calling the police," Lane said.

.   .   .

SHE AND April drove home without speaking and April went upstairs and stayed there till dinner. Spaghetti with marinara sauce: Claire kept cooking good complete meals, kept trying. At the table April spoke when spoken to, then drew back into her sulk. She washed the dishes while Claire sat on the porch with a mug of black coffee spiked with Grand Marnier and watched the kids play kickball. She was learning their names. The McKenna boys. Diana Cook. Nicky Nickerson. The water stopped running in the kitchen, and Claire turned and spoke through the screen door.

"Come out here, April. I want to talk to you."

She wondered what she'd do if April ignored her and went upstairs, but in a moment the door opened and she stood on the porch with her arms folded, looking thoughtfully out into the twilight as if she'd come out alone for a breath of air.

"Sit down," Claire said.

April sighed her sigh and sat down.

"I'm sorry about today," Claire said.

"Don't keep apologizing."

"I won't if you accept the apology."

"All right. I accept it."

"Why are you so hard on me, sweetheart?"

"I'm not."

"I try, April. I really do."

"I know."

Robby McKenna sliced one to the right onto Mrs. Roncetti's porch. The white ball ricocheted around, knocking into porch furniture. Claire thought Mrs. Roncetti would come out, but she didn't. Nicky Nickerson pounded up the wooden steps and found the ball. Nicky made more noise than the ball had, but Mrs. Roncetti still didn't appear. The game went on in the smoky dusk.

"What did you and Lane talk about?" Claire asked.

"Nothing."

"Nothing. You talked about nothing."

"What do I smell in that coffee?"

"A little stiffener. You must have talked about *something*."

"You like him, don't you?" April said.

"Yes. I do."

"Is he going to be your boyfriend?"

"Good Lord, April."

"Good Lord what?"

"He's twenty-two years old."

"So?"

"I could be his mother."

"Let's see. Twenty-two from thirty-seven is fifteen. I don't think so, Mom."

"Almost," Claire said.

She wondered how to stop this, how to get control. It was like losing your brakes or your steering or both, going down a hill. She remembered Stan and Ollie where the Model T's steering wheel comes off in Stan's hands.

"Senator Mallory was your boyfriend, wasn't he?" April said.

The question didn't surprise her. She thought awhile before answering. "Yes," she said, "he was."

"How come you didn't tell me?"

"He was married, April. He was a United States senator and he was a married man."

"I wouldn't have told anybody."

"I know that."

"So why didn't you tell me?"

"I guess I thought you wouldn't like it."

"I know about affairs," April said.

"I'm sure you do."

A car turned onto the street and the kids dropped back on either side to let it pass. The Malones' station wagon. Jack Malone returning from coaching little league. The headlights scoured the pale hedges and black tree trunks.

"Is that why you left?" April said. "Because of the affair?"

"In a way."

"In what way?"

"Don't ask me now, hon. Please."

"You said you'd tell me."

"Someday I will."

"Will you tell me if you have an affair with Lane?"

"I'm not going to have an affair with Lane."

"I bet he'd like to."

"He'll be out of luck then, won't he?"

"I don't know what the big deal is."

"There is no big deal," Claire said.

"Problem, I mean."

"I already told you the problem."

"I don't buy it."

"He's going away in September, anyway."

"So?"

"So that'll be the end of it."

"Where's he going?"

"Detroit. How are you and Kyle doing?"

"Don't change the subject," April said.

"The subject's been talked out."

"I don't think so," April said.

"And I don't want to hear any more talk about affairs, okay?"

"Mom. I'm fifteen years old."

"I'm aware of that," Claire said.

Chapter Six

THERE WAS an empty space in front of Kasselman's Pharmacy. She'd been buying her newspapers at Chamberlain's, letting some time pass, intending to go back when she thought Bernie Kasselman could stand the sight of her again. Tonight the empty parking space struck her as a sign or mandate, and she parked and went into Kasselman's for the first time since David had drowned in the bay.

A young man she hadn't seen before was behind the counter.

"Is Mr. Kasselman around?" she said.

"He's gone home, ma'am."

Ma'am. How old am I getting to look? she thought. She bought a pack of Salems, a *Globe,* and a *Times,* and left them in the car and walked around the corner and up the street to the Kasselmans' house. She rang the bell.

"Oh my God," said Esther Kasselman. "The character as-sassin."

"I just stopped by to see how you were doing," Claire said.

"So you can write another story about us, I suppose. How we're all alcoholics."

"I'm not working now," Claire said.

Esther turned and spoke over her shoulder. "Look who's here, Bernie. Your pretty reporter friend who stabbed us in the back."

Bernie appeared, smiling, behind his wife.

"I just wanted to say hello," Claire said.

"I haven't seen you in the drugstore. I stopped saving your papers."

"I thought I'd give you a vacation from me."

"You didn't have to do that," Bernie said.

"You stand there like you were selling cookies," Esther said. "Come into the house if you want to talk."

"Do," Bernie said.

She followed them down the hall to the living room, with its white rug and back-yard picture window. The clean, empty, daylit room now was odorless of tragedy. Claire sat down. The Kasselmans sat together on the sofa.

"Would you like something to drink?" Bernie said.

"We'd offer you alcohol," Esther said, "but we don't keep any in the house."

"Yes we do," Bernie said. "We have some very nice wine."

"No thank you," Claire said.

"So," Esther said, "what do you want, exactly?"

"She already told us," Bernie said.

"No one at the paper wanted to hurt you," Claire said.

"The boy drank liquor for the one and only time in his life," Esther said. "God forbid you should leave it out."

"She did what she had to do," Bernie said gently.

"Those two boys," Esther said. "I'd like to string them up by the neck."

"No you wouldn't," Bernie said.

"I'd like to blow their brains out."

"I know how you feel," Claire said.

"You got kids?" Esther said.

"A daughter."

"How would you feel if someone wrote about her what you wrote about David?"

"It wasn't me, actually. Someone else wrote the news story."

"Who?" Esther said.

"It doesn't matter," Claire said. "If it had been me, I'd have done it the same way. I would have had to."

"Had to? *Had* to?"

"I'm afraid so," Claire said.

"You know what we don't get?" Bernie said. "Why he got in the car with those two."

"He was hitchhiking," Claire said.

"He never hitchhiked," Bernie said.

"We told that to Chief Williams," Esther said. "He wanted to believe those boys, though."

"They were older than David," Bernie said. "I doubt he'd ever spoken to them. Why would he get in a car with them? Why would he go swimming with them late at night?"

"Why would they lie about it?" Claire said.

"To save their skins, that's why," Esther said. "Cases continued without a finding. No criminal record. I couldn't believe it when I read it."

"It was negligence," Bernie said. "They didn't kill him on purpose."

"I'm not saying they killed him on purpose, but there was something going on. How could he drown and those two idiots not even notice?"

"They couldn't hear him, Esther."

"Why not?"

"I was wondering that myself," Claire said.

"I suppose we'll never know," Bernie said.

"It makes me crazy not knowing," Esther said.

"I don't blame you," Claire said.

.   .   .

HE BROUGHT *Bleak House* the following Sunday. Neither of them had said anything about their encounter on the beach, though they spoke frequently now, in the parking lot coming and going, at the coffee urn, and in a more circumspect way, as professionals, in the newsroom. Nor had any mention been made of the coming Sunday. No plan had been suggested, no invitation issued; they'd all simply shown up, Claire and April first, Lane twenty minutes later, striding along the water's edge with the book in one hand and a rolled towel in the other, cradled like a football against his ribs.

"Look who's here," Claire said, feigning surprise.

"Hi," April said. Even she seemed to understand Claire's need for a pretense of fortuity, of undesign, and had said nothing all week of meeting Lane again.

"Look what I brought you," he said.

It was a thick hardbound book, gray with a black spine. He handed it down to April, who hefted it and nodded, as if its bulk and weight pleased her. Lane spread his towel and sat down.

"Mom read *A Tale of Two Cities*," April said.

"Really?" Lane said.

"What, is that so surprising?" Claire said.

"You read the whole thing in one week?"

"You know," she said, "you really are obnoxious."

"She reads all the time now," April said. "She thinks it'll help with her writing."

"It will," Lane said.

"It must be Harvard that does that to you," Claire said.

"Does what?" Lane said.

"She has a dumb theory about what's-her-name in the book," April said.

"Lucy," Claire said. "Lucy Manet. What I said was, when she finds out what Sydney Carton did, she's going to love *him* more than Charles. Sydney Carton might have saved Charles's life, but he wrecked the marriage."

"She can't love him more if he's dead," April said.

"Oh yes she can."

"It's an interesting idea," Lane said.

"Thank you," Claire said.

"It's a dumb idea," April said.

This time they did not wrestle in the water or touch in any way, but swam sedately out side by side and treaded water and looked at each other without speaking. Then they lay on their towels and dried in the beating rays of the midsummer sun. Beside him on her stomach Claire presented a sinuous profile; shoulders, back, solid upswung hips. He looked at her half-furtively and imagined putting his hands inside the damp bikini. He imagined rolling her over in the sand. He looked out at the horizon, the bending rim of the sea, and thought he could feel the earth's ripe roundness beneath him, he on top of the world in the literal physical sense, so that if he moved he'd be humping it, humping the world itself.

At five o'clock they got up and shook out their towels. The beach was nearly empty. A smoky southwester had sprung up, riffling the steel-blue water. Lane walked them to their car.

"Give you a ride?" Claire said.

"I like the walk," he said. The quiet and privacy of the old railroad bed, the smoky golden light, the soft warm wind on his skin.

Claire shrugged and got in the car. Lane stood at the window and watched her while she found her key and stuck it in the ignition.

"What are you doing tomorrow night?" he said.

Claire removed her dark glasses. She looked up into his face and he into hers, and he saw her light-struck green eyes and the delicate notchings of her crow's feet.

"Tomorrow night?" she said.

"Nothing," April said.

"I have to review the show at the Melody Tent," he said. "I was wondering if you wanted to come. Reviewer gets two tickets."

"I don't think so," she said.

"Why not?" April said.

"It's a good one this week," he said. *"Brigadoon."*

"Why don't you take April? April would love it, wouldn't you, hon? See a live play?"

"I'm going out with Kyle tomorrow night."

"You go out with Kyle every night."

"Show starts at eight," Lane said. "We can be home by eleven."

"Go ahead, Mom," April said.

"Let me think about it," Claire said.

"What is there to think about?" April said.

"April, will you mind your own business?"

"That's fine," Lane said. "Think about it and let me know in the morning. April, I hope you enjoy *Bleak House*."

"I might not read it right away," April said.

They watched him turn and head out alone along the wind-and-sand-swept road with the rolled towel under his arm. He did not look back.

"Why don't you go with him?" April said.

"We'll see."

"You'll see? It's tomorrow night."

"I know when it is, April."

"You want to go, right?"

"I don't know," Claire said.

"Yeah, right," April said.

. . .

He wore a jacket and tie and reminded her of her brothers when they'd dressed up for school dances or away games, the shirt collar tight around the thickish neck, the tie carelessly or inexpertly knotted. But whereas her brothers had looked constrained, straitjacketed, in their tweed and corduroy jackets, Lane's light summer blazer hung loosely on him, decorative and unencumbering and somehow irrelevant, as if he could rid himself of it with a casual shrug.

Claire wore black heels and a black dress to set off the brown of her skin. She wore eye liner and eye shadow and pendant earrings, and when she opened the screen door he stared at her without speaking, as if it had taken him a moment to recognize her. Then he smiled.

"Good evening," he said.

She smiled uneasily and looked away. "Want to see the house?" she said.

April had left an hour ago. Claire stood in the doorway between the kitchen and dining area and the living room while Lane walked around peering at the pictures on the walls, the framed Wyeth and Picasso prints she'd picked out in Georgetown boutiques. The coffee table was piled with newspapers and back issues of *Time* and *Newsweek* and *Cosmopolitan*.

"I like it," he said. "It has a good feel."

"It's a little bare," she said.

He finished his inspection and turned, standing with his hands in his pockets and a knee canted. "You look great," he said. "You look smashing."

Smashing. She'd never heard that one. He stood there looking at her, his gaze all clarity and longing. She was aware now of the stillness, the house empty around them, no kids playing in the street tonight, which seemed odd and unreal. As if the world had stopped turning.

"We'd better get going, don't you think?" she said, but not wanting to move, to set the world in motion again.

"I suppose we ought to," he said.

She found a sweater, left a light on, and preceded him wordlessly out into the still and golden evening. The office Chevy waited in the driveway. Lane opened the door for her. They drove awhile without speaking. Claire lit a cigarette and smoked it down and dropped it out the window.

"What's this show about?" she said.

"Well," he said, "Brigadoon is a little village in the highlands of Scotland. It has a spell on it. It wakes for one day then sleeps for a hundred years. It disappears into the mists, and nothing can touch it, no harm can come to it."

"Except for that one day."

"Not harm, exactly."

"What, then?"

"A couple of Americans come along on the day the village is awake. They're out hunting, and they get lost. They stumble into Brigadoon."

"And fall for two cute girls."

"One of them does."

"So he's got a problem."

"They both do. He can't take her with him because if anyone leaves the village the spell is broken."

"So he stays."

"I'm not going to tell you."

She hadn't been to a play in a long time and had never seen one on a round stage under a tent. The orchestra was in a pit, and the actors entered and exited by different ramps radiating up like spokes from the little stage. They sang beautifully, Claire thought. She knew a couple of the songs. "Almost Like Being in Love," "Come to Me, Bend to Me." So beautiful.

At intermission they bought paper cups of beer at the concession stand and strolled around the big tent in the amber glow of Japanese lanterns. The air was cool and moist and fragrant of pine. The three-quarter moon shone mistily just above the trees.

"It ends happily, right?" Claire said.

"I don't want to spoil it for you," he said.

"You couldn't spoil it for me."

"All right," he said, "it ends happily."

"Good," she said, and, because it now seemed warranted and natural, took his arm. He didn't look at her, didn't seem surprised, and they walked on without speaking, sipping their beer and watching the well-dressed people go by. He looked down at her only once, and when she looked up and met his eye, she felt her heart move.

· . . ·

AFTERWARD he asked her if she wanted to stop for a drink.

"What about your review?" she said.

"No sweat," he said.

"It's after ten."

"So what?" he said.

He took her to a hotel bar overlooking the bay. The room was low and dark and nearly empty. A pianist played unobtrusively, weaving slow, ruminative melodies through the late-night quiet.

Claire ordered a scotch and soda.

"Bourbon on the rocks," Lane said.

"Could I see your ID?" the waitress said.

She didn't look any older than he was. Lane nodded obligingly and reached back for his wallet. The waitress took his driver's license. She met his eye and smiled as she handed it back to him.

"Can you make it a Jack Daniel's?" he said.

The girl turned smartly and went briskly out, twitching in her short, tight skirt.

"She's pretty," Claire said.

"She's okay," Lane said.

"A college girl, I bet."

"Could be."

"She has that look. Refined."

"You were a college girl," Lane said.

"A *junior* college girl. It wasn't exactly Radcliffe."

"You overrate Radcliffe," he said. "You overrate Harvard, too."

The girl came back with their drinks. "Sorry about the ID," she said. "My boss is kind of strict about that."

"It's all right," Claire said, "he likes the attention."

The waitress glanced at her and smiled uncertainly. Lane paid and tipped her fifty cents. She glanced again at Claire and left them.

"What'd you say that for?" Lane said.

Claire looked down into her drink. "I don't know," she said.

Lane picked up his glass, held it up between them. "To the best-looking woman at the show tonight," he said. "Including the actresses."

"Lane," she said.

He sipped his whiskey and put down the glass. "What?"

"There's nothing special about me, do you understand that? Because I'm older, you think I'm special, but I'm not."

"It has nothing to do with your being older," he said.

"Think about it: would you be interested in me if I were your age?"

"I'd be interested in you at any age. Anybody would be."

Compliments. Scott had seldom bothered. Mallory had somehow made it implicit between them that her good looks, the pleasure of her company, were a given, unneedful of mention. Later she understood that he was merely avoiding going on the record.

"Don't," she said.

"Don't what?"

She took a swallow of her drink. "You know what my husband did? He sold insurance, and the only reason he succeeded at it was because he was slick, number one, and too stupid, number two, to have doubts about himself. He had a high school diploma and he beat me up. Twice."

Lane looked away, at the black night over the bay. "I'm sorry," he said.

"It was my own fault. I didn't have to marry him."

"We all make mistakes," he said.

"Not like me. I have a gift for it."

She picked up her glass, took another long swallow. The pianist was playing "It's Not for Me to Say." She remembered Johnny Mathis on the radio and felt a quiet sadness roll through her on the music.

"What happened to you in Washington?" Lane said.

It didn't surprise her any more than it had when April had asked her about her affair with Mallory. Secrets leave their marks on you, their subtle traces.

"You left suddenly," Lane said.

Her downcast gaze moved to her own sun-browned hands. Young hands: she oiled them with Jergens every night and wore gloves in chapping weather. She wondered how many good years she could have with Lane Hillman. Ten? Fifteen? So much about me he doesn't know, she thought. Whereas his life was an open book: Harvard, football, the big loving family, Charles Dickens and William Faulkner. His girlfriends she could imagine without his telling: intellectual types who drank red wine with him in dirty-laundry-smelling dormitory rooms with can-

dle drippings on tables and then fucked him on unmade beds
and said *Oh God* when they came. Afterward they read Shakespeare to each other by candlelight.

"You're different from me, Lane," she said.

"Tell me what happened," he said.

"Then you'll see," she said. "Then you'll know."

"I know what I'll see," he said.

*Then he'll stop. Then this will be over and I can live a normal life
again and find someone finally who's right for me.*

"Ask your sexy friend for another round," she said.

.   .   .

MALLORY was speeding, as usual. What United States senator
didn't speed? Always in a hurry, always running late, and not a
state trooper in the country who would write any of them a
ticket. He drove with one hand, doing eighty, eighty-five, down
the dark, empty Baltimore–Washington Parkway, easing back
only when the wheel of her VW began to jiggle in his hands.

She'd met his plane at Baltimore International. The flight had
been an hour late, delayed waiting for just him, one man more
important than a planeful of people combined. Mrs. Mallory
thought he was still in Boston at a private dinner with liberal fat-
cat friends, idea men, and campaign contributors, where he
couldn't be reached. The plan was for him and Claire to spend
the night or what was left of it at a motor lodge outside the District, a place where an important man could check in with a
companion and count on the staff, right down to the chamber-
maids, to be discreet.

It would be a new experience. They'd been lovers for two
months and had never spent an entire night together—not because of the senator's schedule or family but because of April.

Tonight, though, April was on a class trip, an overnight visit to Williamsburg. Claire had signed the permission slip and mentioned it casually to Mallory, not putting any pressure on him but letting him know the opportunity was there if he wanted it. He did.

She rolled down her window and let the fragrant spring darkness blow over her as she listened to Bob tell her about his day. The fat cats were beginning to lean on him about the war, urging him to back off, let others lead the charge for a while. There was a reaction beginning to build, they said, more and more boys coming home in coffins, good boys from hardworking families who went off uncomplaining to do their duty while college hippies vandalized draft boards and ROTC recruiting offices and shut whole universities down. Working-class Democrats were getting tired of it. There would be defections in November: Democrats for Nixon, if you could imagine such a thing. Not even Bobby Kennedy, if he should carry the convention, could keep them all in the fold.

Claire wasn't expected to talk, just listen. The senator's wife would not, or could not, listen without barraging him with unsolicited advice, carping criticisms of his caution, his innate reluctance to offend. Claire was glad to listen without butting in. And so, over drinks and dinner in Bob's office after everyone had left for the day, or in out-of-the-way restaurants across the Maryland line, she sat quietly while he entrusted his fears, hopes, setbacks, victories, gossip, and secrets to her. The things Claire knew. The power she had that she would never use.

You're tired, she said.

Long day, he said.

A martini and a hot bath is my advice, she said.

A little more than that, I hope.

He shouldn't have been driving. But Claire had never driven him anywhere, and at the airport he'd gotten in behind the wheel without comment, as if he belonged there. He'd slid the seat back to accommodate his long thin legs, then extended his hand for the key.

They passed the broken-down car angled over on the shoulder sometime after one, a big sedan sagging in back and listing to the driver's side. Mallory turned on the radio. He began pushing buttons, looking for a newscast, and the car drifted to the right. The hitchhiker was about a mile from his car, straddling the white line and hanging his thumb out over the road. His skin was black, and he wore black slacks and shoes and a long, dark, loose-fitting coat. He appeared suddenly when they were almost on top of him.

Claire would never forget how slowly he reacted. The autopsy would show that he was high on marijuana and alcohol, and Claire imagined him perceiving the VW's headlights in slow motion, two white orbs swelling out of the flat darkness, mesmerizing him. He just stood there with his thumb out and his leg on the wrong side of the line, refusing to help Mallory not kill him.

Claire saw him first and shouted. Mallory looked up from the radio and spun the wheel, and the car scythed the kid down and ran over him with the right front and rear wheels, then swerved to the left and shot across both lanes before Mallory spun the wheel back, braked, won control, then lost it again as a tire blew. The Bug yawed and nearly capsized; Mallory fought the wheel and again won control, and the car limped to a stop.

The radio was playing an old Sinatra tune. Mallory looked

out blankly into the darkness in front of him. Claire twisted around in her seat. She couldn't see anything. A car sped by, swerving to avoid them. Claire turned off the radio.

Back up, she said.

Mallory turned and regarded her with an odd, appraising expression that was almost a smile. She wondered if he was in shock. He shoved the stick into reverse and looked over his shoulder and backed the car. It rolled swayingly on its pancake tire. Another car tore by and vanished. Mallory kept backing, till they saw the dark shapeless bundle beside the road. They slid past it, then Mallory angled the car so the headlights shone on the body. The boy lay on his stomach with his head tucked down. Mallory killed the engine. He left the lights on.

You wait here, he said.

No, she said, and shouldered the door open. The two of them advanced through the running shafts of the high beams to where the hitchhiker lay in his cheap black raincoat. Mallory knelt and picked up a skinny black wrist.

He's dead, isn't he? Claire said.

Mallory nodded and dropped the lifeless wrist. A car was coming. Claire whirled and waved with both arms but the car shot past and was gone.

Goddamn it, she said.

Take it easy, Mallory said. He stood up.

Oh God, Bob, she said.

I'll have to go report it, he said.

She looked at him. He was very calm. Thoughtful, deliberate in his speech and movements.

One of us has to stay here, he said.

Stay here?

One of us has to. You can't leave the scene of an accident. It's a crime.

I'm not staying here. Not alone I'm not.

You don't want to get in a car with a stranger, do you?

Then we both stay. Flag down a car and get them to send somebody.

I can't take that chance, he said.

What chance? she said. What are you talking about?

I have a duty to report this accident, he said. The only way I can do this is for you to stay here.

I don't understand this, she said. It was wrong, crazy; she knew that but couldn't pin down the flaw, couldn't think the problem through. Mallory was a lawyer. He knew about these things.

I'll be back, he said. Get in the car. Lock yourself in.

You aren't really going to leave me here.

I have to, he said.

She looked down the dark empty highway. Mallory stepped up to her and put his arms around her. She didn't move, was as dead to him as the boy lying beside the road. He did nothing to try to change that; he was already through with her, and it was easy for him. Easier by far than it had been for Scott. It was nothing. She got in the car.

Lock the door, he said. I'll see you soon.

The first car honked at him to get out of the way and tore by without slowing. Mallory stuck his hands in his pockets and watched it disappear. The second car stopped. Mallory jogged to it and got in and slammed the door without looking back.

Claire watched the taillights recede blood-red into the starless night between the low embankments on either side of the Parkway. She doused the headlights, shrouding the dead boy in darkness, but then it occurred to her that the darkened car would look abandoned, inviting some thug to break in, see what there was to steal. She turned the lights back on, and the radio for company. She lit a cigarette.

After a while she started the car and swung it backward till the headlights no longer bathed the slumped heap at the edge of the road. She wondered who he was, where he came from, and where he was going when his car broke down. She wondered if he would be missed. An occasional car went by, fast, and no one stopped or even slowed down. The time passed slowly.

The first policeman arrived a little before two. The flashing lights appeared behind her and the cruiser glided up noiselessly, as if light could drown out sound. It crept in close, lights jumping back and forth. In the mirror Claire watched the big Maryland trooper climb out, deliberate in his fluffed-out trousers and knee-high boots and flat-brimmed Mountie's hat. She turned off the radio and got out of the car.

Ma'am, he said, and touched his hat brim.

There's been an accident, she said.

We know all about it, ma'am. Where's the victim?

Claire pointed. The policeman had a flashlight. He strolled around the hood of the VW through the stream of its lights. She could hear the creak of leather as he moved. He crouched down over the body. Claire wondered where Mallory was and why he hadn't ridden back with the cop. The blue lights throbbed in silent alternating bursts. A car came down the Parkway, slowed, and went on by. The cop stood up. He came around and set the flashlight on the roof of the VW. He reached behind him and pulled out a steno pad.

I have to get a statement from you, ma'am, and then you can go home.

Senator Mallory . . . , she said.

Senator Mallory's gone back to Washington, the way I understand it. Somebody from his staff came out and got him.

Wait a minute, Claire said.

Don't worry, the cop said. Everything's going to be fine.

He told me he was coming back, she said.

It doesn't look that way.

Another cruiser arrived, another pair of pulsing lights.

Excuse me, the policeman said and turned away from her.

Just a goddamn minute, Claire said.

You sit tight, ma'am, he said over his shoulder, and went to meet the new man.

The two of them talked for a while. Claire couldn't make out what they were saying. She could hear their radios spitting static and bursts of unintelligible coughlike words. The policemen finished talking and came toward her out of the blue-lit night. The newcomer touched his hat the way the other had done.

I'm Sergeant Billings, ma'am. We're going to let you go home and get some sleep. Trooper Smith here is going to follow you, make sure you get there in good shape.

I have a flat, Claire said.

We'll change the flat for you, Billings said. Let me just get a look, here.

He went and knelt beside the body. Claire sagged back against her car.

It'll be all right, Trooper Smith said.

I thought you wanted a statement, she said.

We're going to let that ride for now.

Let it ride, she said.

That's the idea, he said.

What does that mean, let it ride?

Sergeant Billings had finished inspecting the body.

Mrs. Malek, he said, right?

Claire nodded.

Just for your information, we found a car down the road with seven plastic bags of marijuana in the glove compartment and enough amphetamines to stock a pharmacy. In the trunk was half a case of malt liquor. What I'm saying is, your story sounds on target.

What story? she said.

The two policemen looked at each other.

According to Senator Mallory, Billings said, the victim was half out in the road. He was acting in an unusual way. Erratic. You couldn't help hitting him.

That's not true, she said.

Again the two men exchanged glances.

Ma'am, Billings said, your boss is putting the hooks in for you. Don't fight it, you know what I'm saying?

He's right, Smith said. Don't fight it.

More gently, Billings said, We got a drug dealer here, that much we know, and from the sound of it, I'll just about guarantee you the lab'll find either alcohol or some kind of controlled substance in his system. I sincerely doubt you were driving recklessly, ma'am.

Wait a minute, Claire said. Hold it.

In the strobe-lashed darkness she could see Billings's flat pale face under the wide hat brim, composed and professional, unreadable.

The only thing that won't be kosher, he said, we're going to remove the senator's name as a witness. I'm not saying I like it, but the word came down and there's nothing I can do about it.

A witness, Claire said. You're saying Bob was a witness and I was driving.

Officially, the senator wasn't here, Billings said.

We need to talk, she said.

Smitty, Billings said, you want to change that tire for her?

Sure thing, Smith said.

Excuse me, ma'am, Billings said, and walked back toward the two cruisers.

Claire followed him. I wasn't driving, she said.

Billings stopped and turned. He eyed her with bland dispassion, almost kindly. It *is* your car, am I right?

I wasn't driving, she said.

Now, Miz Malek, listen to me. It was an accident. It was nobody's fault, and nobody's going to get hurt.

What about him? she said, pointing behind her. He's hurt, wouldn't you say?

It's too late for him, Billings said. It's you we're thinking about now.

But I wasn't driving, she said. Don't you want to know what happened?

Billings looked at her in that composed and easy way. You try to relax, Miz Malek. It'll all be over soon.

What do you mean, *over?* she said.

Just try to relax.

Trooper Smith leaned into the VW and emerged after a moment with Claire's sweater. He came to her and draped it over her shoulders. She pulled the sweater tight around her. Smith took her arm.

You come over here and sit down, ma'am. I'm going to get that tire changed and get you on your way.

A car approached and swung in behind the cruisers.

That'll be the doc, Billings said.

Smith walked Claire across the two-lane highway and off the shoulder, and she lowered herself to the cool wet grass. The medical examiner had gotten out of his car with his black bag. Claire leaned back on her hands and watched him kneel beside the body.

The examination took only a few minutes. The doctor closed his bag and stood up. He spoke quietly to Billings. Smith meanwhile had raised the VW on its miniature jack and was mounting the spare tire. Claire tilted her head back and breathed deeply. She could smell green grass and tilled earth up beyond the embankment where the land stretched away to woods and farmers' fields. The doctor said good night to Billings and went slowly to his car.

She thought of Bob Mallory and remembered with what pride and enthusiasm she'd gone to work in his first senatorial campaign. She'd been thirty, young enough to hope and dream even after what Scott had done to her. A girlfriend who was dating one of Mallory's aides had brought her to campaign headquarters on Tremont Street to meet everybody. The excitement in the crowded, cluttered room was contagious. Jack Kennedy was running for president, the country was on the move, and Claire suddenly did not want to be left behind.

She had a decent enough job typing and answering the phone at Foley, Hoag & Elliot, but here was a life-altering opportunity, the bright promise of history in the making. She did some volunteer work typing and stuffing envelopes. Mallory won, and they hired her as the press secretary's girl Friday. Later they moved her to the legislative department, and then to still another room to be the secretary of the administrative assistant, Mark Fairchild. Then, a few months ago, the senator himself requested that she be transferred to the desk just outside the door to his private office, to be his personal secretary. Claire knew why and did not object.

Be right with you, ma'am, Trooper Smith said.

The doctor had driven away. Billings came across the highway. You okay to drive? he said.

She nodded.

I'm sorry about all this, he said.

She nodded. She didn't look at him.

If I could bring that kid back alive again, I would, Billings said.

So would I, Claire said.

But we can't, he said.

No, she said, we can't.

You take care, Miz Malek, he said.

She stayed home the next morning, drinking black coffee and waiting for someone to call, either Bob himself or Mark Fairchild. At ten-thirty Mark called.

How're you feeling? he said.

How do you think I'm feeling?

We have to talk, Mark said.

So talk.

Not over the phone.

I'm not coming in, Mark.

I guess I'll have to come to you, then.

I guess you will, she said.

She didn't know how he found the apartment. He didn't ask her for directions, just showed up half an hour later, getting slowly out of his BMW and looking around at the treeless neighborhood of two-story pink-brick apartment buildings under the warm blue sky. It was very quiet; kids were at school, adults were at work at the Pentagon or Langley or across the river in the District. Mark sauntered up the front walk, thin and impeccably tailored in a beige summer suit and paisley tie. Claire opened the door before he could knock. He smiled when he saw her. He had a nice-looking boyish face, a bland grin. She stepped back and he came past her and stood with his hands in his pockets, looking around the room.

Nice place, he said.

Who was he, Mark?

Who was who?

The kid we killed last night.

I'd say he got himself killed, Mark said.

Who was he? she said.

Mark leaned forward and stared at Andrew Wyeth's Christina on the wind-blown prairie. You don't really want to know, do you? he said.

She'd worked for Mark for two years. He'd always been easygoing and polite. He'd been patient. Respectful. He kept pictures of his wife and children on his desk.

Who was he? Claire said.

Mark shrugged. His name was Tyrone Moore. He was a thief. A drug dealer. A real lowlife. He had a record as long as your arm.

So it doesn't matter that he's dead.

I didn't say that.

What *did* you say?

Can we sit down, Claire?

She didn't offer him coffee, just threw herself down on the sofa and waited. Mark selected a chair and sat down and crossed his legs. He smiled at her, but his easy manner today had an obdurate and steely quality she'd never seen before, or perhaps had failed to notice.

You get any sleep last night? he said.

No, she said.

You look good, if it's any comfort.

I look good. Jesus.

Her cigarettes were on the coffee table. She leaned forward and lit one. She was wearing jeans, an untucked white shirt, no makeup.

Nothing wrong with looking good, Mark said, watching her.

I take it, she said, you're the one who drove Bob home last night.

You know me, Mark said. Ready, willing, and able.

Did he tell you he was driving? she said.

No, Mark said pleasantly, why would he?

Because it's the truth, that's why.

It was your car, Claire.

I know whose fucking car it was.

Remember how it used to be that women never swore? Mark said.

155

Did you hear me, Mark?

He eyed her a moment. Bland, cagey smile. No one would believe that, Claire, he said.

Want to bet?

Yeah, I'd bet. As a matter of fact, I think you're lucky you're not being prosecuted.

Prosecuted, she said.

Look, he said, and let go of the smile. At this point I don't think it matters who was driving, or who was in the car and who wasn't. The kid's dead. It's over. They're going to throw the case out.

You guys were busy last night, weren't you?

It was a long night for all of us, Mark said.

Especially Tyrone Moore, Claire said.

If I were you, I'd forget about Tyrone Moore.

I don't want to forget about him. Where'd he live?

You open this up, Claire, you'll find yourself in court. Do you want that?

Where'd he live, Mark?

Baltimore.

He have any family?

He had a mother, no father. Now, I want you to listen to me, Claire.

No father, she said. That must have made things easier for you.

Claire. Listen to me. Focus your pretty mind. The senator wants you to take a week off. With pay, of course. Rest up, forget about what happened.

Forget about it. Right.

Take two weeks, if you want. Take a trip. Go someplace quiet.

How old was Tyrone Moore?

Money wouldn't be a problem, Mark said. I've got a bank check in my pocket that'll take care of any financial difficulties about a trip. Fly to Bermuda. Take your daughter.

I'm not going on any trip, Mark.

That's up to you.

I'm not going on any trip, and I don't want your fucking money.

All right, he said. But when you do come back you'll be working for me again instead of the senator. We thought that'd be more comfortable for all concerned.

I bet you did.

To be honest, I hated losing you in the first place. I always thought we made a good team.

She closed her eyes and opened them. Mark sat with an arm hooked over the chair back and watched her.

You know what I think now? Mark said. I think we'd make a better team than you and the senator.

You son-of-a-bitch, she said.

You don't know till you try, Mark said, reddening.

I'm not coming back, Claire said.

Oh? He'd lost the smile now, had misplaced and forgotten it.

Not even to clean out my desk, she said.

You'd better think about that.

I don't have to think about it.

Because, he said, you won't get another job on the Hill. Not even on the Republican side.

I don't want one, she said, and looked at the floor, the brown wall-to-wall carpet that didn't show dirt or stains.

What'll you do? Mark said. Go back to Boston and be a typist?

Maybe, she said.

He stood up. Typist at a law firm, he said. That's what you did before, right? Fetch the guys their coffee?

She could feel tears coming, but she looked up at him, anyway. I wasn't driving, Mark, she said.

He found his smile again. You can always screw your way up the ladder, he said. You'll always have that—right, Claire?

She turned her face as the tears ran down. Mark moved to the door and she heard it open and close with a whump and rap of the brass knocker, sharp and final, the period at the end of the little accident that had killed Tyrone Moore.

.   .   .

NOW THEY sat in the dark in the vinyl-smelling Chevy, looking out at the bay. They could hear the waves, slow and sibilant, on the shore below. The misted moon spread a dull pewter sheen on the water.

"I wanted to go see Tyrone Moore's mother," Claire said. "I called the state police and got the name of the funeral home. The funeral home gave me the address. It was in a real bad section. The kind of place you're going in the fall.

"I was afraid to go there alone, even in the daytime. I asked Mark to go with me. 'One last favor,' I said, 'and then we're even.' I said if he came with me I'd tell Mrs. Moore I was driving. 'Which you were,' Mark said. Then he said he was busy and hung up on me.

"I didn't know who else to ask. I wasn't going to take a girl into that neighborhood. I tried a couple guys I knew who weren't on Bob's staff. I tried a guy I'd dated for a while. I was leaving in a few days, and all of them were afraid or busy or just didn't want to bother. So I never went."

Lane slid over from behind the wheel and put his arm around her. "You didn't do anything wrong," he said.

"I could have tried to make it right," she said. "Gone to the police. Gone to one of the newspapers."

"It was your word against a U.S. senator's," Lane said. "It was your car. There was nothing anyone could do, even if they believed you."

He put his other arm around her, pulled her in, and held her.

"Don't do this to me," she said. "Please."

"I can't help it," he said.

"I'll lose my job. I'll lose everything."

"I love you," he said.

"You can't," she said.

"I already do," he said.

She thought he would kiss her then, but he released her and moved back behind the wheel and started the car. They drove back to town on the King's Highway, winding in and out of the little hollows where the night mist gathered. They passed the funeral home, its big somber sign floodlit beside the road.

"How are you going to write a review at this hour?" Claire said.

"I'll write it," he said.

The kiss came at the end. He walked her to the door and they stood facing each other on the little brick stoop in the orange glow of the outside light. He didn't hesitate, knew she would permit it. The kiss tasted of whiskey, and she was surprised at how easily he gave it, with what knowledge and assurance. He held her afterward and she dropped back on her heels and looked up at him.

"I love you," he said.

"Go home. Please."

"Now you know," he said.

"Now I know."

She stepped inside and closed the screen door and looked out as he went down the flagstone walk to his car. Insects darted and bounced off the outside light; she hadn't heard them until now. Lane got into the car, and she turned off the porch light and closed the inside door. The old car grumbled to life, and the headlights came on and moved backward out the driveway. Claire watched the car disappear around the corner. She wondered if April was awake in the dark and had heard Lane say he loved her, and knew it didn't much matter anymore.

. . .

HIS COPY of *Bleak House* was on her bedside table. Claire propped herself on three pillows and lifted the book onto her lap. On the inside of the cover, in compact but graceful woman's script, was written *For Lane on his birthday, January 10, 1963, from his grandparents, with love.* She opened to her place.

Then the stream of moonlight has swelled into a lake, and then Lady Dedlock for the first time moves, and rises, and comes forward to a table for a glass of water. Winking cousins, batlike in the candle glare, crowd round to give it; Volumnia takes another, a very mild sip of which contents her. Lady Dedlock, graceful, self-possessed, looked after by admiring eyes, passes away slowly down the long perspective . . .

The phone rang. Claire smiled and shook her head.

"I'll take you to Baltimore," he said. "We'll find Tyrone Moore's mother."

"You're out of your mind," Claire said.

"I've got it all figured out," he said. "We'll go next weekend."

"We can't take off together just like that."

"Can we use your car?"

"What would you tell your parents?"

"That I'm driving you to Baltimore."

"Please, Lane. Not tonight."

"You have to," he said. "You have to put this behind you."

"I'll think about it," she said.

"We'll leave early Saturday morning."

"I'll think about it," she said again.

. . .

ON WEDNESDAY night he came home after covering an antiwar meeting at the parish hall of St. Andrew's and found his mother by the fireplace as usual with her book. He got himself a bottle of beer and sat down on the old cobbler's bench that crouched in front of the hearth. His mother marked her place and put the book down. She smiled. Her smile was slow and gentle and spread a milky radiance over her roundish face.

"How was your meeting?" she said.

Lane shrugged. "I counted thirty-three people. They called President Johnson a bunch of names and raised some money. They wouldn't tell me how much."

"What's the money for?"

"They were vague about that. They've got some kind of fund. For expenses for antiwar demonstrations, I suppose. Or speakers, maybe, or films. I don't know."

"I think thirty-three is a good turnout for a town this size."

"I suppose." He tilted the bottle and took a burning-cold slug of beer. "Mom?"

"What, child?"

"Claire Malek came to the meeting with me."

"Two reporters. Gracious."

"I took her to *Brigadoon*," Lane said.

"I know."

"I'm trying to tell you something," he said.

"I don't need to be told," his mother said.

"Is it okay?"

"As long as you're happy."

"Of course I'm happy. I'm happier than I've ever been."

"I'm glad."

"No," Lane said. "You're not."

She smiled gently into the fireplace and did not contradict him.

"Does Dad know?" Lane said.

"Of course."

"He doesn't approve, does he?"

"We worry, is all."

"About what?"

"About what will happen. Not now, but later. She's going to get older, Lane."

"So am I."

"But you'll never catch up."

"It doesn't matter."

"It might someday."

He drank some beer. He leaned over and stroked the silky flank of the sleeping yellow Lab. The dog stretched in her sleep and shuddered pleasurably.

"Mom," Lane said, "I have to tell you something. Claire and I are driving to Baltimore this weekend."

His mother looked at him. "Whatever for?"

Lane held the brown bottle up to the light. He'd killed two-thirds of it. "Well," he said, "she stored some furniture down there. We're going to bring it up in a U-Haul trailer."

"Couldn't she just hire movers?"

He didn't look at her. "It's too expensive."

"It's a long way to go. You'll be stopping for the night, I assume."

"I assume," Lane said.

Headlights swung down the driveway, and they heard the scrape and crunch of gravel under the wheels of his father's car. The dog lifted her amber head and listened, then laid it down again and contentedly closed her eyes.

"I wonder how she knows it's Dad," Lane said.

"Dogs know all kinds of things," his mother said.

"They always know when you're going for a walk," Lane said.

The kitchen door opened, and they heard John Hillman's heavy, almost silent tread. They heard him open the refrigerator. He came into the living room with his briefcase and a bottle of Piels, put the briefcase down, and leaned over and kissed his wife on the mouth. He sat down in his chair.

"They make any news at your meeting?" he said.

"A little," Lane said. "Dr. Vogel called Lyndon Johnson a traitor to his country."

"That's worth printing."

"They were secretive about how much money they raised."

"Well, find out. Call Vogel in the morning."

"He won't tell me."

"It's public record. Don't let them put you off like that."

"Lane's driving to Baltimore this weekend," his mother said.

His father looked at him.

"He and Claire Malek. To pick up some furniture."

"What furniture?" his father said.

"Just some furniture she left down there," Lane said.

"And whose idea was this?"

"Mine."

"Your idea to take a divorced woman to Baltimore."

"She can't do it alone," Lane said.

"Where were you planning to spend the night?"

"I don't know. A hotel."

"The two of you in a hotel."

"Separate rooms," Lane said. "What's wrong with that?"

"Have you thought of the expense?" his mother said.

"What's so expensive?" Lane said.

"Hotels," his mother said. "Nice ones, at least."

"Well," his father said, "I hope you know what you're doing."

"I know what I'm doing," Lane said.

"I'm not so sure of that," his father said. He sat hunched with his bottle in his fist, staring moodily at last winter's banked ashes. Lane looked at him and knew that the discussion was over.

Chapter Seven

HE GAVE no outward sign that he cared or even knew that she was going away overnight with his son. There was no difference in the way he looked at her or spoke to her, or in the brusque notes he left on her typewriter. His silence on any subject but her work, so impenetrable and absolute, felt to Claire like a rebuke, as perhaps it was, but there was also a certain comfort in his unaltered courtesy and patience, his absolute professionalism. At least here, in the workplace, he could overlook what was about to happen, if not forgive it, and would overlook it afterward. He was not a vindictive man.

They left before sunrise. The roads were awash in lavender shadow, the birds were waking, and the air was cool and clear as springwater. He waited for her by the white picket fence in front of the house and heard the car's soft mutter a long way off.

It grew rapidly to a liquid and slightly tremulous hum, and then the yellow Camaro appeared from around the bend in the road, and in it Claire's face, her smile when she saw him standing by the road with his overnight bag as if he were waiting for a bus or taxi.

She pulled over. She wore a red-checked shirt with the sleeves rolled, and white slacks and sandals.

"You ought to be driving a sports car," he said. "A Corvette." With the top down and the wind in her jet-black hair.

"Tell me something," she said. "Are you one of those guys who has to drive when he's with a girl?"

"Only if she asks me," he said.

"Then I'm asking," she said.

The roads were empty. He ran the stop sign at the end of the street, bumped across the railroad tracks and swung through the intersection by Dimmock's without touching the brake. They passed the Amvets Hall, the Knights of Columbus, the cemetery and Turner's Ice Cream and got on the highway. Not a cloud up ahead of them, just hard luminous blue. Claire turned on the radio and found "Midnight Train to Georgia."

"This okay?" she said.

"Sure."

They drove over the sky-high arch of the bridge and down Route 44 through the leafy towns above New Bedford. They got onto Interstate 95. The sun rose and whitened the highway. There was traffic now; lone drivers and highballing eighteen-wheelers and cars whose back seats were full of kids.

"I'm almost finished with *Bleak House*," Claire said.

"Who's your favorite character?"

"Lady Dedlock, of course."

"After Lady Dedlock."

"It isn't Esther Summerson," Claire said. "She's too sweetsie."

"How about Mrs. Bagnet?" Lane said.

"No," Claire said, "the detective, Mr. Bucket. He makes me laugh."

"He reminds me a little of Paul Williams," Lane said. "The amiable exterior."

"Mr. Bucket doesn't come on to women," Claire said.

"Mr. Bucket has other things on his mind," Lane said, smiling.

"Williams was okay last time I saw him. He was actually very helpful."

"Lady Dedlock reminds me of you," Lane said.

"Yeah. A deep, dark secret in her past."

"That isn't why," Lane said.

They crossed tiny Rhode Island, entered Connecticut, and stopped for breakfast along the Turnpike. They ordered take-out. Claire paid and they got back on the road.

"A personal question," Claire said. "What'll you do if they draft you?"

"They won't draft me while I'm in VISTA."

"But afterwards."

"I've filed as a CO."

"CO?"

"Conscientious objector." He looked at her. "Does that bother you?"

"Why should it?"

"A draft dodger."

"I don't believe in the war, either."

"There's no guarantee I'll get the 1-O status. The draft board can always say no."

"Then what?"

"I don't know."

"Go to Canada?"

"I just don't know," he said.

The Connecticut Turnpike raveled out ahead of them, straight and endless-seeming, over lush green countryside broken here and there by a working farm or huddled town. It brushed the edges of the smoggy cities of New London, New Haven, and Bridgeport, affording glimpses of the hazy sun-silvered ocean. Near the New York border they left I-95 and drove west. They crossed the Hudson on the Tappan Zee Bridge while far below white sails drifted like shavings of ivory on the dark blue water. They drove down into New Jersey.

"I'm beginning to wonder if this is such a hot idea," Claire said. She'd been silent awhile.

"Too late now," Lane said.

"No it isn't."

"Yes," he said, "it is."

"It really wasn't fair to bring you into it."

"I brought myself into it."

"Yeah, but you don't know what you're getting into. This is a bad neighborhood we're going into. They don't like white people coming around. Stokely Carmichael and Rap Brown and that bunch have got them stirred up."

"Don't forget," he said, "I went to college in a city."

"You went to college in Cambridge."

"Cambridge isn't a city?"

"Not like the Baltimore ghetto."

"We'll be all right," Lane said.

They stopped for lunch on the Garden State Parkway. You

could feel the massive presence of New York City off to the east, an emanation of heat and energy, of acrid city air.

"Why do they call it 'the Garden State'?" Lane said.

"Because of the farms."

"What farms?"

"I guess they're out there somewhere," Claire said.

They bypassed Philadelphia on the Pennsylvania Turnpike and rejoined I-95 in West Chester. By two-thirty they had left Delaware and were advancing through the gentle hills of Maryland, past red barns and cornfields.

"What if Tyrone Moore's mother isn't home?" Claire said.

"We'll ask around, find out where she is."

"Ask around. We're going to get ourselves shot."

"No matter what happens," he said, "you're going to be glad you came down here."

The sun had fallen from the meridian and tumbled halfway down the sky. The air changed, grew warm and blossom-scented. Southern air. The low hills now were littered with tract houses, and pretty soon Baltimore stood on the horizon, a dull steel-gray, the sky pale above it. Claire opened her purse. She took out Tyrone Moore's address and a map of the city.

"We want Gay Street," she said, unfolding the map. "I guess the first thing is to get on I-83."

"Tell me where to turn," he said.

"Maybe we ought to wait till morning," she said.

"What for?"

"We'll be fresher. It'll probably be safer."

"Let's get it over with," he said.

They entered the city, left the downtown area and were soon lost in a grid of shadeless one-way streets lined with brick rowhouses and windowless taverns and corner stores with metal lattice that could be drawn across the display windows at night. There wasn't much traffic. People sat on brick stoops fanning themselves with folded newspapers. A woman in a maid's uniform waited for a city bus.

"Lock your door," Claire said, locking hers.

Lane looked at her. He shrugged and pushed the lock down.

"It isn't any good unless you roll your window up," she said.

Sweat already plastered his shirt to his back. He rolled the window halfway up. Claire studied the map. She looked at the street signs.

"Tell me what to look for," Lane said.

"Gay Street."

"I know that. What else?"

"Orleans. Or Monument."

"Here's Monument," he said.

"What are we on now?"

"North Carolina."

"Shit. We're going the wrong way."

"I'll ask somebody," he said.

"Better be careful," she said.

He pulled over and double parked in front of a laundromat where two young men stood talking.

"Not them," Claire said.

"Why not?" Lane said.

"All right, but watch yourself," she said.

He left the engine running and got out and slammed the door. The two men stopped talking and watched him come toward them. They were both lean and good-looking and well dressed. One of them wore lime-green slacks and a green cashmere sweater with no shirt under it. The other wore a rasp-berry silk shirt. They eyed Lane neutrally and waited for him to speak.

"Could you tell me where Gay Street is?" he said.

They looked at each other. "You sellin' somethin'?" said the man in green.

"I'm looking for somebody," Lane said.

Their gazes moved out past him and fastened on Claire, who watched them through her dark glasses from inside the car.

"Who you lookin' for, exackly?"

"A Mrs. Moore. She had a son named Tyrone."

"Tyrone Moore. Name's familiar."

"Tyrone, yeah, he that gangbanger got hisself kilt on the Park-way ain't too long ago."

"That's the one," Lane said.

"What you want with his mother?"

"I just want to talk to her. You know where she lives?"

"You said Gay Street, man."

"Right."

"Then you know where she live at."

"I don't know where Gay Street is," Lane said.

"Don't you, now."

"No," Lane said.

"You sure you ain't sellin' nothin'?"

"I'm sure."

"Buyin', then."

"No," Lane said.

"He a cop, Munro," said the one in the silk shirt.

"I'm not a cop," Lane said.

"Who that lady with you?" the one called Munro asked.

"She a lady cop," the other said.

"No," Lane said.

"Ain't neither one of you cops?"

"We aren't cops, and we aren't selling anything."

"Tell him where Gay Street at," Munro said.

"You want North Gay or South?"

"The six hundred block," Lane said.

"Shit, y'all could walk there," said Munro's partner.

He gave the directions and Lane thanked both of them and got in the car.

"First they thought we were drug dealers," he said. "Then they wanted to know if we were cops."

"You should have said yes."

"I don't want to be a cop," Lane said.

Gay Street was lined on both sides with parked cars. Big cars; not fancy, necessarily, or well maintained, but big. They found the address, a brick rowhouse with mustard-yellow trim, but there was no place near it to park, the cars solid along both sides of the street as far as they could see. Lane drove slowly on, through a cross street, through another, and found a space halfway down the next block. He backed in and killed the engine.

"Lock up," Claire said.

The sun was drawing down toward the building tops, but it was still hot in the street. The air was breathless and sticky and laced with a sharp smell of cinder. A young woman, hardly more than a girl, sat on a stoop in the warm shade with a baby in her arms. She watched Lane and Claire get out of the car. Lane said hello, and the girl nodded. Claire took his arm and they walked back toward Tyrone Moore's mother's rowhouse.

It was very quiet. Cars rolled by intermittently, moving leisurely, and here and there people sat alone or in pairs on the little stoops. Most of them were old, with gray-black faces and irritable gazes that followed Lane and Claire with silent and faintly hostile interest. Lane nodded to them, but they did not say hello.

They crossed the first side street. A police car came up Gay, and the two cops saw Lane and Claire and pulled over to the curb next to a fire hydrant and waited for them with the engine idling.

"What's up?" the cop behind the wheel said pleasantly. He wore a short-sleeve shirt and his elbow hung out of the open window. Both men were young. Both were white.

"How do you mean?" Lane said. Claire still held his arm.

"How do I mean? I mean what's going on. Maybe you're lost, for instance."

"We aren't lost," Lane said.

"You kind of look it, you know what I mean?"

"We're on our way to see somebody."

"You with the welfare office?"

"It's a private matter," Claire said.

The cops looked at her, running their gazes up and down.

"If I were you," the driver said to Lane, "I'd be careful."

"I'm being careful," Lane said.

"And you're sure you're not lost."

"I'm sure," Lane said.

The cop nodded and then took another look at Claire. He put the car in gear, and the cruiser swung out and glided away, slow, up the empty street.

"I wonder what that was all about," Lane said.

"I'll tell you what it was about. They think that if we don't work for the welfare department, we're either lost or crazy."

"They ought to mind their own business," Lane said.

"Let's find Mrs. Moore and get the hell out of here."

They walked on. Claire's sandal heels struck the pavement in distinct rapid clicks that echoed off the sides of the houses. They crossed the second side street. At the end of the block stood a corner store, a dark little place opening onto the intersection. The door opened, shaking a small toneless bell, and three full-grown boys came out, and then two more. They noticed Lane and Claire and stopped. They'd bought food in the store, sweet rolls and slices of ham, and they folded the ham on the rolls and ate and watched Lane and Claire come toward them.

"Just keep walking," she said quietly.

But they were blocking the sidewalk, and Lane stopped with Claire on his arm. Her grip tightened, her fingers squeezing, digging.

"What you want, white folks?" one of the boys said. He wore thick glasses and a denim jacket over his T-shirt despite the heat, and he was built like a pro halfback, with flat hips and a V-shaped upper body. He seemed to be the leader.

"We're looking for Mrs. Moore," Lane said. "Tyrone Moore's mother."

"Tyrone Moore dead," said a smaller boy with café-au-lait skin and a scowling expression of overdone, almost comical malevolence.

"We know that," Lane said. "We want to talk to his mother."

"His mother a 'ho'," the impish one said.

"Maxie, shut the fuck up," said the kid in glasses.

"Fuck you, Bobby," Maxie said.

"We don't care what she is," Lane said. "We want to talk to her."

"Y'all sellin' weed?" Bobby said. He tore off a bite of sweet roll and ham.

"We aren't selling anything," Lane said.

"Whyn't y'all gimme five dollars?" Maxie said. He pushed the last of his roll into his mouth.

The store door opened, jingling the bell, and a man in an apron came out. "What's all this?" he said.

"White folks here lookin' for Tyrone Moore's mama," Bobby said.

"She don't live round here no more," the man said.

"Are you sure?" Lane said.

"Sure I'm sure. What you want with her, anyhow?"

"Do you know where she went?" Lane said.

"Went down South where her family's at, what I heard."

"I told 'em she a 'ho', Mr. Thomas," Maxie said.

"Boy, what you know about it?" Mr. Thomas said.

"Know all I got to know," Maxie said, "and I ain't no boy."

"I was you," Mr. Thomas told Lane, "I'd get on out of here."

"Lane," Claire said, "let's go."

"Lane?" Maxie said. "That his name, Lane?"

"Y'all go back where you come from," Mr. Thomas said, "'fore these boys do you bad."

"We ain't gonna do 'em bad, Mr. Thomas," a tall boy said, grinning. He wore a gray sweatshirt lopped off at the shoulders. His long pale brown arms hung at his sides.

"I'll do 'em bad, they don't gimme five dollars," Maxie said.

"Don't say I didn't tell y'all," Mr. Thomas said, and went back into the store.

"Lane," Maxie said. "Sound like a honkie movie actor."

"Let's go, hon," Claire said, and gave Lane's arm a tug. "Please."

"It's half a block," Lane said. "Let's go make sure."

"Come on, white folks," Maxie said. "We show y'all where the house is at."

"We know where it is," Lane said.

"Show you anyway," Maxie said.

"Believe we will," Bobby said.

All seven of them crossed the side street, Claire still clutching Lane's arm, the boys surrounding them like captors or an escort, it wasn't clear which. They moved in a group down the block, filling the sidewalk.

"Miz Moore ain't gonna be there," Maxie said.

"I believe you," Lane said.

"What you goin' for, then?" Maxie said.

"He want to see with his own eyes," Bobby said.

Then, behind them, a boy said, "I like watchin' you walk, lady."

"She fine," said another.

"You can sit on my face, you want to," the first one said.

Lane turned on him, breaking loose from Claire. It was the tall kid in the cutoff sweatshirt.

"Don't," Lane said.

"Don't what?" He was taller than Lane. He looked him in the eye and faintly, coldly, smiled.

"Don't talk like that," Lane said.

Claire had his arm again, gripping it now with both hands. "Lane," she said. "Never mind."

"Talk how I want to, motherfucker."

176

"Shut up, fool," Bobby said.

"He gettin' all bad with me, Bobby. I'll whip his white ass."

"What you expect, you talk that trash to his old lady?" Bobby said.

"I was just jivin' 'em."

"Just jivin' 'em," Bobby said.

"It's all right," Lane said.

"See that?" the tall one said. "We cool, ain't we?"

"Sure," Lane said.

"Damn," Maxie said, "I wanted to see 'em fight."

"Let's go, white folks," Bobby said. "The house right up here. Ain't gonna find Tyrone's mama, though."

The boys waited while Lane and Claire went up the steps and into a dark vestibule with tin mailboxes and doorbells on the wall. Names were Scotch-taped beside the doorbells. WIGGENS. JONES. ROBINSON. HUNTER. COFFEY. RAINEY.

"Damn," Lane said.

Claire folded her arms and leaned back against the wall. She closed her eyes.

"Are you sure her name was Moore?" Lane said.

"Yes."

"Maybe someone in the building knows where she went."

"The man told us where she went."

"That was just something he heard," Lane said.

He pressed the button beside WIGGENS, choosing randomly. He pressed it again, and a door opened somewhere inside and they heard footsteps plodding toward them. A low, thick female voice spoke to them through the door.

"Who is it?"

"I'm looking for Mrs. Moore," Lane said.

"She don't live here no more."

"I'm trying to find out where she went," Lane said.

"You the poh-leece?"

"No."

The door opened and a stout, very black woman in a cotton dress and bedroom slippers eyed them morosely. "She in Macon, Georgia," she said.

"Macon, Georgia?"

"That's right. She got folks down there."

"Well," Lane said. "Thank you."

"You sure you ain't the poh-leece?"

"I promise," Lane said.

Three of the boys were sitting on the porch steps. Bobby and Maxie were perched on the hood of a car with their legs dangling. The three boys got up and moved to the sidewalk as Lane and Claire came out.

"Now you believe us?" Maxie said.

"God*damn* it," Claire said.

"We did our best," Lane said.

"Done your best at what?" Maxie said.

Claire closed her eyes, pinching off tears that ran glistening down her cheeks. Lane put his arm around her, and she turned and hid her face against his shoulder. The boys looked at each other but didn't say anything. Claire sniffed and stepped back and wiped her eyes with the back of her hand.

"You had to try," Lane said.

"Try what?" Maxie said.

"What's this about?" Bobby said.

"It's personal," Lane said.

"Somethin' 'bout Tyrone, I bet," Maxie said.

"Y'all knew Tyrone?" Bobby said.

"No," Lane said.

A police car turned the corner and came up the street at a slow prowl. Lane guessed who the two cops were. They saw him and Claire and pulled over and double-parked. Bobby and Maxie popped down off the car hood. Claire gave her eyes another wipe with her shirtsleeve. The cop who was driving, the one who had spoken to them before, got out of the cruiser, leaving the engine running.

"Still here," he said.

"We were just leaving," Lane said.

"I wonder if you and the lady have any form of ID," the cop said.

"Why?" Lane asked.

"I'd like to look at it, that's why."

He stepped up onto the sidewalk and the boys melted back, regarding him closely but without fear, as if he were dangerous only if you took your eye off him. Lane drew out his wallet. He handed his driver's license to the policeman. The cop looked at it.

"Massachusetts," he said.

"That's right."

"What are you doing down here?"

"I already told you."

"You didn't tell me anything." He returned the license, holding it between two fingers like a playing card.

"ID, ma'am?" he said.

"It's in the car," Claire said. "In my purse."

"And where's that?"

"Down the street."

"You from Massachusetts?"

"Yes," she said.

"You two related?"

"We're friends."

"You know these boys here?"

"Boys?" Maxie said.

"We just met them," Lane said.

"Just met them," the cop said.

"A few minutes ago," Lane said. "They've been helping us."

"Helping you do what?"

"Look," Lane said, "we came down here to look somebody up. She's not here. Now we're going home."

He'd started forward as he finished speaking, and the cop stopped him with a hand on his chest. "Wait a minute," he said.

Lane looked at him. Claire moved to his side and took his arm.

"I see you around here again," the cop said, "you're going to talk to me. You understand?"

"I understand," Lane said.

The cop removed his hand. He turned and looked around at the boys. "I got my eye on your black asses, too," he said.

They watched him get into the police car. He said something to his partner and the two of them laughed. The car continued up the street in the same slow, watchful way as before.

"Bastards," Lane said.

"That ain't nothin'," Bobby said.

"He called us 'boys,'" Maxie said. "Y'all hear that?"

"What you come down here from Massachusetts for?" Bobby said.

"It's a long story," Lane said.

"It's me," Claire said. "I wanted to speak to Mrs. Moore. I wanted to tell her I'm sorry."

"Sorry 'bout Tyrone."

She nodded.

"Y'all did know Tyrone, then."

"I knew him," Claire said.

"Where at?"

"Don't ask me," she said. "Okay?"

Bobby looked at her. The pale light flashed on his glasses. "Okay," he said softly.

For a while no one spoke or moved. A car went by. From a second-story window across the street floated the thin airy tenor of Smokey Robinson.

"You say you parked up the street?" Bobby said.

Lane nodded.

"We'll walk you to your car," Bobby said.

.   .   .

THEY DROVE back in the heat and glare of the urban early evening, and this time found their way without getting lost. Claire lit a cigarette. She watched the rowhouses slip past.

"You okay?" Lane said.

"I guess so. You?"

"Sure."

"I shouldn't have brought you here."

"I wanted to be brought," he said.

They got on the interstate and drove awhile in companionable silence, alone with their thoughts, but not alone. Long shadows had crept out, and the light, outside the city, was golden. The wind coming in through the window turned sweet again and cooler. At twilight they left the highway and followed signs to a Holiday Inn. The parking lot was huge and nearly empty. Lane parked in front of the motel, and they sat in the country stillness and looked at the featureless modern building with its red-carpeted entrance and cheerful marquee: HAPPY HOUR 4:30–7. He had never checked into an American hotel by himself. He had never signed a register except in pensions and cheap hotels in Italy, Switzerland, and France.

"Lane," Claire said.

He looked at her.

"What are you going to do when you get in there?"

"What do you mean?" he said.

"At the desk," she said. "What are you going to say?"

"That we want a couple of rooms," he said.

Claire didn't say anything. Lane waited. He didn't move.

"You want to get a single?" Claire said.

"If you do," Lane said.

"That doesn't sound very enthusiastic," she said.

"Of course I do," Lane said. "I just don't want to push you."

"Don't want to push me? We wouldn't be here if you hadn't pushed me."

"About this, I mean."

Claire nodded and was silent a moment. "Before you say yes, you better think about it," she said.

"I don't need to think about it."

"It's going to make things harder. Do you understand that?"

"No," he said, "I don't."

She laid her head back and looked at the blue eastern sky. She'd taken off her dark glasses. She looked tired and sad and very lovely.

"I told myself I wouldn't," she said.

"You don't have to," he said.

"I know," she said.

He took her hand. "Tell me what to do."

"Ask for a double and register us as Mr. and Mrs. Lane Hill-man."

"They won't say anything?"

"They might think it, but they won't say it."

Lane carried his bag and hers into the motel. He set them down and signed the register while Claire waited in an armchair across the flagstone lobby, sitting with her legs crossed and her purse in her lap. The clerk was a pale, slack-faced young man not much older than Lane. He glanced at Claire a couple of times while Lane wrote in the book, then pushed the room key toward him and looked at her again.

"Room 73, sir," he said. "Get off the elevator and go left."

The room was air-cooled and as clean and impersonal as if it had never been used. It was his first modern generic hotel; with his parents and grandparents he'd always stayed at older places rich in ambience and history. The Copley, the Algonquin. He put the bags down and sat on one of the double beds. Claire drew the curtain back from the wall-length window and stood looking out over the twilit countryside rolling back toward the city. The air-conditioner droned windily.

"There's a dining room in the hotel," Lane said, and knew immediately how irrelevant it sounded, how inadequate to the moment.

"I'll want a shower first," Claire said.

She stood motionless at the window with her back to him, swayed thin-waisted and graceful against the lambent peach sky. It was August now, and the long days, the lingering mother-of-pearl twilights, were behind them. Even Lane could feel it. He waited, and after a while she turned and smiled, and brought the smile to the bed, all melancholy gone, traceless, like a garment she'd shed. She sat down and took his hand.

"Just so you know," she said, "I'm on the pill."

He nodded.

"I bet you never had to worry about birth control, did you? I bet all your little college tricks were on the pill or had IUDs."

"There were only two."

"That's all?"

"Why do you call them 'tricks'?"

"Don't pay any attention, sweets. I'm being catty."

He lifted her hand to his mouth and kissed it. "How come you're on the pill?" he said.

"Because it regulates my period and makes the cramps hurt less. Why do you ask?"

"I was just wondering."

"You didn't think I was sleeping with anybody?"

"No."

"You did," she said. "Just for a minute."

"I did not."

"Why do men worry about that so much? I don't think Scott ever trusted me."

"I trust you."

"Who the hell would I be sleeping with?"

"No one," he said and kissed her gently, the two of them sitting side by side on the edge of the bed. She closed her eyes, opened them, and smiled.

"I love you," he said. "You're the first."

"Am I?"

"The one and only," he said.

She looked at him contentedly but without surprise, like a queen to whom he'd sworn eternal fealty, then kissed him once lightly, sealing the pledge, and got up. Lane watched her go into the bathroom and turn on the light and look the place over. She turned and stood in the doorway and began unbuttoning her shirt.

"Come here," she said.

He stood up slowly. Claire peeled back her shirt and dropped it on the floor. Lane took his shirt off, and they undressed, watching each other. Claire stepped out of her underpants. She moved to the shower, turned it on, and adjusted the temperature. She looked at him over her shoulder, dropping him a knowing half-smile, and extended her hand. Lane took it, and they stepped hand in hand, like playmates, into the shower.

He'd memorized every inch of her in the two-piece bathing suit, but it's different with nothing on, the imagination can never make that short final leap. She was buttermilk-white where the suit covered her, and her uncupped breasts looked smaller, and her hips broader and higher up her body, making her leggier and shorter-waisted and too good to be true. The hot water and scented motel soap washed away the tension and road weariness, and they kissed and caressed, discovering each other, until Claire felt behind her and turned off the shower.

They made love on top of the bedspread in the soft current of the air-conditioner. She let him know when it was time for him to enter her, and he came too quickly and it was over. She hugged him hard, as if he'd done something marvelous or heroic, and he rolled back and looked up at the low white motel ceiling.

"Damn," he said.

She raised herself on her elbow. "Lane, honey, there's a few things you have to learn."

"I know," he said.

"Not about sex. About women."

"What?" he said.

She smiled and didn't answer. She leaned in and kissed him, then got up and moved unshyly around the room and found her purse. She dug out a cigarette and came back and smoked it sitting up beside him with one leg out straight and the other cocked sexily. Lying beside her, free to touch her, use her, Lane felt drunk. He felt expansive, grateful, light-headed.

"You're beautiful," he said.

"Not beautiful," she said. "Ingrid Bergman and Audrey Hepburn are beautiful."

"So are you," he said.

"I guess the eyes of love are blind," she said.

"Not my eyes."

"Who said that, anyway? Shakespeare?"

"Must have been."

"You don't know?"

"It sounds like *A Midsummer Night's Dream.* In that one a beautiful queen falls in love with a yokel who has a donkey's head."

"Why?"

"You mean why does she fall in love with him, or why does he have a donkey's head?"

"Both."

"It's all done by magic. Everything gets straightened out in the end."

"Aren't you smart," she said. She rubbed out her cigarette. "Want to get some dinner?"

"Not yet," he said.

She looked down at him. "No?"

"Not yet."

"Oh my," she said, and slid down beside him.

He put his hand on the warm smooth curve of her hip. "I hope this time'll be better," he said.

"You'd better stop worrying about that," she said.

.　.　.

THE DINING room was almost empty by the time they got there. They drank manhattans to celebrate and got high and held hands on the table.

"You were terrific today," she said.

"You know what I loved?" he said. "The way you kept taking my arm. It was like a current running through me. A kind of energy, but calm, almost peaceful."

She closed her eyes, opened them, and smiled. "I'm glad we kept going," she said. "You were right: we had to go to the house and be sure."

"Do you think Mrs. Moore was really a whore?"

"Could be."

"The kids were nice, once you got to know them," Lane said.

"I liked Bobby," she said.

"I liked Maxie."

"I think Maxie had a couple of screws loose."

"You can't blame them for being hostile. Look at the way those cops acted."

"Weren't they beauties?" Claire said.

"No wonder black power is the thing now."

"I'm going to worry about you in Detroit."

"You'd worry more if I were in Vietnam."

"You aren't going to Vietnam. Don't even talk about it."

"I'd go if I believed in it."

"I know you would."

"My father was in the Marines in World War II," Lane said.

"My brothers were in the Korean War," Claire said.

"I don't know if that war was right or wrong."

"My brothers didn't worry about it."

They were the last to leave the dining room. The lights had been turned on and the waitresses were setting the tables for breakfast. Lane took Claire's hand and they rode the elevator up without speaking. They chain-locked their door, shed their clothes on the floor, and made drunken love under the covers. Lane had been looking forward to a long night of lovemaking, but he fell asleep and it was morning when he woke, and the bed was empty beside him.

The bathroom door was closed. The window curtain was drawn back, and the sky was lead-gray and low. He waited, and after some minutes Claire came out of the bathroom brushing her hair. She looked rested. She was wearing the red-checked shirt from yesterday, unbuttoned, and nothing else. She smiled and sat down on the bed, brushing her hair.

"Somebody passed out last night," she said.

"It was the manhattans."

"I'm glad you slept," she said.

"I'm not," he said.

He watched her brush her hair. A leg was tucked under her and her head was tilted to one side, and as she pulled the brush through her lustrous black hair she seemed to know, to understand, how beautiful she was at this moment, how desirable. She didn't flaunt it; it simply *was,* and she knew it. Lane almost hesitated to touch her, as you would a priceless and fragile work of art. He reached slowly and put his hand on her leg. Claire went on brushing.

"I'm going to give you money," she said, "and you can pay the bill."

"I wish you'd let me pay half," he said.

"We've been all through that," she said.

"I still don't like it."

"A deal's a deal," she said. "But I want you to pay, so the clerk won't think I'm buying you, like poor Patricia Neal in *Breakfast at Tiffany's.*"

"You'd never have to buy anybody," he said.

"When I'm old and gray, I might."

"Never," he said.

His hand still rested on her leg. Its warmth seemed to flow upward into his curved palm and beyond. He moved the hand down between her thighs, then up under her shirt, over her hip to the soft flesh above the hipbone, and around and up the graceful sweep of her back. She lowered the hairbrush.

"I don't know," she said. "I'm a little sore today."

"Sore?"

"From being out of practice."

"Oh," he said.

"Of course," she said, brushing again, "there are other ways."

Lane looked at her, and she paused in mid-stroke and regarded him thoughtfully.

"Didn't your college girls ever do that for you?" she said.

Lane, beginning to understand, shook his head.

"I'm glad," Claire said.

She put down the hairbrush. Lane moved over. Claire took off her shirt and threw the sheet back and swung her legs up onto the bed. "Just relax," she said. "Pretend you're floating." Lane lay back. Claire knelt beside him. She ran a cool hand up his chest, then folded herself down over him. Lane closed his eyes and waited, as in a lovely and unprecedented dream, for what was going to happen.

.   .   .

AFTER THE trains stopped running from the Cape to New York, they had driven to Pennsylvania to visit his grandmother. Lane was older now; he helped with the driving. Coming home, he would see the estuarine marshes around Fall River and New Bedford and know he was in his own corner of New England. The marshes stretched out pale green, intersected by still, ditchlike streams that coiled back on themselves as they wandered in from harbor and inlet. In the distance, when the woods parted, you could see the ocean in its different moods.

Lane wasn't glad to see the marshes today. He drove gloomily, watching the wet highway come at them, resenting every mile.

"Where will we make love?" he said.

"Be patient, sweets. Take it a day at a time."

"Where?" he insisted.

"You leave that to me," she said.

Darkness was closing in when they stopped in front of his house. The front rooms—Lane's bedroom downstairs, Lizzie's up—were unlighted. Lane turned off the engine and put his arm around her.

She glanced at the house. "We'd better not," she said.

"They're going to know anyway," he said.

"I suppose," she said.

"They won't care," he said.

"Your parents will, and I wouldn't blame them."

"Why?"

"Why? Because I'm thirty-seven years old, I'm divorced, and I have a fifteen-year-old daughter. That's just for starters."

"I love you," he said. "I love everything about you."

"Then you're crazy."

"Crazy as hell," he agreed.

She looked at him and smiled. "You have to promise me one thing," she said.

"All right."

"No one at the office can know, except your father. No flirting at work. No touching."

"Are we going to sneak around? Never be seen together?"

"I don't know," she said. "I haven't thought that far."

"I have," he said.

"I have more to lose than you do. Do you understand that?"

"I want to go out with you. See a movie. Have a drink."

"One day at a time," she said.

She let him kiss her, then they got out of the car. He pulled his bag from the back seat and set it down on the sidewalk and kissed her again, and after a moment she pushed him gently away.

"Thanks," she said.

"For what?"

"For coming with me. For everything."

She got into the car on the driver's side. She reached down and moved the seat forward. She started the car and looked up at him.

"Hey," she said.

"What," he said.

"You're the first guy."

She was gone, the engine's purr and the wet swish of tires dying away to nothing before he understood.

Chapter Eight

SHE WONDERED IF she'd overdressed. Sunflower-yellow chiffon cocktail dress, spike heels, the pearl necklace Mallory had given her and which she'd decided to keep because he owed her something, and why not pearls? She'd put her hair up. Studying herself in the full-length mirror, she twirled, swirled her skirt. From the hall came the nasal wail of Bob Dylan. "Stuck Inside of Mobile with the Memphis Blues Again." That funny twitch in his voice.

April appeared in the doorway. She'd put on the nice peach sweater Claire had found for her at Filene's, with her white slacks and sandals. She folded her arms and looked sullenly at Claire in the mirror.

"What does it mean, April?" Claire said, watching herself.

"'Stuck inside of Mobile with the Memphis blues again'? Is it some kind of symbolism?"

"Stop admiring yourself," April said.

"Go brush your hair."

"I already brushed it."

"Brush it some more."

"God," April said, "you'd think we were going to Buckingham Palace or something."

"It's a courtesy when people invite you to dinner not to go looking like a slob."

"I look like a slob. Thanks, Mom."

"April, just go brush your hair, will you?"

"Why do I have to go to these people's house, anyway?"

"Because you were invited."

"No, *you* were."

"We both were. One night not seeing Kyle isn't going to kill you."

"It wouldn't kill *you* to go without me tonight."

"Will you go brush your goddamn hair and act your age?"

"Act my age? What about you?"

She turned and strode out and slammed the door. Her sandals clacked on the bare hardwood floor of the hallway. Her bedroom door slammed, and "Stuck Inside of Mobile" swelled to a roar.

"Jesus H.," Claire said.

She sighed, opened the door and went down the hallway. There was no lock on April's door. Claire turned the knob and walked into the gale of music. April was lying on the bed reading *The Wind in the Willows,* or pretending to. Lane had loaned it to her. Claire went to the record player, which squatted on the floor, leaned and lifted the arm, careful not to scratch the LP. April shot her a look, then resumed reading.

"April," Claire said.

April turned a page.

"All right," Claire said, and snatched the book from her hands, shut it with a loud clap, and threw it—because it belonged to Lane—harmlessly into a soft chair. April folded her arms and glowered at the far wall.

"What age am I acting?" Claire said.

April didn't answer or look at her.

"What age?" Claire said. "Twenty-five? Nineteen? Two-and-a-half?"

April sighed and still didn't look at her. Claire sat down on the edge of the bed.

"What do you want me to do?" she said. "How do you want me to act?"

April shrugged.

"If you're going to criticize," Claire said, "you could at least back it up with something."

"Never mind," April said. "Forget it."

Claire looked down at the floor. The dark-blond wood was scuffed smooth and varnishless by the feet of boys and girls grown now, of adults long dead.

"How can I forget it when my daughter tells me I'm acting like a child?"

"You told me I was acting like one."

"You were being difficult, April. Is it so goddamn hard to go have dinner with a nice family?"

"No, it's not so goddamn hard."

"Why do you insist on swearing, April?"

"Why do you?"

"Because I was brought up in a house full of men with dirty mouths."

"All the more reason not to."

"You're right," Claire said. She looked at her watch. "We're due there in ten minutes."

"What are you so uptight about?"

"I'm not."

"Yeah. Right."

"It's hard, April. I don't know what his parents think."

"Who cares what they think?"

"They're nice people. I don't want to hurt them. Not to mention that Mr. Hillman's my boss."

"If they don't like it, why'd they invite you to dinner?"

"They invited *us* to dinner. I think it was Lane's idea."

"Are you having an affair with him?"

Claire looked out at the sun-gilded leaves of the oaks. "An affair. That's such a funny way to put it."

"Are you?"

"What if I asked you if you were having an affair with Kyle?"

"For pete sake, Mom."

"It's just a funny question when you love someone."

"I wouldn't go so far as to say I love Kyle."

"No?"

"You are having one with Lane, aren't you?"

Claire looked away. "I'm very fond of him, April."

"Cool," April said.

"You think so?"

"Very."

"Well. We'd better get going. We're supposed to be there now."

"I have to brush my hair," April said.

"Leave it. It's fine."

"Leave it and be a slob, you mean."

"Am I going to pay for that remark for the rest of my life?"

"Probably," April said, and jackknifed forward and pivoted off the bed.

.   .   .

HE WAS in the yard playing football with a half-dozen little boys from the neighborhood. Claire eased the car down the sloping gravel driveway. She and April got out slowly and stood and watched Lane toss a pass to a stocky towhead of perhaps eight or nine. The boy got under the ball and tried clumsily to hug it as it spiraled down. It grazed his chest, hit the ground, and bounced away, end over end. Lane grinned. He looked over at Claire and April. He was wearing a maroon-lettered Harvard Athletic Department T-shirt.

"Evening, ladies," he said.

The little towhead put his hands on his hips and hung his head disconsolately, the way boys and men do wherever games are played.

"Nice try, Patrick," Lane said.

"He can't catch squat," said an older boy.

"Don't listen to him, Patrick," Lane said.

Claire gave April a little prod, and they moved toward the gray weathered house with its slant roof and chimneys. The boys watched them come across the lawn. Claire held a bouquet of summer flowers. Her dress glowed flame-yellow in the oblique light of the sun.

"Game's over, guys," Lane said.

"We won," said a boy.

"I don't remember it that way," Lane said.

"Twelve-nothing," the kid said. "You didn't even score."

"Toss me the ball, will you, Greg?" Lane said.

Greg picked up the football and pushed a wobbly pass, which Lane pulled in with one hand. I bet he was good, Claire thought. I bet he was as good in his way as Scott ever was.

"Night, everybody," Lane said.

The boys drifted off in several directions, looking back once or twice over their shoulders. Lane gave April a hug, and she returned it awkwardly, angular and unpliant in his embrace. He surprised Claire with a brief kiss on the mouth, then took her arm and moved with her toward the house with April walking behind them.

"You didn't have to bring flowers," he said.

"I had to bring *some*thing," she said.

"She's very uptight," April said.

"Relax," Lane said. "They're all going to love you."

They climbed the steps of the small brick porch with its white wooden railing. Lane opened the screen door and stood aside, letting them into a cluttered sunlit kitchen. At the stove stood his mother. She wore pink and green floral culottes, had blue eyes like Lane's, and was moonfaced and beautiful.

"I'm Sally," she said.

"This is Claire," Lane said, "and April."

"I've heard so much about you," Sally Hillman said.

Claire offered her hand. Sally put down two singed potholders, wiped her hands on her culottes, and gave Claire's a gentle squeeze.

"These are for you," Claire said.

"*Gracious,*" Sally said, as if it were a jewel Claire had brought her, an enormous diamond.

Lane looked around for a place to put his football.

"Nice to meet you, too, April," his mother said.

"Same," April said.

"I hope you like meatloaf. It's Lane's favorite. Lane, get a vase for these beautiful flowers."

The dog padded in, wagging her feathery tail. April's face lit up prettily, and she dropped to one knee and stroked the Lab's head and back.

"That's Tasha," Sally said.

"Hi, Tasha," April said.

"Lane, get Claire a drink. April, we have Tab and Sprite and ginger ale."

"Want a bourbon, April?" Lane said.

"Sprite, please," April said.

"Lane, get April a Sprite."

"I don't think we have any," he said.

Then Mr. Hillman appeared in the doorway. He had an empty glass in his hand. He still wore his white shirt and loosened necktie.

"Well," he said.

April came slowly to her feet.

"Dad," Lane said, "this is April."

"Hello, April," he said.

"Hi," she said.

"This is very nice of you," Claire said.

"Heavens," Sally said, "we wanted to."

"I love your house," Claire said. "It must be very old."

"It's a mess, I'm afraid," Sally said.

"Want a bourbon?" Lane said.

"Not too strong," Claire said.

"Where are the girls?" Sally said.

Lane went into the pantry and came out with three glasses. He opened the refrigerator. "I don't see any Sprite," he said.

"I'm sure we have some," his mother said.

"How about a ginger ale?" Lane said.

"Fine," April said.

"Lane *said* you were pretty," Sally said.

"I'm afraid I'm overdressed," Claire said.

"In this house, anything goes," Sally said.

Lane broke ice cubes out of a tray. He snapped open a can of ginger ale and uncapped the Old Crow.

"Lane, I don't want your football on my counter," his mother said.

Lane handed April her ginger ale. "You sure you don't want a little bourbon in that?" he said.

"Very funny," April said.

He gave Claire her drink and winked at her.

"Did you find a vase?" his mother said.

"I've only got two hands," Lane said.

"Sweetheart, did you see the beautiful flowers Claire and April brought us?"

"They're very nice," Mr. Hillman said.

"Where are the girls?" Sally said.

"Lane," his father said, "why don't you show your guests to the living room."

"And call the girls," his mother said.

The living room was long and low and smelled of mildew and old wood and flowers. Claire and April sat together on the sofa. Lane went to the foot of the stairs and called his sisters down. He sat down on the low, narrow bench in front of the fireplace.

"Why didn't you tell me not to dress up?" Claire said.

"I didn't know you were going to," Lane said.

"You could have said something."

"Said what?"

"Mom," April said, "will you stop being so uptight?"

"Thank you, April," Lane said.

Claire glared at him.

"Relax," Lane told her.

"You aren't helping," she said. "You aren't, either, April."

"You're lucky you have a dog," April said.

"We've always had one," Lane said.

His sisters appeared, first Lizzie, then Jessica and Meg together. They shook hands politely with Claire and April, then found seats here and there around the long room. Mr. Hillman came in with his glass refilled, and then Lane's mother, smiling radiantly, the sun at the center of her family.

"Meg," Lane said, "you and April'll be in school together next year."

"Meg can show you the ropes," his mother said.

The two girls didn't look at each other. April smiled politely.

"I bet you're a good student," Claire said.

"Not that good," Meg said.

"I'm not, either," April said.

"April, that's not true," Claire said.

April sent her an irritated glance but didn't say anything.

"I hear you had an interesting time in Baltimore," Sally said.

Claire blushed and glanced at Lane.

"Mom's a master of the non sequitur," he said.

"Lane told us about those policemen," said Lizzie, the oldest daughter. She had a long, pretty neck; a long, earnest face.

"They were something," Claire said.

"Someone ought to report them," Jessica said. She had softer lines than Lizzie and a quiet air, a dreaminess.

"I don't think it would do any good," Lane said.

"I'd have been petrified in that ghetto," his mother said.

"Well, I wouldn't have wanted to be there by myself," Claire said.

"Oh, but Lane said you weren't afraid at all," Sally said.

"Well, I was."

"Whatever made you store furniture in a place like that?" Sally said.

"She didn't know what kind of place it was," Lane said.

"You'd never actually been there, then," his mother said.

"The movers had," Lane said.

"This is very confusing," his mother said.

"It is, a little," his father said.

"Why didn't you have everything shipped straight up here?" his mother said.

"She didn't know she was going to end up here," Lane said.

"I think it was brave of both of you," Lizzie said.

"We all think *that,* child," her mother said.

At dinner Claire was seated next to Lane. She tried not to

look at him, was afraid of what his family would see in her face when she did.

"Isn't this meatloaf good, April?" she said.

"You better agree with her, April," Lane said.

"The secret," his mother said, "is to use really cheap ground beef. The cheaper, the better."

"I wouldn't broadcast it, Mom," Meg said.

"Why not? Claire might want to make it for Lane sometime."

"I don't think I'd dare," Claire said.

"You always buy cheap food," Meg said. She turned to April. "She used to put powdered milk in with regular to save money. It was gross."

"Some people live on powdered milk," Lizzie said.

"Yeah, in the slums of Bombay," Lane said.

"We used to be a little hard up," Meg explained to April. "The house was a wreck."

"It wasn't *that* bad," Lizzie said.

"I don't think this house could ever be considered a wreck," Claire said. "Isn't it nice, April?"

"We live in kind of a dump," April said.

"April, we do not," Claire said.

"Remember when she used the soap powder?" Jessica said.

"It's a family legend," Lane said. "She mistook soap powder for powdered milk."

"You mean laundry detergent?" April said.

"It was in a jar on the counter," Sally said.

"She mixed it with our milk," Lane said.

"Claire," his mother said, "this happened *years* ago. I don't know how anyone even remembers."

"You drink soap, you remember it," Lane said.

"I think it's great you can laugh about it," Claire said.

Later, Sally said, "Lane was exhausted when he got back on Sunday."

"He went to bed at seven," Meg said.

"Are we back on Baltimore?" Lane said.

"I hope you found a decent motel after your hideous experience," his mother said.

Silence. Claire heard Lane breathe in beside her.

"I told you what we found," he said.

"A Holiday Inn, I think you said."

"About five times," Lane said.

"They're very comfortable, *I* think," his mother said. "We love Holiday Inns, don't we, sweetheart?"

"They'll do," said Lane's father.

"They even have them in Europe now," Lizzie said.

"Now," said Sally Hillman, "who wants apple crisp?"

. . .

Mr. Hillman got up before the dessert was finished. He kissed his wife and said good night to Claire and April and was gone, crossing the lawn in the gathering dusk with his briefcase under his arm. They heard the car start and roll up the driveway. A few minutes later there was a knock on the front door, and Lizzie popped up and carried her plate into the kitchen.

"It was very nice to meet you," she said. "I'll see you soon, I hope."

"I hope so, too," Claire said.

April helped Meg and Jessie clear the table. Then a horn honked out front, and Jessie said good-bye and left.

"Why don't you show April your room?" Sally said to Meg.

The two girls eyed each other.

"You want to?" Meg said.

"Sure," April said.

They disappeared up the stairs.

"We'll do the dishes," Lane said.

"Claire doesn't want to do *dishes,*" his mother said.

"I'd be glad to," Claire said.

"You go sit down and I'll bring you a beer," Lane said.

He took her a glass and a bottle of Piels, then came back and turned on the radio. The Stones were singing "As Tears Go By." He opened the dishwasher.

"Lane."

She stood at the sink looking out at the back yard, the black trees and the softer darkness filling in around them.

"What?" he said.

"They know we slept together in Maryland."

"No they don't."

"They do."

"So what?" he said.

She bowed her head, standing gracefully with one knee bent and her hands on the edge of the counter. Lane turned her gently and held her.

"They don't want me here," she said.

"That's crazy," he said.

"No," she said, "I could feel it."

"How 'bout it?" said the disc jockey. "An oldie! A knockout nifty from the past! Here's Ed Townsend . . ."

The song entered the room like a deep river of blue light, slow, sweeping them up irresistibly in its coils. Lane took her hand and danced with her.

For your love,
I would do anything . . .

Claire shut her eyes and rose on her toes and molded herself
against him. She could smell the laundered cotton of his T-shirt
and the clean, earth-warm essence of his skin. She could feel the
heat of his young body.

For your kiss,
I would go anywhere . . .

"Lane," she whispered. "Come over later. April's going out."
He touched his tongue to her cheek. "You bet," he said.
A saxophone played, sensual, weaving itself like an iridescent
ribbon through the song's blue glow. Lane slid his right hand far-
ther, deeper, down her back. She could feel him now, hard
against her thigh.

More foolish I grow,
With each heartbeat . . .

"We could go outside," he whispered. "There's an old founda-
tion of a barn."
And for a moment she considered it, a quick disheveling fuck
in the out-of-doors, flop down in the cool wet grass and pull her
skirt up. She would come in seconds, would explode.
"They'll think we're out walking," he whispered.
"No," she said. "We can't."
"Come on," he purred.
"We can't," she said again, but again she thought about it,

even imagined hoisting her skirt and shinnying up him right here in his mother's kitchen. But then the song ended, and the dance, and Lane held her another moment, squeezed her hard, and let her go.

"'For Your Love,'" said the DJ. "Gone from the charts, but not from the hearts!"

They looked at each other. Claire swallowed. Lane smiled.

"You go on home," he said.

"The dishes . . ." she said.

"I'll do the dishes."

"Hurry," she said.

. . .

SOME NIGHTS, after April had gone to bed, they made love under a lilac bush behind the house, where an ell and the back hedge hid them from passersby. Only someone venturing into the yard could have seen them, and Claire was very sure that wouldn't happen. Not in this staid neighborhood, where everyone minded their own business and you never saw anyone who didn't belong.

If she didn't go out with Kyle Bagwell, April went to bed at ten-thirty or eleven. They would wait until her light went out and they could no longer hear her shifting around in bed, give it another ten minutes to be sure, then creep outside with a couple of mothball-smelling wool blankets. The August nights had turned cool. They undressed quickly and hurried to lie down between the scratchy blankets. On her back, Claire could look up past the low-hanging boughs of the old lilac and see the stars and the vague swirl of the Milky Way. Once, opening her eyes in the sweet lassitude after orgasm, she saw a shooting star beyond the ridge of Lane's shoulder.

On the nights that April went out, they would go upstairs and undress each other by the chalky light of the streetlamp outside Claire's bedroom window. Their bodies were brown, lustrous as copper, and a glowing oyster-white where their bathing suits covered them. Lane wanted to learn, and she wanted to be the one who taught him, so she moved him around, moved herself around, sat him on a chair and herself on his lap, made love to him half-dressed, and took him into the shower and the bathtub. She put him on his back and salaamed down to him on her knees as she had that first morning in the motel room, and afterward he kissed his way up her leg and repaid the favor, improvising, teaching himself as he went.

Afterward, in bed or between the blankets under the lilac, they talked. She told him all about Scott, and about her father and mother. She told him of her lifelong fight with Violet. She talked about her early boyfriends, and the courses she'd taken at Dean Junior. She found she could talk freely even about Bob Mallory, and anything else under the sun.

Weekends they went to the beach. On Monday night they dressed up and went to the Melody Tent using Lane's reviewer's tickets and afterward stopped at the hotel bar where she'd first opened her heart to him. One Saturday it rained, and they went to the matinee at the Empire and held hands, and Lane told her about coming here as a kid to see John Wayne and Audie Murphy, and how before the Saturday matinees Harold Crocker, the school janitor, would put on shows with his ventriloquist's dummy, Butch, practicing up for his vain dream of appearing on the *Ted Mack Amateur Hour.* They ate at a restaurant, Claire insisting on Dutch treat.

In the office they avoided each other so fastidiously that it occurred to both of them that the unnaturalness of it would arouse suspicion, and so they went back to talking in the old way, kidding and even flirting a little. Claire's only rule was that there be no touching, and she wouldn't let him walk her to her car at the end of the day. Lane agreed reluctantly.

Time moved along, and August was half gone. One night they came out of the Irish Pub on Main Street and stood face-to-face with Fred Purdy and his wife Dot, who had taught Lane ninth-grade English. Fred regarded the two of them with unsurprise. Dot smiled her quick vivacious smile. Lane had known her all his life. His first memory of her was at the Fourth of July parade, when she'd held his hand and walked him and her son Eric up Main Street, both dressed in their cowboy outfits.

"Evening," Fred said pleasantly.

Lane gave Dot a hug. He hadn't seen her in a while.

"This must be Claire," she said.

The two women shook hands. Dot looked at her with her head tilted in an attentive and appraising way that Lane remembered from the classroom. "I think it's terrific the way you've caught on at the *Covenant*," she said.

"Well, I'm trying," Claire said.

"They're always hiring these smart young kids," Dot said, "and how often do they work out, Fred?"

"Not often enough," Fred said.

"Dot was my English teacher in ninth grade," Lane said. "I first read *A Tale of Two Cities* in her class."

"You had a lasting effect, believe me," Claire said.

"Is the music in there worth the cover charge?" Fred said.

"There is no cover," Lane said.

"Then the price is right, I'd say," Fred said.

"You're leaving soon," Dot said.

"Couple of weeks," Lane said.

"You take care of yourself," she said.

Claire was silent afterward in the car, watching the darkened Main Street stores go by.

"What?" Lane said.

"I didn't want that to happen," she said.

"It doesn't matter," Lane said.

"Think Fred'll tell people in the office?"

"Fred? He'd be the last one to gossip."

"It's funny," Claire said. "If I were the man and you were the woman, no one would think twice."

"That's right," Lane said. "Look at Cary Grant and his wife. What is she, fifty years younger?"

"Something like that."

"Frank Sinatra and Mia Farrow," Lane said. "Prince Andrew and Natasha."

"Who are they?"

"They're in *War and Peace*."

"Be serious, Lane."

"I am."

"Maybe we ought to stay home. What if we ran into Ruth Engle? The whole office would know in a day."

"So what?"

"So you're going to Detroit in two weeks. I'll still be here."

"You're my girl," Lane said. "I want to take my girl out, I'll take her out."

"Doesn't the girl get a say in this?"

"She's overruled," Lane said.

. . .

OVERRULED. A few nights later they went to the early show at the Empire. A gentle rain was falling when they came out. They stood under the marquee and watched the cars go hissing by with their wipers flapping.

"Buy you a drink," Lane said.

"Pressing our luck, aren't we?"

"You like swing music, right?"

"Why do you ask?"

"Come on," he said.

He'd never been in the place, but he'd seen the ads. There was a parquet dance floor, and the tables had red cloths and candles under red glass, creating a racy bordello atmosphere. The music was provided by a trio who were down from Boston for the summer. The ads claimed that they played the Copley, among other places, in the off-season. Tonight the lounge was less than half full, weekends being the big nights, and the trio played in an abstracted and listless fashion, going through the motions. No one was dancing.

They chose a table close to the dance floor and ordered a Black Russian and a bourbon. The waitress was older than the usual college summer help. She had a beauty spot below her left eye and wore a black miniskirt and black tights and heels. Lane watched her as she went to get their drinks.

"Don't strain your eyes," Claire said.

"No strain," he said.

"What is this, the Playboy Bunny Club?"

"This trio's supposed to be famous. I heard one of them played with Benny Goodman for a while."

Claire's gaze had wandered past him and out across the room. "Oh my God," she said.

"What?" he said.

"Turn around."

He did, and saw Paul Williams in the shadowy candlelit distance. He was sitting beside a pale-skinned bleached blonde, heavily made up and clearly past her prime. They were with a group of men and women at several tables that had been pushed together in a row near the wall. Williams was comfortably out of uniform in a shortsleeve madras shirt. The blonde said something into his ear and Williams laughed.

"That isn't his wife," Lane said.

"Why am I not surprised?" Claire said.

The band was doing "Mack the Knife." Lane took another look over his shoulder. "The guy in the green shirt owns the Sea View," he said. "The fat one built the new golf course."

"They look like real charmers," Claire said.

"A lot of money in the group," Lane said.

"I say we drink up and get out of here," Claire said.

Williams had seen them by the time the waitress brought their drinks. Claire didn't look at him, but she knew he was watching her, could feel the light and heat in his eyes. When they'd nearly finished their drinks and she thought they'd be able to leave with no more interchange with Williams than a distant passing wave, a friendly smile, he stood up, eyeing the two of them, smiling. Claire looked away. Williams picked up his drink, said something in the blonde's ear, and came toward them across the empty dance floor.

"Lane, let's get out of here," Claire said.

"Relax," he said, but it was too late anyway. Williams was at the table smiling a brittle, drunken smile that Claire had seen on other male faces, a cold smile that always meant trouble.

"Well," he said. "What the hell is this? A little office romance? A little rendezvous?"

"Hello, Paul," Lane said.

"You've been holding back on me," Williams said.

He looked around and found a chair and dragged it to the table. He sat down and placed his drink in front of him: gin or vodka with a sodden wedge of lime and ice cubes melted down to platelets. The trio had moved into "So Rare."

"So," Williams said, "what's the good word?"

"About what?" Lane said.

"Anything," Williams said. He looked at Claire, at Lane, and back at Claire, swinging the boozy grin back and forth.

"I can't get over this," he said. "I cannot fucking get over this. Are you two an item, or is this a one-night thing?"

"What's an item?" Claire said.

"It isn't a one-night thing," Lane said, "not that it's any of your business."

"Hey, I'm your *friend,* Lane," Williams said. "I'm your buddy."

"Speaking of friends," Claire said, "is that Mrs. Williams you're with tonight?"

"Now I bet you know the answer to that," Williams said. "I bet young Lane here already told you that isn't Mrs. Williams."

"It looks to me like she misses you," Claire said.

"She'll wait," Williams said. "You know who that is, Lane? Betty Winslow. Billy Winslow's ex-wife. She said you went to school with her daughter."

"Donna Winslow?" Lane said.

"Is it a one-night thing, or are you two an item?" Claire said.

"Me and Betty?" Williams said. "Let's just say she's a friend of mine. Like everyone else at that table. Like you and Lane. Matter of fact, why don't you two come join us?"

"We're about to leave," Claire said.

"Anything new on the Jane Clifford murder?" Lane said.

"Lane, you ask me that every fucking day."

"I haven't mentioned it in over a week," Lane said.

"Well, let me tell you. I think O'Neill's ready to give up. The girl got in a car with a transient. Didn't leave any footprints. Eddie's spinning his wheels. You know Eddie, right? Not very bright, but persistent as hell."

Claire looked across the room. Williams's blonde, Betty Winslow, watched him with vague apprehension as she listened with half her attention to the woman beside her, as a mother would glance repeatedly at a child down by the water's edge, or in the vicinity of a strange dog. *Why are we women such fools?* Claire thought.

"I only met O'Neill that one time in your office," Lane said. "He seemed pretty smart to me."

"Take my word for it," Williams said.

Claire wished Lane wouldn't be quite so cordial to him. She took out a cigarette. There was a book of matches on the table; Lane reached for it, but before he could tear a match, Williams had produced a lighter. He thumbed it open, lit it, and held it for Claire, cupping the flame in his small meaty hand and watching her as she leaned forward and sucked in her cheeks. She sat back again and turned and blew smoke into the air. Lane pocketed the matches. Williams capped the lighter with a flick of his thumb and in the same motion lowered and shoved it into his pocket, smooth as a movie cowboy holstering his six-shooter.

"Let me ask you something," Claire said without thanking him. "Do you try less hard when it's a stranger that gets killed? A stranger with no important connections, I mean. No money, no power."

"What are you saying?" Williams asked.

"I just said it," Claire said.

"Claire, that isn't fair," Lane said.

"Tell you what," Williams said, ignoring Lane. "Why don't you come dance with me and we'll talk about it."

"I don't think so," she said.

"Tough broad you got here, Lane," Williams said.

"Broad?" Claire said.

"You better learn to assert yourself, kid. A girl like this, you got to rein her in."

"This is making me sick," Claire said.

"You hear what I said, Lane?"

"I heard you."

"A girl like this'll take you to the cleaners, you don't assert yourself. She'll hang you out to dry, buddy."

"Maybe she doesn't want to," Lane said.

"Maybe she does and you don't know it."

"Maybe you ought to mind your own business," Lane said.

"Lane, honey, let's get out of here," Claire said.

"Time to go, Lane," Williams said.

"I'll go when I want to," Lane said.

"Hear that?" Williams said to Claire. "He'll go when he wants to."

"Tell you what," she said. "Why don't you and I have that

dance? We dance, then you go back to your table. How does that sound?"

"Wait a minute," Lane said.

"Sounds good," Williams said.

"You don't have to dance with him," Lane said.

"Maybe she wants to," Williams said.

"I'll be right back, sweetheart," she said.

"Sweetheart?" Williams said. *"Sweetheart?"*

He lifted his glass and drained it with a quick roll of his wrist. He slapped the glass down and rose and squared his shoulders. Claire rubbed out her cigarette and stood up.

"Lane . . ." she said.

"Enjoy your dance," he said.

It was too late now, there was no going back, and she let Williams take her hand and lead her onto the empty dance floor. She glanced over her shoulder at Lane and saw him tip his glass up and drain it. He wouldn't look at her. The band was playing "Memories of You." Williams wrapped his arm around her and scooped her against him, and they began to move to the measured beat and sway of the music. His hand sweated warmly. His arm was very strong, locking her against him. He smelled of liquor and after-shave. They danced.

"I think I pissed off your boyfriend," Williams said.

"What were you trying to prove?" she said.

"I wasn't trying to *prove* anything. What do I need to prove?"

"Lane likes you. What do you want to push him around for?"

"Maybe I'm interested in his woman."

"I'd forget about her if I were you."

"Maybe I can't."

"Maybe you'll have to. Where's your wife tonight?"

"She's where she wants to be. At home."

"How about your kids, are they at home, too?"

"Probably."

"And how long do you think you can behave like this and stay chief of police in this town?"

"You know what the department looked like before I got here? You know what kind of law enforcement this town was getting? You're talking to a pro, kiddo."

"And you think that entitles you."

"I think what I do when I'm off-duty is my own business. Isn't he a little young for you?"

"Leave him alone," Claire said.

"What do you want a kid for, can't even look out for himself?"

"He can look out for himself."

"Sure he can."

"You might find out the hard way."

"I'd eat him for breakfast, and you know it."

"No," Claire said, "I don't."

"Let's talk about you and me."

"There's nothing to talk about."

"There might be. Give it a chance."

"Not in a million years," she said.

"I'm patient," Williams said.

The pianist ran the song out, and the saxophonist and drummer finished on his cue. The set was over. Thin applause rattled across the dance floor. The three musicians got up and filed quickly out of the room. Williams unlocked his right arm, and his hand, as he brought it down, brushed Claire's backside.

"I'll see you to your table," he said.

"You said you'd go back after the dance."

"After I see you to your table."

She turned her back on him and clicked across the parquet in her high heels. Williams followed her. Lane was in the middle of paying for another drink. The waitress looked at Claire and at Williams.

"Everything okay here?" she said.

"Everything's fine," Lane said.

Claire didn't sit down. "I want to go," she said.

"I just paid for this drink," Lane said.

"Please," she said.

Williams put his hands flat on the table and leaned down toward Lane. "I'll take her home," he said.

Lane's chair went over as he came to his feet. The room went silent. The waitress didn't move.

"You touch her again and see what happens," Lane said.

"Lane," Claire said, "that's what he wants."

"What'll happen?" Williams said softly, his pale eyes shining avid and bleary. "What'll happen, Lane?"

End it, Claire thought. *Now.* She reached down for Lane's untouched glass of whiskey, and as he took a step sideways, moving to get around the table at Williams, she stepped between the two men, cutting Lane off, turned with the glass in her hand and dashed it at Williams with an upward toss that caught him full in the face, ice cubes and cold liquid, as sudden and stunning as a right cross. His face tightened and he shut his eyes, but he held his ground and did not even turn his head. The room was as still as a church. Williams opened his eyes, his face dripping, and smiled.

"Cute," he said.

A man in a yellow blazer, a frown of authority stamped on his face, bustled in from the next room. "Can I help you folks?" he said.

"It's all right, Harry," Williams said. "Just a friendly disagreement."

The manager looked at him. "Are you all right, Chief?" he said.

"I'm fine," Williams said. "The lady here just bought me a drink."

People began to speak again, conversing in whispers and murmurs that grew quickly to a low hum of blended voices. Williams wiped his face on his shoulder.

"How about I buy all three of you a drink?" Harry said, looking anxiously from one to the other.

"We were just leaving," Claire said.

She grabbed her purse and took Lane's hand and pulled. Lane jerked his hand free but followed her, across the parquet, through a doorway and out of everybody's sight at last, then past the bar and the restrooms and out into a warm, steady-falling rain.

"Lane," she said.

He didn't answer. He didn't open the car door for her. They drove out of the parking lot. The windshield wipers swished and slapped.

"Lane," she said, "listen to me."

He didn't say anything.

"You want to get in a fight with the police chief?" she said. "What the hell would that prove?"

"It might prove that I can take care of myself," he said.

"Jesus," she said. "You sound like Scott."

"What do you want me to sound like, the Pope? The bastard insults me, I'm supposed to sit there and take it?"

"Now you do sound like Scott."

"At least you respected Scott."

"Don't, Lane. Don't do this to us."

"What did you dance with him for?"

"Use your goddamn head. What do you think I danced with him for?"

"I'm using my head and I don't see it. You know how I felt watching that?"

"No worse than I felt doing it."

"I wonder," he said.

"Lane, for God's sake. I danced with him to get rid of him."

"It worked, didn't it?"

"Is that my fault?"

"He's laughing at me," Lane said. "He's sitting there with his friends laughing about how my girlfriend saved me."

"And it really matters, right? It really matters what those morons think."

"You wouldn't have dragged Scott out of there."

"Will you forget Scott?"

"Some guy came on to you with Scott there, you wouldn't have danced with him and you wouldn't have thrown a drink at him. You'd have let Scott take care of it."

"That's right, I would have, and you know why?"

"I know why. Because he's a man and I'm a kid."

"And you believe that's what I think."

"Damn right I do."

"Well, fuck you, Lane Hillman."

They were silent the rest of the way. The porch light burned feebly in the rainy gloom, and the house was dark inside. Lane left the engine running. The rain was coming down harder. It beat on the car roof and rustled loudly in the trees.

"Stay in the car," Claire said. "I wouldn't want you to get wet."

He shrugged. "Whatever you say."

"Good night," she said without looking at him, and swung the door out and took off her high heels and ran through the rain to the kitchen door. Lane watched her scamper up the porch steps carrying her shoes and let herself into the house. The kitchen light came on. He backed out, turned the corner, and floored it.

A preliminary pause, then the Chevy sprang forward with a smooth deep roar. He turned onto the empty rain-swept Shore Road and accelerated to eighty before the impulse died, shriveling like a flame in a hard wind. He let the car coast down to thirty and crept home, across the railroad tracks, on under the rain-shedding trees. He braked for his driveway, slowed to an almost-stop, but then drove on.

The lamplit sidewalks along Main Street were deserted now. The marquee of the Empire had been turned off. Lane drove very slowly. He didn't know what he was going to do, or didn't think he did, till he came to the corner by the telephone office, where he turned and drove again toward the water, finishing a circle that brought him back where he'd begun.

The porch light had been turned off, but the kitchen light burned, and the light in her bedroom. He parked in the driveway and left the headlights on. It was raining hard again. It came down silver in the white light of the headlights. A minute passed, and another, and as Lane finally opened the car door, she burst out of the house, flitted down the brick steps, and came running, shoeless, through the savage rain.

He opened the passenger door for her. She wriggled in and slammed the door. Rain streaked her face and glistened on her jet-black hair.

"I'm sorry," he said, and held her.

"I didn't love Scott enough to do that for him."

"I know," Lane said.

"I never loved any man enough."

"I'm stupid, aren't I?"

"Very," she said.

"A dope."

"A total dope."

They kissed. The rain drummed overhead.

"Where's April?" he asked.

"Asleep."

"It'll be a little wet under the lilac."

"But not in the car," she said.

He turned the lights off. "I've never made love in a car," he said.

"I'm glad," she said.

.   .   .

HIS FATHER put down his coffee cup and looked out at the old pear tree.

"You say she threw a drink," he said.

"He asked for it," Lane said.

"Asked for it how?"

"He was drunk. He wasn't the Paul Williams you know."

"How smart do you think it was to put yourself in that situation?"

"What situation? We went into the Harbor Lounge for a drink."

His mother came out of the kitchen in her bathrobe. "It sounds to me as if he was being completely obnoxious."

"He wouldn't leave our table," Lane said. "He was trying to take Claire away from me. She thought I was going to start something with him. She threw the drink to keep the two of us from fighting."

"Fighting with the police chief," his father said.

"What was I supposed to do?" Lane said.

"You can't get into these situations, Lane. You simply can't."

Lane got up and took his plate and coffee cup into the kitchen. He wondered if he'd ever step into this room again without hearing echoes of "For Your Love."

"You know Lane wouldn't start trouble," his mother said.

"Claire wouldn't either," Lane said, reentering the dining room.

"Do you think you really know this woman?" his father said.

"'This woman'?" Lane said. *"This woman?"*

"Sweetie, of course he knows her," his mother said.

"I want to talk to the two of you first thing this morning," his father said.

"All right," Lane said.

"First thing," his father said.

. . .

HE LED the two of them to Lane's grandfather's tenantless office and closed the door. He sat down behind the desk. Claire sat where she had the day he'd interviewed her for the job. Lane dragged a chair from the corner.

"So," Lane's father said, "what happens now?"

"I don't know," Lane said.

"You'd better think about it."

"It was my fault," Claire said.

"It was not," Lane said.

"I don't care whose fault it was. The question is, how are you going to cover the police if you're having public run-ins with Paul Williams?"

"I'll get the news from the captains," Lane said.

"No. You'll get it from Paul."

Lane shrugged. "I'll try."

"Claire, you're going to be covering police when he leaves. I haven't got anyone else."

"I understand."

"You don't have to like Paul, but you have to deal with him."

"He's going to get himself fired if he keeps this up," Lane said.

"Maybe, maybe not," his father said.

"I told you he was with Mrs. Winslow last night. Not to mention trying to pick Claire up."

"I'm interested in the news, not his night life."

"His night life's going to get him fired," Lane said.

"Did you hear me?" his father said.

"I heard you."

"Your first stop this morning'll be the police station," his father said.

. . . .

THE DOOR was open, and Mrs. Woodling watched him come up the front steps from her perch behind the desk.

"He wants to see you," she said.

"Who does?"

"Santa Claus," she said.

I'm not going to miss you, Lane thought.

"The chief," she said. "He told me to send you in soon as you got here."

The state police detective, O'Neill, was coming out of Williams's office. He stopped in the doorway and looked thoughtfully at Lane.

"The reporter," he said.

"Good morning," Lane said.

O'Neill nodded and went on, and Lane entered Williams's sunny office with its flags and framed citations and glass-topped desk. The chief was sitting back in his swivel chair as usual with his hands clasped over his gut. His face was as empty of last night's drunken belligerence as the azure sky the day after a howling tempest.

"Lane," he said. "Come on in."

Lane stood warily just inside the door.

"That O'Neill," Williams said. "He won't quit. Now he's thinking there might be a connection between the Clifford murder and the Kasselman drowning."

"You wondered that yourself at one point."

"Before those boys confessed. Not anymore. Sit down, Lane."

Lane came forward and sat down in front of the desk with his notebook.

"Eddie's grabbing at straws. You got to know when to quit. It's a question of resources. How are you going to spend your time, your manpower?"

Lane nodded. Williams spun his chair and looked out at the

pond, the patient swans. He spun back and dropped forward and spiked the desk blotter with his elbows.

"I guess I owe you an apology," he said.

"Yeah, sort of," Lane said.

"Let's face it. I acted like a total asshole. Christ, if you'd taken a swing at me, I wouldn't blame you."

"You wanted me to," Lane said.

"No I didn't. Not really. Christ, you're my friend."

"I thought I was," Lane said.

"Face it, I was plastered. I don't even remember half of it. I danced with her, right?"

Lane nodded.

"She threw a drink in my face."

"She was pretty upset," Lane said.

"Protecting you," Williams said. "I like that. Girl's got guts."

"She didn't want me to fight with you. Where would it have gotten either of us?"

"Nowhere."

"My father blames me as much as you," Lane said.

"You told him."

"I had to."

"I guess you did."

"He said I have to get along with you. Claire, too."

Williams looked at him. "She's ripshit, isn't she?"

"She's pretty upset."

"You're a lucky bastard, Lane."

"I know."

"The age difference doesn't bother you?"

"Not at all."

"What is it, eighteen, twenty years?"

"Fifteen."

"Fifteen," Williams said.

"It's not so much."

"No, I guess not. Listen, tell her I'm sorry, okay?"

"All right."

"I'll tell her myself, if I ever see her."

"You'll see her. She's going to be covering police after I leave."

"Is she, now?"

"You have any news for me?"

"A little. You tell anyone else besides your dad?"

"Nobody."

"It's up to you who you tell. I can't stop you, right?"

"I don't intend to tell anybody."

"It's the sauce," Williams said. "I get on the sauce, I get crazy. I got to stop drinking, is what I got to do."

"Far as I'm concerned, it's over," Lane said.

"You're a hell of a guy, Lane, you know that?"

Chapter Nine

HE WAS in the back shop slipping papers when O'Neill came in looking for him. The press run hadn't ended, and the old Duplex filled the back shop with its rhythmic, smothering din. As he worked, Lane looked out the window and saw Manny Dutra stagger down the steps of the concrete loading platform with papers stacked to his chin. Manny heaved the pile into the back of a station wagon. The drivers were all women, housewives earning a little extra money. They stood in the dusty lot in the sunshine chatting quietly while they waited for Manny to load up their cars. Lane didn't notice O'Neill or Ellie Whiting until Ellie touched his arm.

O'Neill stood behind her, not much taller. A little black cigar was clamped unlit in his narrow, thin mouth. His black eyes watched Lane.

"Mr. O'Neill here to see you," Ellie said.

Lane nodded, and Ellie saw that it was all right and waddled away. O'Neill picked the cigar out of his mouth.

"How 'bout we go someplace private," he said. He didn't seem to raise his voice, but he could be heard perfectly over the roar of the press.

Lane led him back past the press, past the little line of men waiting for papers, and into his grandfather's office. He closed the door, shutting out the noise, and went around behind the desk and sat down. O'Neill sat down facing him in the wooden armchair. Lane wondered how such a runt could become a state cop. On a waiver, maybe. He wore a polo shirt and baggy khakis, and he looked like a tough little tavern owner, say, who'd come down to the Cape from Dorchester or South Boston for some bottom fishing, a couple of nights in a motel with the wife.

"What can I do for you?" Lane said.

O'Neill didn't answer. He was looking at the picture on the desk of Lane's grandmother and her collie, Cookie. Lane remembered Cookie.

"May I?" O'Neill said, speaking with the little cigar lodged in the corner of his mouth and reaching for the picture.

"My grandmother," Lane said.

"Good-lookin' broad," O'Neill said past the cigar.

"I guess she was at that," Lane said.

"She alive?" O'Neill put the photograph down.

"Sure."

"Then say *is,* not was."

"Is," Lane said.

"How 'bout your grandfather?" O'Neill said.

"He's alive."

"Doesn't work anymore, though."

"Sometimes he does. They're in Nova Scotia right now. They go up there in the summertime. Down to Florida in the winter."

"Must be nice," O'Neill said. He took the cigar out of his mouth and looked at it.

"How come you don't light it?" Lane said.

"I gave up smoking. Ever smoke yourself?"

"No."

"You drink, though."

Lane hesitated. He wondered where this was going. "Sure," he said, "I drink."

"You drink at the Harbor Lounge," O'Neill said, "am I right?"

"I did once. Why?"

"Broad threw a glass of whiskey at Paul Williams over there a couple nights ago. She was with you, am I right?"

Lane nodded.

"Let him have it in the face."

"How'd you know about it?" Lane said.

"I go in there sometimes. My wife and I like the music. I don't dance, but I like to listen, have a few pops. I know the owner. He was telling me about it."

"Paul apologized," Lane said. "I'd forgotten all about it."

"Why'd she throw a drink at him?" O'Neill said.

"He was bothering us."

"Bothering you."

"He'd had a few, you want to know the truth."

"He was drunk," O'Neill said. "He was bothering you. And yet I hear she danced with him."

"She didn't want to."

"Didn't want to? Bad idea to dance with someone when you don't want to. Gives 'em the wrong idea."

"I know," Lane said.

"This is the reporter broad we're talking about, am I right? The one was out there at the funeral home that day we were doing those postmortems."

Lane nodded.

"She your girl?"

"You could say that."

"Gorgeous broad," O'Neill said. "How old is she, she tell you?"

"She's older than I am, if that's what you're getting at."

"Early thirties, maybe?"

"She's thirty-seven," Lane said.

"You're shittin' me."

"No," Lane said.

"She's almost Paul's age, then."

"Probably."

"What'd he do that made her throw a drink at him? Pinch her ass? Stick his tongue in her ear?"

"Just said things."

"Like what?"

"That she needed to be reined in. That I wasn't up to that."

"You wanted to pop him one, I bet."

"She beat me to it."

"Stand-up broad," O'Neill said.

"You aren't going to mention this to Paul, are you?"

"I don't think so. It'd embarrass him, you know? A broad throws a drink at a cop and he doesn't smack her, it's embarrassing."

"He isn't a bad guy," Lane said. "He likes the ladies, but so what?"

"Likes the ladies," O'Neill said. "His wife wasn't there, was she?"

"No."

"He was with somebody, though."

"Betty Winslow. I don't know if he brought her, or just met her there."

O'Neill looked at the cigar, contemplating it as if wondering what to do with it next. "You know," he said, "there's a lot went on this summer I don't understand."

"Like what?"

"Well, for instance: We got a homicide and no clues. Not just no clues, but some of the fuckinest questions. Riddles, you know?"

"Riddles?"

"Sure. Girl was laid but not raped. She'd been in the salt water, and where do they find her? The woods."

"The salt water?"

"There was sea salt on her skin. In her hair. Not on her clothes, though, except what had rubbed off. She'd been in the water, but her clothes hadn't."

"I wonder why Paul didn't tell me this."

"He didn't think it was important. Like he said, the girl went to the beach every day. Swam, laid in the sun. If she doesn't take a shower, the salt's still there when she gets whacked. She could have swam the day before. Who knows?"

The press had stopped, Lane realized. He wondered if the run was over or if they'd had to put on a new roll of newsprint. Outside of this little room life went on as usual, the men slipping papers and talking baseball, the newsboys pedaling away down the avenue laden with their heavy canvas shoulder bags.

"The thing is," O'Neill said, "on the same night the girl gets it—same fuckin' night, now—we got a drowning where two older boys take a younger boy skinny-dipping that they never spoke two words to in their life. Explain that one to me."

"They picked him up hitchhiking," Lane said.

"He never hitchhiked."

"Why else would he get in their car? They didn't force him."

"No, they didn't force him, and that's one of the mysteries. I don't know why Paul went so easy on 'em. Me, I'd have leaned on 'em a little. Pressed charges if they didn't talk."

"They talked," Lane said.

"They talked, but they didn't talk enough. Paul should have realized that."

Lane looked at him. O'Neill had a youthfulness about him: the black curls, the small hands. He wasn't stupid, though. Paul was wrong about that.

"Those kids didn't kill Jane Clifford," Lane said.

"That's right," O'Neill said. "They didn't have time to kill her. That's what's making me nuts, here. The pathologist says the girl died between two and three in the morning. The kids were home by then."

"Why would they lie if they didn't kill her?"

"I didn't say they lied. I said they left things out."

"Why?"

"Think about it. The girl's with them, let's say. Maybe the kid's with her, maybe that's why he gets in the car. They go swimming. One of the big boys screws her. Maybe they both do, it wouldn't surprise me these days. They're so busy with the girl they don't notice when their little buddy tries to swim to Spain. So he drowns, and now they're scared shitless. Then it gets worse. They drop the girl off, wake up in the morning, and find out she got whacked. Bad enough they got a kid drowned, now they got a second cadaver connected to them. A fuckin' homicide. They think about it awhile and decide to split the difference: tell about the kid, which was an accident, and leave out the girl."

O'Neill slid the cigar into his shirt pocket. He placed his hands on his hard, squat thighs and looked at Lane.

"I got to ask you a personal question. Your girl—Claire Malek, right? She ever show any interest in Paul Williams?"

"Absolutely not."

"No offense, but a broad doesn't always tell you these things."

"This one would," Lane said.

"Before you were dating her, maybe."

"No."

"Never responded to his interest in her, is what you're saying."

"She responded," Lane said. "She threw a bourbon in his face."

"And he hasn't contacted her since then. Hasn't called her, hasn't stopped by her house."

"No, for Christ sake. Why don't you ask her?"

"Sometimes it's better not to worry 'em."

"Worry them about what?"

"She live alone?"

"She's got a daughter. Worry them about what?"

"How old's the daughter?"

"Fifteen. Are you going to tell me what this is about?"

"You stay over at her house?"

"Why?"

"Do you?"

"No."

"Good for you. With her daughter in the house, you know? Some guys don't give a shit. Some mothers."

It was still quiet beyond the varnished door. The press run was over.

"I wish you'd tell me what's going on," Lane said.

"It's these fuckin' mysteries," O'Neill said. "I hate 'em. They keep me awake nights."

"With Claire, I mean. And Paul."

"That's one of the mysteries. A married guy, couple of kids. Chief of police. Comes on to a broad and gets a drink in his face at a public place. Isn't that a mystery?"

"I don't see why."

"The guy's been a cop for twenty years. Spotless record."

"So what?"

"I don't know so what. If I did, it wouldn't be a mystery."

He drew the cigar from his pocket and put it in his mouth, and Lane knew the interview was over.

"You aren't going to tell me anything, are you?" he said.

"Isn't anything to tell. I'm just asking questions. That's what cops do. They're nosy bastards, like newspaper reporters."

"Maybe I haven't been nosy enough on this one," Lane said.

"I'll let you know, anything happens," O'Neill said.

. . .

THAT NIGHT they walked the beach under a creamy half-moon. The waves fell softly. There was a nip in the air, a whisper of September, and she knew how short their time was.

"Lane," she said, "what did that detective want?"

"O'Neill? Just to talk."

"About what?"

The lights of a trawler, laboring out toward Georges Bank, moved slowly and silently on the moonlit darkness of sea and sky.

"He thinks Jane Clifford might have been there when David Kasselman drowned," Lane said.

"What gave him that idea?"

"There was saltwater on Jane's body. She'd been swimming, at some point."

They walked slowly, hand in hand, in the wet firm sand just above the wave line.

"What do you mean, 'at some point'?"

"The saltwater might not mean anything. She might have swum that afternoon, or even the day before."

"A girl takes a shower after she's been at the beach."

"This one was a hippie. Maybe she didn't take showers."

"Why did O'Neill want to talk to *you* about all this?"

"I don't know," Lane said.

"You asked him?"

"Sure I asked him. He's a different kind of cop from Paul Williams. He keeps things to himself."

Sometimes it's better not to worry 'em.

Worry them about what? he said, but O'Neill never told him.

"You were with him a long time," Claire said.

"It takes him a while to get to the point."

"It takes you a while, too."

"I *have* gotten to the point," Lane said. "That's all there was to it."

They climbed the jetty by the herring run and picked their way out, hand in hand, over the round boulders, and sat down on a flat-cut slab of stone and looked at the moonlight shimmering out to the horizon. Beneath them the water sloshed gently against the rocks. They kissed, and Claire worked her hands under his shirt and warmed them on his back.

"Maybe I won't go to Detroit," Lane said. "Maybe I'll stay here and live with you and April."

"You have to go," she said.

"Will you come visit me?"

"If I can," she said.

"Of course you can. It's an hour-and-a-half flight from Boston to Detroit."

"That's not bad."

"And then I'll be home for Christmas."

"No promises, sweets."

"I will, though," he said.

"Good," she said, and tilted her face up close to his, a burnished heart in the pale moonlight, and he looked at her a long moment before he kissed her, and never forgot it.

. . .

HE WAS sitting at her kitchen table on the following evening nursing a beer while Claire cooked dinner for the three of them. April came down and said she wanted to go to the library.

"We're about to eat," Claire said.

"Kyle's coming over soon," April said.

"Good. Then Kyle can drive you to the library."

"I'll drive her," Lane said.

Claire turned from the stove. "She does *not* need to go to the library this instant," she said.

"We'll be back in ten minutes," Lane said.

"You know, April, it wouldn't hurt you to take no for an answer once in a while," Claire said.

In the car April said, "Mom is *so* uptight."

"How are things with you and Kyle?" Lane said.

April shrugged. "Okay."

"Just okay?"

"He's a little immature sometimes."

"Boys mature slower than girls," Lane said.

"He is *so* hung up on his car. Obsessed."

"Well, boys like cars."

"Did you?"

"I wasn't so much the car type. I was too busy playing sports."

"That's a turnoff, too," April said.

"Listen, April. I want to ask you a favor."

"Like what?"

They were on Main Street now, not far from the library. Lane drove very slowly.

"The police chief has sort of a crush on your mother," Lane said.

"That's disgusting," April said.

"Why? He can't help it."

"Kyle calls policemen 'pigs.'"

"Chief Williams isn't a pig, he's just a little indiscreet. You know what 'indiscreet' means?"

"What's the favor you want?" April said.

"You do know what 'indiscreet' means."

"Yes. What's the favor?"

"If he calls her, or stops by, I want you to let me know."

April looked at him. "Why?"

"He's got a family. He's in a prominent position. I don't want him to get in trouble."

"That's his problem," April said.

"I might be able to say something to him. For his own good, you know?"

"Mom'll tell you if he pesters her."

"Maybe not right away. I want to know as soon as he calls or sees her."

"You're not telling me something," April said.

Lane parked along the curb in front of the gray stone library. April didn't get out.

"There's nothing to tell," Lane said.

"Nothing? *Rien? Nada?*"

"Will you do this for me, April?" Lane said.

"I guess."

"And not tell your mother?"

"I feel like a spy."

"That's a little dramatic," Lane said.

"He might call and I wouldn't know about it," April said.

"He might."

"I feel like a spy."

"Just do it, okay?"

April shrugged. "All right," she said.

"Promise," Lane said.

"All *right,*" she said. "Can I go get my book now?"

"Sure," Lane said. "What are you reading?"

. . .

HE SPOKE to her, and she got up with her notebook and pencil and sat down beside his desk. His stiffness and reserve as the days dwindled down toward Lane's departure alternately infuriated and exhausted her; it was as if they spoke to each other through shatterproof glass by telephone, as is done in prison visiting rooms, and if she should ever turn the conversation personal—protest, apologize, explain, entreat, or swear her good intentions—he would simply hang up and leave her voiceless and out of reach, denying her any chance of coming to an understanding, of conciliation. So she waited for a crack to appear in his ironclad civility, in the invisible wall between them. Waited and did her work, silent, and burning, too, with the desire to excel, to prove her worth in this, at least.

"I just got a call from the town busybody, Abner Peck," he said. "He says Paul McCartney's on Furnace Island."

"Paul *McCartney?*" Claire said.

"Isn't he one of the Beatles?" Ruth Engle said.

"The cute one," Claire said.

"Abner says Moose Rebello and his crew were over there doing some work on the big house, and they saw him playing croquet with the Rossiters. Give Duncan Rossiter a call."

"He's unlisted," Ruth said.

"Then you'll have to do some legwork," Mr. Hillman said. "Start with Moose Rebello."

"Moose," Claire said.

"Charles," Mr. Hillman said. "You'll have to track him down at work."

She found the Rossiters' file in the graveyard. Duncan Rossiter was an art dealer. His wife Virginia had been cochair of the hospital fund drive for several years and was on the board of the Sierra Club and the NAACP. They spent their summers on Furnace Island, their winters in New York and London. In the photographs they were youthful, photogenic, with an aura about them of glamour and ease.

She found Charles M. Rebello, Building Contractor, in the phone book and got his wife, who said Moose was working on a house north of town. Claire got directions and shouldered her purse and gathered up her notebook and a couple of pencils.

"Good luck," Lane said.

"It's a front-page story, if you can get it," Mr. Hillman said.

"I'll get it," she said.

It was late morning, windless and clear under a high radiant sky. Rebello and the two young men who worked for him were framing a house up a dead end off the King's Highway. He stood in the middle of the bare plywood floor with a hammer in his hand and watched Claire come up the grassless, lumber-strewn yard in her dress and heels. His men had perches on sloping rafters, silhouetted against the sky. They stopped hammering and looked down at Claire.

"Mr. Rebello, right?" she said.

He nodded and spat past his shoulder.

"Claire Malek with the *Covenant*. I hear you guys saw Paul McCartney on Furnace Island a couple days ago."

"No comment," Rebello said.

"No comment?" Claire said. A plank had been laid from the ground to the deck. Claire walked up it, gingerly, on her high heels. "No comment when you've already told half the town?"

"I did like hell."

"But you did see Paul McCartney."

"I didn't say that."

"You implied it."

"We got work to do, lady."

Claire looked around and saw a sheet of plywood resting across two sawhorses. She walked over to it and sat down, boosting herself up backward, and let her legs swing. Rebello looked at her legs. He bit a thumbnail.

"Off the record," she said.

"What the hell, Moose, why not?" said one of the men overhead.

Claire took her dark glasses off and wiped them on the hem of her dress. She gave her head a toss and pushed the hair back from her face and put the glasses back on.

"Come on, Moose," she said.

"Moose, it ain't like we're the only ones seen the guy," said the voice above them.

"A lot of people know about it," Claire said. "What day did you guys see him?"

"Friday," said the voice.

"He was playing croquet, I hear," Claire said.

Moose sighed. He tossed his hammer down. He dug a pack of Marlboros from his tight-fitting jeans, shook out a cigarette, and offered it to Claire. She accepted it and he lit it for her, then lit one for himself. He sat down on the deck with his back against a vertical stud and his legs out straight and his ankles crossed.

"This is off the record," he said. "You don't tell *nobody.*"

"Not a soul," Claire said.

.   .   .

SHE HAD a sandwich and a cup of black coffee at Chamberlain's.

"How's Lane doing these days?" Beth Weeks asked her.

"Fine," Claire said.

243

"I haven't seen him all summer," Beth said, watching her.

"He's been pretty busy," Claire said.

"I bet," Beth said.

There was an old phone booth at the back of the drugstore. Claire shut herself in and called the office. Mr. Hillman had gone home for lunch. Claire asked Ellie Whiting to put Lane on.

"Moose Rebello says there's a woman named June Pires who cleans for the Rossiters," she said. "He says she goes out there three times a week."

"I went to school with June," Lane said.

"I need to talk to her."

"Stay there. I'll make a couple of phone calls."

She went back to the counter and ordered another coffee.

"Lane tells me you're engaged," Claire said.

Beth dropped her a smirk. "Afraid so," she said.

"Congratulations," Claire said.

"Same to you," Beth said.

Claire looked at her. She knew. Claire shrugged and smiled, not unkindly. She finished her coffee and called Lane back.

"June's working at her uncle's vegetable stand today," he said. "You know where Bayberry Road is?"

It was a twenty-minute drive. June Pires was reading a magazine inside the shed-roofed vegetable stand beside the road. She was a Cape Verdean girl, penny-brown, with broad shoulders and a generous figure. Behind the vegetable stand a cornfield ran back toward the woods.

"I really shouldn't talk about it," June said.

"Lane Hillman says hello," Claire said.

June smiled, pushing wrinkles up her nose, her forehead. "You know Lane?"

"He's at the newspaper this summer."

"We were in home room together all the way through. We're close together in the alphabet, you see. H and J. How's that boy doing?"

"He said you'd talk to me."

"You know, I really don't know much. I just saw Mr. McCartney for a few minutes."

"What was he doing?"

"I'll lose my job out there, the Rossiters find out I talked to you."

"They won't find out," Claire said.

. . .

SHE WAS back in the office at two.

"I'm on a roll," she said.

"What have you got?" Mr. Hillman said, and she thought she saw the faint glimmer of a smile.

"According to June Pires, Rossiter brings the help back from the island in a little motorboat. She said if I hang around Blue Harbor in the late afternoon, I'll probably catch him."

Mr. Hillman looked out past the tracks. "Better get over there, then," he said.

The harbor was a natural cove with a single narrow dock extending out perhaps thirty feet. Sailboats floated peacefully at their moorings. Out beyond the opening you could see the glittering bay and the low jade hills of Furnace Island a half mile out. You could make out a dock, and the dirt road wending up over the first hill toward the Rossiters' compound.

The harbormaster's shack was open but empty. There was no sound but the ripple of water along boat hulls and a chirr of insects. Claire bought a Coke from the machine by the harbormaster's shack. She sat down in his canvas chair, wishing she'd brought a book or newspaper. After a while she went up the hill and got in her car and turned on the radio. The third or fourth song was "Nowhere Man," and she wondered if Paul McCartney could be listening to himself over on the island. She smoked a cigarette, smoked another, then walked back down the hill. The canvas chair was in shadow now; she moved it into the sunlight and sat down and watched a sailboat pass, heeling over in the wind. The breeze had brought with it the late-afternoon haze that Lane so loved. The smoky southwester, he called it. It turns the world into an old faded photograph, he said.

At quarter to four an open car or jeep came down the dirt road on Furnace Island, raising the white dust behind it. Claire stood up and shaded her eyes. The car stopped at the dock and several people got out. They piled into a small white boat, and in a moment Claire heard the snarl of an outboard motor. The boat squirmed forward and took off, its flat bottom skimming, slapping, the choppy water. A Boston Whaler with a lot of horsepower.

It crossed in a couple of minutes, slowed abruptly, and slid into the harbor and past the sailboats. Duncan Rossiter was at the wheel, easily recognizable from his pictures. His two passengers were swart Portuguese or Cape Verdeans. One of them stood up to fend off, and Rossiter killed the engine and let the Whaler drift in.

Claire walked out onto the dock, careful in her heels. One of the passengers looped the hawser around a piling and swung the boat in.

"Mr. Rossiter," Claire said.

Rossiter squinted up at her. He was as young as she was, maybe younger. He wore a bathing suit and unbuttoned safari jacket and wraparound dark glasses.

"At your service," he said.

"Claire Malek with the *Covenant*," she said.

"Thanks for the lift, Mr. Rossiter," one of the men said, and stepped up onto the dock.

"See you tomorrow, Herbie," Rossiter said.

"See you tomorrow, Mr. Rossiter," said the second man.

The two of them nodded at Claire and clumped away down the dock carrying their lunch boxes. Rossiter stood in the Whaler with his hands on his hips. He cocked his head over and eyed Claire in an inquiring but good-natured way.

"How can I help you?" he said.

"I'm doing a story about Paul McCartney's visit," Claire said.

Rossiter smiled suavely. "Who's he visiting?" he said.

Claire lowered herself to the warm planking. She took off her shoes and sat with her legs dangling above the water, at eye level with Rossiter.

"I don't need to see him necessarily," she said. "I could get the story from you."

"What story?"

"How long he's here for, how he spends his time. His connection with you. Stuff like that."

Rossiter studied her, still smiling. "I'm trying to figure out who you've been talking to," he said. "Someone who works for me, obviously."

"It's all over town," Claire said.

"That's a bit of a lie, isn't it?"

"Not a lie. An exaggeration, maybe."

"How long have you been working for John?" Rossiter said.

"Since June. How do you know McCartney?"

Rossiter came forward in the Whaler, stepping over the seats. He climbed lightly and athletically onto the dock and sat down beside Claire.

"I know a lot of people," he said.

"Really," Claire said.

"You can't meet Paul," he said. "I promised him no press."

"I told you I didn't need to meet him."

"Suppose you don't use the story till Paul leaves?" he said.

"Depends when he's leaving."

"Day after tomorrow," Rossiter said. "You use the story Friday."

"It's a deal," Claire said.

"John going to go along with that?"

"Sure," Claire said.

"I don't want every lunatic and teenage girl in New England hopping a boat to Furnace Island," Rossiter said.

"I don't blame you," Claire said.

.   .   .

SHE COMPOSED the lead in her head as she drove back to the office. *Not all of the Beatles were in town this week, but one of them was.* Light, but not cute or sly. Put some fun in the story, write it for adults and teenagers alike. She was smiling when she walked into the newsroom. On a roll.

"I saw Rossiter," she said. "I got everything."

"Congratulations," Lane said.

She sat down by Mr. Hillman's desk. "There's only one thing," she said. "McCartney's leaving day after tomorrow. I told Rossiter we'd hold the story till Friday."

Mr. Hillman thought about it, then nodded slowly. "I guess that's all right."

"It was the only way he'd talk to me," she said.

"As a rule, you don't want to make those agreements."

"No," she agreed.

He nodded and groped in his shirt pocket for his cigarettes. "Good job," he said.

She looked at him, startled, but he'd already turned back to his typewriter. Claire smiled anyway. "Thanks," she said.

He nodded and did not look at her.

. . .

SHE WAS alone in the building by the time she finished writing. She proofed her story, left it on Mr. Hillman's desk, and went out and locked the door behind her. She drove down the avenue beneath the elms, through the intersection by the gas station, and past the village green. There was no place to park in front of Kasselman's, so she turned onto Pleasant Street and parked around the corner.

As she was getting out of the car, a big, quiet, dove-gray Ford Crown Victoria came up Pleasant. She waited for it to pass before she crossed the street. The Crown Vic slowed and stopped, and Paul Williams smiled at her with the sun in his face.

"How are you?" he said.

"Okay," she said carefully.

Williams was in uniform. Gray, like the unmarked car. An American flag patch was stitched on the shoulder.

"Did Lane ever apologize for me for that business at the Harbor Lounge?" he said.

"Don't worry about it," she said. "We all got a little carried away, I'd say."

"I guess we did at that." He eyed her, squinting against the sun. "I've got some news, if you're interested. Big news."

"About what?"

"Jane Clifford."

A car turned the corner and passed between them. Williams watched it disappear, then swung his level gaze back to Claire.

"You interested?" he said.

"Sure."

"They found another body at the same crime scene. Negro male in his late twenties. Gunshot wound to the head. He was found a hundred yards from where the Clifford girl was found. Looks like a double murder."

The police radio crackled chaotically; Williams leaned over and turned it off.

"Some kids found him, just like they found the other one. I got the call about twenty minutes ago. Eddie O'Neill's out there, and a guy from forensics. Eddie didn't want me to say anything yet. The Boston papers'll be down here like bees on honey when they hear the racial angle."

Another car came around the corner, a girl in a VW Bug. Williams watched the Bug scoot by.

"You want to take a ride out there with me?" he said.

"Now?"

Williams shrugged. "You could follow me."

Claire looked at her watch. Six-thirty.

"I just thought tomorrow being Tuesday, you might want to jump on this," Williams said.

Claire looked down the shaded street, past the Kasselmans' high hedge. "I should call Mr. Hillman and let him know," she said.

"Why? He'll just give the story to Lane."

"He might not."

"Why risk it? Anyway, I don't have time for you to be explaining things to John on the phone. Unless you want to find your own way out there."

Again she looked down the street, meandering away out of sight beneath the trees.

"Come on," he said. "I'm giving you a scoop. You'll beat the Boston papers."

"Can I run into Kasselman's and get my newspapers?"

"Hurry up," he said.

He watched her cross the street, then backed the Crown Vic over to the side of the road. Claire went into the drugstore and grabbed a pack of Salems. Bernie Kasselman reached down and brought up her *Globe* and *Times* from under the counter.

"How's my girl?" he said.

"Bernie, I wonder if I could make a quick phone call."

"Come on around," he said.

April answered on the first ring. "Where *are* you?" she said.

"I'm at Kasselman's drugstore. April, listen, I just ran into the police chief. There's been another murder."

"No *way,*" April said.

"The police chief's going to take me out to the crime scene."

"The police chief?"

"I'm going to follow him out there."

"Follow him out where?"

"Near where the girl was killed. Jane Clifford. They think it was a double murder."

"I think you ought to come home," April said.

"This is my job, sweetheart. I'm a newspaper reporter. Fix yourself some supper if you want. I'll be home soon."

"Mom . . ."

"I don't have time, April. I'll see you later."

Bernie was chatting with a customer over the counter. "Everything all right?" he said.

"Big story," Claire said.

"What happened?" Bernie said.

"I'll tell you about it tomorrow."

She went out with her newspapers under her arm. Williams watched her come around the corner. "I was about to leave without you," he said.

"I had to get cigarettes," she said.

"Bad for you, you know."

"I know," she said.

"Let's go," Williams said.

Chapter Ten

SHE FOLLOWED him out Main Street, away from the village green. They left the old store blocks behind them and passed the ivied brick fire station and the telephone office. They passed St. Patrick's Church, the old-age home, and the rec building. Some filling stations, the Dairy Queen, and finally the General Swift Motel, where Claire had spent her first nights here a lifetime ago. They drove on past the new shopping plaza where she'd eaten her lonesome suppers, and out through the once-rural outskirts of town past filling stations, miniature golf, an auto parts outlet, and the A & W Root Beer where, Lane said, the girls used to come out on roller skates and serve you in your car.

Williams drove with his elbow out the window, casually and confidently and fast. Claire stayed with him, driving more recklessly than she liked. After a few miles the country became wilder, more open, with here and there a frame house or filling station or vegetable stand sitting alone with fields and woods behind it. They passed a cranberry bog and an auto salvage yard where derelict cars slumped like dead things in a weedy lot. They passed a small and beautiful white-clapboard church with a little graveyard beside it.

The road hit Route 110 about seven miles out of town. Claire knew that Jane Clifford had been found along Route 110, but not where. She stuck close to the gray police car, which was speeding now, the road running arrow-straight, bordered on both sides by scrub woods with here and there a business that could survive the remoteness—a discount liquor store, a veterinarian's office, a maker of custom signs. In a few places roads had been bulldozed into the woods for future development—raw, yellow-dirt ribbons leading nowhere.

The sun was below the trees now, and Claire took off her dark glasses. Another mile, and Williams put on his left turn signal and slowed. They waited for an oncoming car to pass, then swung across the left lane and onto a rutted dried-mud road so narrow that brush and low branches clawed and slapped at them as they passed. Ten yards ahead of her the Crown Vic wormed through the forest dusk, lumbering over potholes.

It amazed her now that Jane Clifford's body, not to mention a second, had ever been found in all these empty woods. She tried to calculate how far they'd come, guessed a half-mile, maybe more. They went on, slower now. Williams watched her in the rearview mirror. He was looking more at her now than at the road and was no longer in a hurry, and suddenly it began not to add up. She slowed to a crawl that barely lifted the speedometer needle. Williams noticed right away and slowed, too. She stopped, and he stopped, too.

She sat a moment with the motor running. Williams watched her in the mirror. The woods were growing darker by the minute. She sat still and listened. No sound of human voices, of cars and police radios; just a vast darkening emptiness. Williams watched her, patient and unmoving, and with the suddenness of a thunderclap she knew.

She cried out and shifted violently into reverse and turned in the seat and mashed the gas pedal, the Camaro yawing and fish-tailing with the brush swiping its sides. Williams shifted too and chased her backward, more skilled than she, calmer, the Crown Vic slithering quietly and relentlessly back, closing on her. She could barely see now. She felt for the lights and couldn't find the knob. The Crown Vic's fender struck hers, struck again, and again, and Claire turned in a fury and screamed at him, and the Camaro missed a bend in the road and plowed backward into the woods, the thick brush, up and over a bush which held it clear of the ground, rear wheels spinning now, whining in the dry leaves. She didn't give up yet, but put it in first and tried to power clear of the bush and ram him, but the Camaro took a short froglike hop and stalled, and it was over.

She cranked the window up and locked both doors. Williams shut his engine off and got out deliberately and portentously, the way cops do when they pull speeders over. He came toward her slowly and tried the door. He leaned down sideways and tugged up his pant leg and drew a gun from a holster that was strapped to his calf. With the handle of the gun he broke out the glass. He knocked away the spider-webbed fragments and reached in and unlocked the door.

"Out," he said.

"When I was in Kasselman's," she said, "I called Lane and told him I was coming here with you."

Williams smiled. "There's no phone in Kasselman's."

"I used the store phone."

"I don't think so," he said. He put the revolver uncocked to her cheek. "Out," he said.

Her eyes rolled to look at the gun. Its barrel was very short, and she could smell oil and an acridness she knew must be gunpowder.

"He'll be here any minute," she said.

"You think I'm afraid of Lane Hillman?"

"He'll bring that detective. O'Neill."

"Get out of the car," Williams said, and gave her a prod with the gun.

She swung her legs out.

"Wait," he said.

Holding the gun to her face and keeping his eye on her, he dropped the other shoulder and felt for her leg. He found it and ran a callused hand down her bare thigh and calf and slowly up again.

"Yes," he said. "Yes, I do like that."

He felt the leg all over, front and back, slow, then stood up straight.

"It's nice you don't wear stockings," he said. "You don't need them, either. You wouldn't even need them in the wintertime."

"Please," she said.

"Please what? I thought the big football star was coming to save you."

"He is," she said.

"On your feet," Williams said.

"He said he was going to call O'Neill. He said it right away."

"On your feet. Now."

She rose slowly and unsteadily on the hard-baked, rutted mud and stood facing him, as tall as he in her high heels. He moved the gun barrel down her cheek, stroking, caressing, and with a deft sudden thrust pushed the barrel inside her mouth where she could taste its sour bitterness of metal and oil, its coldness. She struggled reflexively and tried to spit the thing out, but he grabbed a fistful of hair and held her head as if he were feeding her, pushing the sour-tasting snub-nosed muzzle deeper in.

"If only I'd known you were in the market," he said. "If only I'd known you were so hard up you'd screw a college boy."

The roots burned where he gripped her hair. She closed her eyes, waiting for the explosion, the atomizing of her skull and brain, sudden fiery death. She was afraid to move, to breathe.

"Now I want you to take your dress off," he said.

She opened her eyes and rolled them to look at him. He looked very serious now, and his eyes were luminous with a colorless, otherworldly light, and she knew he was going to kill her.

"Take it off or I'll blow the back of your head off," he said.

It no longer occurred to her that she could choose between obeying and disobeying; the world of choices and volition lay out beyond these lightless woods and was lost to her forever. Somehow, still with the gun in her mouth and Williams gripping his fistful of hair, she reached back with shaking hands and unhooked her dress. Williams withdrew the gun and released her and stepped back to watch her undress. She reached back again and unzipped the dress. She shucked it over her head and dropped it on the ground. The night air was cool on her skin, and she'd never felt so naked. Williams watched her, attentive and businesslike. She looked away and thought of April, of Lane, and her eyes filled.

"I didn't think you'd cry," Williams said. "I thought you'd be different."

"I'm not crying," she said, weeping.

"Yes you are," he said. "You talk smart, throw a drink in a man's face, and screw college boys, but you aren't any different."

He unbuckled his belt with his left hand and pulled it off with a slither and snap of leather.

"And lie to me," he said.

She looked at the belt in his hand. "I never lied to you," she said.

"You sound like Janie. 'I never lied to you, Paul.' Little drug addict. Little hippie nymphomaniac screwing high school boys. What is it with you women? You and your boys. 'I was afraid you'd be jealous,' she said. Goddamn right I was jealous. I could have arrested the little hippie bitch for murder. Get that underwear off."

No choice. She reached into the curve of her back and unfastened her bra and stood bare-breasted before him. He looked at her and nodded. She thought he would touch her, but he didn't.

"The rest of it," he said.

"Please," she said.

"Now."

No choice. She stepped out of her shoes and slid her underpants down, and as she bent over naked in this grotesque parody of undressing for a lover, she heard the car.

It was no more at first than if God were teasing her, distant and faint and too good to be true. She'd grown used to the idea that she was going to die here, had traveled beyond hoping for deliverance. But the car came on, fast, slashing recklessly through the brush, its deep smooth rumble swelling in the still and empty world of these woods. Claire froze, half-crouched with her underpants around her knees, and in another moment the convergent running beams of its headlights lanced the dusk, and the gloom was alive and gaudy with the flashing blue lights of a police car. It skidded to a stop, yawing sideways with a crash of brush, its headlights blinding her. She heard the static squawk of its radio.

Williams had turned. Claire pulled up her underpants and covered her breasts with her arms. Williams faced the police car, stamped dark and blocky against the white glare. She saw O'Neill get out of the car and stroll toward them holding his palms up to show he had no weapon and advancing in a threatless and even friendly sort of way, as if he'd stopped to see if he could help them change a tire.

"Ma'am," he said easily, "get over behind your car, will you?"

She stepped sideways, barefoot, still covering herself, and stumbled against the hood of the Camaro. She wondered if she would faint, fall; leaning on the car, she worked her way around the hood, holding on to it like a cripple, and collapsed on the ground, into the brush and dead leaves, and huddled there in the dark shadow of the Camaro.

"Stay there, Eddie," she heard Williams say.

"Let's talk about this, Paul."

"There's nothing to talk about."

"There's always something to talk about, Paul."

"Not anymore, Eddie."

"Put the piece down, Paul."

"You take care of yourself, Eddie."

"Don't do that, Paul."

"I have to, Eddie. You know that."

"We'll talk about it," O'Neill said. "We'll—"

The gunshot smote her ears and reverberated away in the night, and she thought O'Neill had been shot and that she was going to die here after all. She remained sitting and thought again of April and Lane but distantly this time, numbly and without tears. She hoped he wouldn't rape her. She hoped he'd shoot and not strangle her, and thought how this might be easier somehow if she'd been a better Catholic. Then she felt a hand on hers and looked up, and it was O'Neill.

"You can get up now," he said.

She grasped his hand and he drew her gently to her feet. Her legs wobbled, held. Williams lay in the road on his stomach, arms and legs sprawled awkwardly, the back of his head broken and dark with blood. She looked away, hugging herself, and thought how in their shapelessness and anonymity all dead bodies must look pretty much the same.

"Try not to look at that," O'Neill said.

He leaned over and picked up her dress and bra. He averted his face and handed them to her, then turned his back while she dressed. She could hear the crisp yawp of his radio. He took her arm and led her past the body to his car. Another car was coming, fast. O'Neill stopped and listened.

"That's not a cop car," he said.

The headlights shone through the trees, and the car bore down on them out of the semidarkness and slammed to a stop behind O'Neill's cruiser, and in the smoky gloom she recognized the office Chevrolet.

The door flew open and Lane ran to her. O'Neill got out of the way as he threw himself against her, scooped her nearly off her feet, and hugged the breath out of her. O'Neill gave them a few moments, then took him gently by the shoulder. Lane held her a moment more, then stepped back and saw the body.

"What happened?" he said.

"It's over," O'Neill said. "Everything's under control."

Lane looked at Claire and she turned her face from him.

"What happened?" he asked again. "What the hell happened here?"

"Come on," O'Neill said.

He got between them and took each by the arm and moved them to the Chevy. "Sit in the car," he said. "Relax a few minutes. I got two more officers on the way and then we can get out of here."

They got into the car. O'Neill left them, got into the cruiser, and spoke quietly on the radio. Lane put his arm around her, and in a flat, lifeless voice she told him. He listened without moving or speaking, and when she was done, he rocked forward and put his face in his hands.

"It was my fault," he said.

"It was mine," she said. "I wanted another big story."

"I didn't warn you," he said.

"You didn't know."

"Yes I did," he said, and lurched up out of the car.

"Lane," she said. "*Lane.*"

But he didn't answer her, didn't stop. O'Neill was sitting in the cruiser with the door hanging open. The overhead light was on, and he was writing on a steno pad. The roof strobes flashed silently back and forth, dyeing Lane an iridescent blue.

"The officers'll be here in a couple minutes," O'Neill said.

"Why'd you do that?" Lane said. "Why'd you tell me not to warn her?"

O'Neill looked at him. "Did I say that?"

"You said it's better not to worry them."

"It usually is. Believe me."

"Why?" he cried, and slammed his fist down on the car roof.

"It's done," O'Neill said. "Better let it go."

"Let it go?" Lane said. *"Let it go?"*

He turned, and his eye fell on the body, thick and shapeless with its outflung arms and legs, its blood-matted hair.

"You son of a bitch," he said.

O'Neill got out of the car.

"You sick son of a bitch," Lane said. "You sick bastard."

O'Neill turned him by the arm. "He can't hear you," he said.

"I know," Lane said, and bent over with his hands on his knees and vomited on a roadside bank of moss.

. . .

O'NEILL drove her back in the Camaro with its gun-broken window. Lane drove behind them in the Chevy. Behind him, in O'Neill's cruiser, was a grave and very young state trooper, hatless but otherwise in uniform. O'Neill drove with one hand. He took a cigarillo from his shirt pocket and stuck it in his mouth without lighting it.

"I got to take you to the hospital," O'Neill said.

"No," she said.

Her window was open. She looked out at the house lights, the dark trees.

"It's a rule," he said.

"I don't care," she said.

The wind coming through the window was pleasantly cool on her tear-streaked face. It wasn't as dark as it had seemed in the woods; the sky was a watery indigo, and the moon was rising above the trees.

"If he took advantage of you, I got to take you to the hospital," O'Neill said.

"Took advantage of me," Claire said. "He did that all right."

"Sexual contact, I'm talking about."

"I know what you're talking about."

"Of any kind."

"No," she said.

"Nothing?"

"Nothing," she said.

She watched a kid in bib jeans pump gas into a big Skylark while the owner of the car leaned back against it and combed his hair, smoothing it back with his left hand and following with the comb. His date sat in the car looking bored.

"The contact was his gun," Claire said.

"How do you mean?"

"He put it in my mouth. He raped me with it."

O'Neill waited a polite moment. "Put the gun in your mouth and then what?"

"He told me to undress. Do I have to talk about this?"

"A little bit," O'Neill said. He drove awhile in silence. Claire looked out the window. "Who would have thought?" O'Neill said. "Two years I've known Paul. He was a good cop."

"I think he killed Jane Clifford," Claire said.

"I think so, too."

263

"He said she liked to screw high school boys. He said it made him jealous."

"A guy like Paul'll always find a reason to do what he's going to do," O'Neill said. "Know what I'm saying?"

"No," she said.

A group of teenage girls stood around a kid in his twenties straddling a motorcycle in the parking lot of the A & W Root Beer. The kid was holding forth, the girls all listening raptly.

"Paul didn't do anything funny to himself, did he?" O'Neill said.

Claire looked at him. *He has to ask these questions,* she thought. *He has no choice.* She resumed gazing out the window. "No," she said.

"Kept his own clothes on," O'Neill said.

"Yes," she said.

"Then we can forget it," O'Neill said.

He was silent for a while, leaving her alone with her thoughts. They were on Main Street now. O'Neill drove slowly. She looked up and saw the evening star glinting above the white steeple of St. Patrick's.

"It was my fault what happened to you," O'Neill said. "I took my eye off the ball just long enough."

"It doesn't matter," Claire said.

"He wasn't dating you, was the thing. I was more worried about another lady he *was* dating."

"You don't have to explain," Claire said.

"It'd help if you'd accept my apology," O'Neill said.

"I accept it."

"Lane Hillman's blaming *himself,*" O'Neill said. "It wasn't his fault."

"I know," Claire said. She watched a man come out of the Village Café. He stopped and reached back and slapped his hip pocket to make sure he had his wallet, then walked on.

"I thought he'd killed you," she said.

"Excuse me?"

"When I heard the shot. I thought Williams had killed you."

"He wouldn't have done that," O'Neill said. "It wouldn't have fitted."

She directed him to her house, and they turned into the driveway with Lane behind them and the young cop behind him. Kyle Bagwell's Triumph was parked to the side, half on the grass. The outside light was on. April came out onto the porch and stood with her arms folded, as if she were cold. Kyle came out and stood behind her. They watched Claire get slowly and stiffly out of the car.

"Mom?" she said.

Claire moved unsteadily toward her, as if she were dizzy or very drunk. Lane caught up with her and took her arm. O'Neill followed, bringing Claire's purse. The young trooper sat stone-faced in the state cruiser.

"Oh God," April said. "Oh my God, what happened?"

"It's all right, sweetheart," Claire said.

"She had a scare," Lane said, "but it's all right now."

"What kind of scare?" April said.

"Everything's fine now," Lane said.

"*Tell* me."

"Why don't we all go inside?" O'Neill said.

April looked at him, and then at Claire. She opened her mouth in a silent scream and came down off the porch and threw herself on her mother. "Oh God," she said, "oh God, oh

God, oh God," while Claire held and rocked her, thinking how nothing would ever be the same again.

. . .

SHE SAT in the deep, springless, cigarette-smelling sofa between Lane and April. Kyle sat on April's other side. O'Neill sat facing them on the edge of the soft chair across the room. The two table lamps had been turned on. The lamps cast a drab yellowish light.

"The case is closed, as far as I'm concerned," O'Neill said. "There isn't going to be any trial, obviously."

"I'll have to write something," Lane said.

"Why?" April said.

"The chief of police killed himself," Lane said. "You can't keep that out of the paper."

"You can keep Mom out," April said. "It's your paper."

It all sounded trivial to Claire, of no moment. It was as if she'd died and were her own disembodied soul hovering in the room and listening to talk of things that could no longer concern her. She felt for Lane's hand and drew it into her lap.

"I'll keep her out," Lane said, "if you'll agree to it."

"Fine with me," O'Neill said.

"He went off alone and committed suicide," Lane said.

"Your editor going to go along with that?" O'Neill said.

"The editor's my father."

"I know that. He going to go along with it?"

"I think so."

"Well, it'll be easier on Paul's wife this way," O'Neill said. "His daughters, too, I imagine."

"What about the Boston papers?" Lane said. "They're going to look into this."

"They'll take what I give 'em," O'Neill said.

"I appreciate it," Lane said.

O'Neill put his hands to his knees, preparing to rise.

"How'd you know it was Paul?" Lane said.

O'Neill kept his hands on his knees. "I wonder if these kids want to hear this," he said.

"We aren't kids," April said.

O'Neill looked at her. "I was using the term loosely," he said.

"Go ahead and tell it," Claire said.

O'Neill nodded and relaxed again. "That incident in the Harbor Lounge started me thinking. I did some checking. Turns out that six months before he left the force up in Brockton a girl was found strangled in an abandoned building. A schoolteacher. Case never solved."

He paused and looked at Claire.

"Do you want to hear this?" Lane asked her.

Claire nodded. She held Lane's hand tightly.

"He goes up to New Hampshire, as you know," O'Neill went on. "A chief now. Three months before he applies for the job down here, a high school cheerleader disappears. She was never found."

He removed the cigarillo from his shirt pocket and looked it over.

"There was no known connection between him and the victims, but there wasn't one either between him and Jane Clifford except that he ate sometimes at the diner. He was very careful. With you, ma'am, he got very careless. He got careless and I got stupid."

"So did I," Lane said.

"Didn't I tell you to stop that?" O'Neill said.

"I can't," Lane said.

"When you're feeling better, ma'am, you'll talk to him," O'Neill said.

"Yes," Claire said.

"Why'd he kill all those people?" April said.

O'Neill looked at her. "It's April, right?"

April nodded.

"You don't want to know, April."

"Yes I do," April said.

"Let's just say he was the jealous type," O'Neill said.

"Jealous of whom?"

"Couple of high school boys."

"Kenneth Earle and Mike Sullivan," Lane said.

"She never knew them but that one night," O'Neill said. "They picked her up a block from the diner and talked her into going to the fair."

"And she was the reason David Kasselman got in the car," Lane said.

"She was the reason they stopped for him. Girl was the milk of human kindness."

"So Paul met her later," Lane said. "After the drowning."

"The kids dropped her off at the boarding house. They didn't see her go inside, but maybe she did. The landlady didn't hear her, but maybe she did go in. I imagine Paul was waiting for her. I imagine he saw the boys drop her off."

"The boys talked to you," Lane said.

"I told 'em I had enough to arrest them as accessories to murder. That'll usually do it."

Again O'Neill put his hands on his knees and this time pushed himself to his feet. "You folks have heard enough of this," he said.

Claire let go of Lane's hand, and he stood up. The two men shook hands, the one tall and fair-skinned, the other Irish-dark and squatty.

"Thanks," Lane said.

"You did real good, Miz Malek," O'Neill said.

"She's a brave girl," Lane said.

"Damn straight," O'Neill said.

He went to the doorway and turned.

"I don't know if it'll help," he said, "but I think maybe he wanted to be caught. They do, sometimes. They're like a junkie who wants to kick a habit: they need help, and the only way you can help them is to catch them. I think maybe Paul wanted to be caught this time. I think that's why he was so careless."

"How's that supposed to help?" April said.

O'Neill eyed her mildly. "I don't know," he said. "Maybe to know he didn't hate her."

"What good is that?" Lane said.

"None, I guess," O'Neill said. "You feel better, ma'am, okay?"

.   .   .

IT WAS Lane who spoke first.

"I have to go home and tell my parents," he said.

"No," Claire said.

"I have to," he said.

"Call them," she said.

"I have to talk to my father about leaving you out of the story. I can't do that over the phone."

"You'll come back," she said.

"Of course."

"I want you here tonight."

"I know," he said. He lifted her hand to his lips. "I won't be long. I'll pick something up for dinner."

"I can do that," Kyle said. His voice was thick and logy, of a piece with his pallor and sleepy eyes, his mop of tousled hair. "I can get pizza half-price where I work," he said.

"Good man," Lane said.

He kissed her and was gone, and Claire went upstairs and peeled off her dress and stuffed it into the hamper. It was navy with white polka dots, and she knew she'd never wear it again. She would wash it and give it to Goodwill or the Salvation Army if she didn't simply throw it out with the garbage. She took a long shower, soaping and resoaping herself, then put on jeans and the red-checked shirt she'd worn to Baltimore.

She poured herself a scotch and went out on the porch and sat. In a few minutes April came out and sat down close beside her and silently took her arm. It had gotten dark long ago. The lights burned in the small houses up and down the street. Claire thought of the people in them, her neighbors, watching TV, listening to a ball game, putting their kids to bed. She thought of how innocent they were, how oblivious of evil. She wondered where she'd gone wrong, what act or acts of blindness or stupidity or arrogance had landed her in the empty woods with a psychopath. Following him, yes, but it went back further than that, it went deeper. It went to the very essence of her character.

"Are you okay?" April said.

"A little shaky," she said.

"Mom?"

"What?"

"Did he . . . ?"

"Did he rape me? No."

"Was he going to?"

"I don't know. He might have just wanted to look at me."

"Look at you?"

"He made me undress, April."

April turned and put her arms around her. Claire set her glass down, and they held each other. Crickets chirred in the hedges, and the night rang huskily with their steady, mingled voices. Claire could feel the scotch, lightening her and putting a shadowy distance between the recent past and the immediate present. She saw now that her life would be divided forever into two parts, two existences. Nothing the same, ever again. April released her and wiped her eyes with the back of her hand.

"Is Lane going to sleep with you?" she said.

"I want him near me, sweetheart, do you understand?"

"Sure."

"It has nothing to do with sex."

"I know."

"Sex is the last thing I'm thinking about. I wonder if I ever will again."

"You're going to get all better, Mom."

"I wonder."

"I promise," April said.

. . . .

KYLE CAME back with two huge pizzas and a six-pack of Coke and refused to take any money for them. "It's on me," he said, and Claire smiled and almost began weeping again.

Then Lane returned, bringing his overnight bag and a six-pack of beer. Claire met him at the door and hugged him long and hard while April took the beer from him and put it in the refrigerator.

"My father said yes about the story," he said. "I'll write it first thing in the morning."

She nodded, her head still on his chest.

"He wants you to take the day off tomorrow," he said.

She nodded again, and bit her lip.

It was Claire's idea to eat on the sofa, in the dark, in front of the TV. She was too tired and empty for talk of any kind, yet dreaded solitude, silence.

"What do you want to watch?" Lane said.

"It doesn't matter," she said. "Anything."

"Try the eight o'clock movie," Kyle said.

Lane knelt in front of the set and found the movie. It was the old western, *Shane.*

"Is this okay?" he said.

"Sure," she said.

They watched the movie, tearing off wedges of pizza and drinking Coke and beer out of the can. Claire had seen *Shane* years ago and remembered its stark cinematography, its midnight-blue skies and yellow prairies. Lane and April were pressed against her on either side, warm and familiarly fragrant. She ate a pizza slice and didn't finish her can of beer. After a while she lay down, curled up like a child with her head in Lane's lap, her knees pressed against April's hip, and closed her eyes. She could hear the movie distantly, as if it were going on somewhere above her. Lane stroked her hair, and without opening her eyes she knew he looked down at her from time to time, could feel him watching over her.

"This is hokey." Kyle's sleepy voice, disembodied at the other end of the sofa.

"April," she said, opening her eyes, "do you and Kyle have enough room?"

"We're fine," April said.

"I'm getting squished," Kyle said, and she wondered if he was complaining or joking.

"Enjoy it, Kyle," Lane said.

She closed her eyes again. Lane stroked her hair.

"I can't stand that little brat," Kyle said. He was talking about the boy in the movie, little Brandon De Wilde.

"Shut up, Kyle," April said.

They watched the movie. Claire lay with her arm wrapped around Lane's waist and her head still in his lap. She drifted, nearly slept, then heard a frantic neighing and stamping of horses, the measured slaplike sounds of a Hollywood fistfight. She opened her eyes, saw Alan Ladd and Van Heflin slugging it out in the corral. It wasn't like the real thing; no blood, no split skin and broken teeth. She closed her eyes and remembered how, when he was about sixteen, her brother Kevin had beaten up a neighborhood boy named Stephen McNally on the side-walk outside their house. Kevin had hit him again and again, until the poor boy's face was bloody and disfigured and he dropped to his hands and knees and tried to crawl away. Kevin then had kicked him in the ribs. Claire, who was thirteen, had grabbed Kevin and tried to pull him away, and he'd shoved her off the curb so hard she'd fallen, bloodying a knee.

She opened her eyes and looked up at Lane.

"Are you okay?" he said.

"I was just remembering something," she said.

"We're about to get the big showdown between Shane and Jack Wilson."

But she wasn't interested, and she closed her eyes and snuggled back down. Lane touched her cheek, ran a cool finger down its curve.

"This is *so* hokey," Kyle said.

"Kyle, don't be a snob," April said.

"This is one of the great scenes," Lane said, and she knew by the slant of his voice that he was looking down at her.

Her mother had come out that day. Claire had forgotten that. Kevin was following Stephen McNally as he crawled away, leaning down close to his battered face and taunting him. He spat on him, kicked him. He didn't see Violet coming. She was running now. She grabbed him by the arm, spun him off his balance, and stood between him and Stephen. Kevin staggered, caught himself, and stared at her stupidly, as if he couldn't place her. He looked suddenly confused, unsure of what was happening.

What's wrong with you, Kevin? Violet said. What the *hell* is wrong with you?

Then she'd gone to Stephen and helped him to his feet, hauling him up by the arm. Don't crawl, Stevie, she said. Don't crawl for him or anybody.

Claire opened her eyes. Lane smoothed her hair back from her face, and her gaze moved out to the TV screen, where Shane was riding sadly away into the blue night, toward the distant snow-capped mountains. The little boy called to him from the boardwalk. *Come back, Shane. Mother wants you* . . . Shane kept riding, growing smaller and smaller. The music swelled. The End.

"Bedtime," Lane said decisively.

"I better get home before my parents freak out," Kyle said.

"You're going to help me with the dishes first," April said.

"I am?" Kyle said.

Claire sat up and Lane took her hands and pulled her to her feet. She climbed the stairs slowly, leaning on the bannister. She took another shower and put on a cotton nightshirt and crawled into the double bed and waited for Lane, leaving the bedside lamp on. She did not want to be alone in the dark.

After a while she heard the kitchen door bang. She heard April and Kyle talking outside, their voices hushed and intimate and indistinct. Lane came up the stairs, light on his feet. He came into the bedroom with his overnight bag, the same one he'd taken to Baltimore, and sat down on the edge of the bed.

"Will you be able to sleep?" he said.

"I don't know. I doubt it."

"My father's blaming himself for what happened. That lecture about how we had to get along with Paul."

"All you good men blaming yourselves."

"If I'd just said something to you. Told you what O'Neill said."

"Don't, hon. It just makes it worse."

"I can't help it," he said.

"You have to," she said. "For my sake."

April and Kyle were still talking.

"What does she see in him?" Claire said.

"He's okay," Lane said.

"Yeah. I shouldn't complain."

"You weren't," Lane said.

She lifted his hand and laid the warm dry palm against her cheek where the gun had traced its line, left its invisible scar.

"I was never afraid of Scott," she said. "Even when he hit me. He was a bully, and he knew it, and so did I. He knew he couldn't change my contempt for him, no matter how many times he hit me. This was different. I was terrified. I'd have done anything he said."

She looked up at the plaster ceiling with its whorls and ridges. Lane held her hand.

"It destroys something in you," she said. "Like being maimed or crippled, only it's your spirit and not your body."

"You'll get better," he said.

"I don't see how," she said, and tears came, blurring her vision, running warm down her cheeks.

Lane pulled her up against him.

"I can't go to Detroit now," he said.

"Yes you can. You have to."

"I can't leave you," he said.

"You have to, sweetheart."

The door of Kyle's Triumph shut with a tinny slam. The engine started, idled while he and April talked some more, and then the little car muttered away.

"Maybe you should come with me," Lane said.

"You know that wouldn't work," she said.

April came up the stairs, sandals clacking. She stood in the doorway. Claire had lain down again. Her cheeks still glistened in the lamplight.

"Are you okay, Mom?" April said.

"I'm fine, hon."

"Kyle won't say anything, will he, April?" Lane said.

"Nope."

"Not even to his parents?"

"He can't stand his parents," April said.

She clacked away down the bare hallway, and after a while they heard the bathroom door shut and the shower come on.

"I don't have any pajamas," Lane said.

"I know," Claire said.

"I'm thinking about April," he said.

"I'm not going to worry about it tonight," Claire said.

. . .

HE SLEPT soundly beside her. The luminous hands on the bed-side clock showed the time creeping up toward midnight. Then it'll be yesterday that it happened, she thought. A different date on the calendar, a different time frame. More and more days would intervene, and then months and then years, and eventually it would be like looking at it through the wrong end of a telescope, the event appearing tiny and pain-depleted down the long corridor of time. Maybe. Or maybe it would move up the corridor with her, forever undiminished, stalking her to the bitter end.

A car passed, its engine rumbling through a rusted-out muffler. Down the street a front door banged. A dog barked in the distance. Lane slept peacefully. She could make him out in the thin light of the streetlamp. She watched him sleep while her own heart beat wakefully.

At twelve-fifteen April padded in. She stood by the bed. Claire raised herself on her elbow.

"I can't sleep," April whispered.

"Why don't you read for a while?"

"I want to be with you."

"We're pretty full here," Claire whispered.

"There's room."

277

Lane stirred, growled voluptuously in his sleep. Lane in his BVDs, but what did that matter tonight? Claire slid over against him, and April threw the covers back and crawled in, bony and flower-fragrant in her clean cotton nightgown. Claire lay on her back, wedged between the two of them. Lane slept on.

"I love you, Mom," April whispered.

"I'm glad," Claire said.

April drew a long breath, and Claire felt her daughter's tight-wound body unclench and melt downward in sleep. Like a kitten or puppy. And now the two of them slept on either side of her, April knobby but weightless, Lane solid and unbudgeable. Claire had no room to turn over or extend an arm or bend a leg, but that was all right.

After a while the craving for a cigarette stole over her. Impossible: she couldn't get up without waking at least one of them. She closed her eyes, immediately saw the grinning face of Paul Williams, and opened them with a start. In high school they'd made her read *Hamlet* and memorize the famous soliloquy: *To sleep, perchance to dream* . . . Terrible dreams awaited her, and she fought sleep when it began to take hold at three in the morning. She dropped off finally into a shallow doze, chaotic with rapid, edgy, but not terrifying dreams. The dreams tired, did not rest her. She would wake, find Lane and April beside her, and plunge once more the short distance down into that enervating half-sleep.

At first light she woke fully. She shook April gently. April rolled onto her back and opened her eyes.

"I'm going downstairs," Claire whispered. "You go on back to your own bed now."

April nodded groggily, got up, and shuffled out with her eyes half-open. Lane slept on. Claire got up carefully. She covered Lane's shoulders and dressed herself in the shirt and jeans she'd worn last night. She crept downstairs and made coffee.

She poured a mugful, lit a cigarette, and called her mother. The phone rang and rang. Claire sat down at the kitchen table and looked out at her car in the gray dawn. There was nothing left of the driver's window; Williams had broken out every last shard. She remembered how methodical he'd been about it, how unhurried. Another car she would have to get rid of.

"For Christ sake," her mother said. "It's the middle of the night."

"Ma, can you come down here?"

There was a long pause. "When?" her mother said.

"Now. Today. I need you, Ma."

"Need me for what?"

"To be here." She closed her eyes and took a deep breath. "Somebody tried to kill me yesterday," she said.

"Tried to *kill* you? Is that what you said?"

"Will you come down, Ma?"

"Who tried to kill you?"

"A crazy man. Ma, just come down, will you?"

"I think I better," her mother said.

Afterward, Claire went out on the porch with her coffee. She watched the day break over the trees and rooftops, gradually infusing the gray world with color. The sky hardened to summer-blue. The sun rose above the trees and hurt her eyes. She picked herself up and went back inside. A few minutes later April wandered into the kitchen, still in her nightgown.

"Good morning, sweetheart," Claire said.

"Can I have some coffee?"

"No," Claire said.

"I slept about two hours," April said, and pulled down a mug.

Claire closed her eyes. They were dry and gritty with fatigue. What did it matter if April drank coffee? She looked out at the new summer day.

"I talked to Grandma a little while ago," she said.

"What did *she* want?"

"She didn't want anything. I called her. I asked her to come down."

April looked at her. She held her mug of coffee with both thin dark hands. "Why?" she said.

"Because I need her," Claire said. "She's coming down today."

They could hear Lane moving around upstairs. He went into the bathroom. The pipes shook inside the wall and the shower ran.

"Another thing, April. I'm thinking I might go away with Lane for a few days."

April didn't say anything.

"For the weekend," Claire said. "It'll be our last chance."

"Is that why Grandma's coming?"

"I told you why Grandma's coming. I need my mother right now."

"Some mother."

"I know," Claire said. "Will you be nice to her if I go away with Lane?"

April shrugged. "I'll try," she said.

. . .

SHE POURED coffee for him, and he sat looking out the window, and she knew he was thinking about the story he'd be writing as soon as he got to the office.

"Lane," she said, and put her hand on his.

He looked at her, and now she saw the old longing in his eyes, but softened by what had happened to her.

"I was thinking we might go away this weekend," she said.

"Go away?" he said.

"If I could just get away from here. Just for a couple of days."

"That's not a bad idea," he said.

"I was thinking of Nantucket or Martha's Vineyard," she said.

"You know, that's not a bad idea at all."

"Do you think your father would give us Friday off?"

"He might."

"We don't have to," she said.

"Let's," he said. "Why not?"

She looked down at her hand on his. "Only if you want to," she said.

"I'd give a thousand dollars for the chance," he said.

Chapter Eleven

HE GOT THERE early and found his father alone in the news-room. John Hillman looked up and nodded but didn't say any-thing, so Lane didn't either. He went straight to the graveyard and found Paul Williams's envelope and took it to his desk.

"Should I call his wife?" he said.

His father thought a moment. "I guess you'd better," he said.

"Who else?" Lane said.

"I think he had a brother somewhere."

"I don't want to make a hero out of him," Lane said.

"It's either that or tell the truth," his father said.

"Yeah," Lane said, "I suppose it is."

Police Chief Paul L. Williams, who took over the department two years ago and brought it into the modern era, died last night of a self-

inflicted gunshot wound. The suicide was witnessed by State Police Detective Edward T. O'Neill, who had followed Chief Williams down a lonely dirt road in the woods off Route 110. Chief Williams was 43.

Detective O'Neill declined to speculate on a motive on Chief Williams's part, or to say why he'd followed him. It was, Detective O'Neill said, a matter of some urgency. Chief Williams had turned off the radio in his police cruiser and could not be reached. Detective O'Neill said he spotted Chief Williams turning off Route 110 onto the little-used dirt road near where the body of Jane Clifford, the Oregon woman murdered early this summer, was found. Detective O'Neill said that the matter he wished to discuss with Chief Williams had nothing to do with Miss Clifford and could have played no part in the Chief's suicide.

Paul Lansdowne Williams was born in Haverhill in 1925. He attended public schools in Haverhill and

It was easier to write than he'd thought it would be. There was even a certain satisfaction in it; it was as if, in rewriting history, he was not ignoring but was actually shaping, inventing, the truth. Officially, in the eyes of the world, Williams had never been near Claire last night, and he imagined that as a kind of defeat for Paul, a negation of his triumph over her.

His father proofed the story without once marking it, then got up in his deliberate way and pushed it through the slot into the back shop for one of the linotypists to pick up. Lane watched him. He knew there was something still unsaid and that his father might not wish to wait, or be able to. Returning to his desk, his father looked at him, sternly and yet ruefully, too, as if they were both at fault this time.

"Never again," he said.

Fred and Ruth looked up, saw that it was a matter between father and son, and went back to what they were doing.

But I had to, Lane thought. I had to.

. . .

HER MOTHER got out of her car and walked slowly toward the house carrying an expensive leather suitcase. Claire came out onto the porch and down the steps. Her mother stopped and put the suitcase down, and Claire went to her slowly and hugged her.

It was awkward at first. Her mother's embrace was stiff, cautious, as if she'd never learned to mold her body to another woman's. But then Claire smelled her mother's perfume and remembered it from long ago, and the subtle pressed-flower fragrance of her skin and the cigarette smoke in her hair, and a noiseless sob broke from her and she clung to her mother with all the desperation of a frightened child while at last Violet held her tight and patted her shoulder and kissed her about the ear.

"It's all right, Clairie," she said. "It's all right, it's all right, it's all right."

They separated finally and Claire wiped her eyes and smiled the wan ghost of a smile. She picked up the suitcase and took her mother's arm.

"Who attacked you, Clairie?"

"Come on in and I'll tell you about it."

"Because, Clairie, we're not going to fuck around with civil liberties and suspended sentences and all that shit. We're going to put the son of a bitch *away*."

Claire wondered if April had heard this, and how many of the neighbors. "You like the house?" she said.

"It isn't much from the outside," her mother said.

. . .

HIS MOTHER sat at the kitchen table cutting green beans that had come from her garden. Lane took a clean bowl from the dishwasher and filled it with raisin bran. The mullioned windows were ablaze with the evening sunlight. Lane got a carton of milk from the refrigerator and sat down.

"I take it you aren't having dinner with us," his mother said.

"I'm sorry," Lane said, and dug into the cereal.

"I hope you'll have dinner with us *once* before you leave."

"Of course I will."

He ate and watched her work. She had pretty hands, shapely and lightly tanned.

"Is Claire feeling any better?" she said.

"A little. Her mother came today."

He shook more cereal into his bowl.

"That isn't much of a dinner," his mother said.

"It's fine," Lane said. "By the way, Claire and I might go away this weekend."

"Oh?"

"We're thinking of going to the Vineyard."

"We'll miss you," his mother said.

"Do you think Dad would give us Friday off?"

His mother broke a bean in half. *Snap.* "He might," she said.

"I thought you might put in a word for us," Lane said. "Explain to him how Claire needs to get away. From a woman's point of view, I mean."

"I think your father understands that."

"I guess he does," Lane said.

"He feels terrible about what happened."

"I know," Lane said.

"It wasn't easy for him, you know, to cover up the truth in the paper."

"I know," Lane said.

"You're lucky your grandfather isn't here."

"I know."

"Did you thank him?"

"I haven't had a chance," Lane said. He got up and put his empty bowl in the sink. He put the milk away.

"Don't stay out too late," his mother said, as she'd been doing for ten or more years, as long as he'd been leaving the house at night, saying it now in full awareness that he was free to come home whenever he pleased, but preserving the ritual for ritual's sake and the continuity it afforded.

"Will you say something to Dad?" Lane said.

"If you want me to," she said.

.   .   .

VIOLET's black Mustang sat in the driveway behind the Camaro. Claire and Violet and April were eating supper in the kitchen. The sun was on the other side of the house, and the small room swam with dusky shadows.

Lane would have known Violet O'Brien anywhere. She had her daughter's heart-shaped face and her supple curves. She put down her fork and looked Lane over.

"You're right, Clairie," she said. "He's a good-looking boy."

"This is my mother," Claire said.

"Nice to meet you, Mrs. O'Brien," he said.

"Robichaud," she said. "*Ms.* Robichaud."

"What's this?" Claire said.

"Women's liberation, Clairie. You don't have to keep a creep's name anymore. You should think about that."

"Think about what?"

"Going back to your maiden name."

"Then I'd be O'Brien. A creep, remember?"

"That's true," her mother said. "You're in kind of a no-win situation. Lane, sit down and join us. Have a hamburger. We're eating fancy tonight."

"You want one, hon?"

"He wants one," April said.

"Push over, April," Violet Robichaud said.

April scraped her chair sideways and Lane pulled a chair from the corner and sat down.

"So I hear you're turning my little girl into a newspaper reporter," Violet said.

"She's turning herself into one," Lane said.

Claire was at the stove now, frying Lane's hamburger.

"How are you feeling?" Lane said.

Claire turned, answered with a shrug.

"She took a nap," April said.

"Did your father say anything about your story?" Claire said.

"No," Lane said.

"I'll have to thank him," Claire said.

"Thank him for what?" her mother said.

"They left Mom out of the picture," April said.

"They should have," Violet said.

"He killed three girls, Ma. We left that out, too."

"So what? He's dead, who cares?"

"Ordinarily," Lane said, "you want to tell the whole truth."

"I keep thinking about the Kasselmans," Claire said. "What they'd say if they knew."

"Who are the Kasselmans?" Violet said.

"Just some people, Ma."

"Well, that narrows it down," Violet said.

"This is a little different," Lane said. "Your name wouldn't have been printed, remember."

"Why not?" April said.

"Because it was a sexual assault," Claire said.

"I thought he didn't touch you," Violet said.

"I thought so, too," April said.

"I told you what he did, Ma. I told you too, April. And I don't want to talk about it anymore."

"All I can say is, you got quite a town down here if a guy like that can get to be the chief of police."

"He had a split personality," Lane said. "No one knew about his dark side."

"Can we please not talk about him?" Claire said. She turned the stove off and shoveled the hamburger out with a spatula.

"You want coleslaw?" she said.

"He wants everything," April said.

"How come you don't get fat, you eat two dinners?" Violet Robichaud said.

. . . .

THEY SAT in the dark and watched the police riot in the streets outside the Democratic convention in Chicago. The Siege of Chicago, Norman Mailer would call it. The police fought in lines, advancing slowly and attacking in sudden violent gusts, clubbing and scattering the demonstrators.

"They're just kids," Claire said.

"Well, they shouldn't make such pests of themselves," Violet said. "What are the cops supposed to do, let 'em close the city down?"

"I ought to be there," Lane said.

Violet looked at him. "What the hell for?"

"He's against the war, Ma."

"So what?" Violet said.

"I ought to be doing something," Lane said.

"You'll be doing something," Violet said. "You'll be lucky you don't get killed. Those colored neighborhoods are like war zones these days."

"Not quite," Lane said.

"At least you're not a hippie, Lane. These goddamn hippies, it'd be good for 'em to go to Vietnam."

Claire sighed but didn't say anything. Violet was Violet, and you couldn't expect her not to be. She's my mother, Claire thought, my *mother,* and she took Violet's thin cool hand and held it.

"You want anything, Ma? A beer?"

"Lane'll get me one," she said.

He found a Bud in the refrigerator. When he went back to the living room, John Chancellor was recapping the events of the last hour from the quiet of the TV studio.

"It's okay you don't go to Vietnam, Lane," Violet said. "Why get your head shot off for a bunch of Communists and Chinese?"

"They aren't Chinese, Ma."

"Lane knows what I mean," her mother said.

"I get the general idea," Lane said.

The coverage had moved to the convention, where someone they didn't recognize was giving a droning, listless speech that nobody seemed to be listening to.

"Your father avoided the service," Violet said. "Maybe it's the dumbbells that go and fight. Look at Joey and Kevin."

"It depends on the war," Lane said.

"Claire's father avoided World War II," Violet said. "How's that for not doing your duty?"

"I'd have gone in World War II," Lane said.

.   .   .

He left early. Claire walked him to his car.

"Now I know where you get your sass," he said.

"I was afraid she might flirt with you and make a fool of herself," Claire said.

"She was fine," Lane said.

"You don't mind her political views?"

"I'm not sure what they are," he said.

"I don't think she is, either."

He put his arms around her, but gently, carefully, as if she'd broken a bone or dislocated something. She laid her head against him.

"It's going to take me a few days," she said.

"I know," he said.

"Can you be patient?"

"Sure."

"I want you to stay home tomorrow night, anyway. Have dinner with your family."

"Why?"

"Because you're going to leave home forever next week."

"All right," he said.

"Promise me," she said.

"All right."

She kissed him gently but lingeringly, then stepped back and smiled sadly up at him in the darkness.

"It's okay if I'm not ready for a while?"

"All I want is your company," he said.

"I don't think that's quite true, sweets."

"Almost," he said.

. . .

SHE WAITED till Lane was out of the office, then rose from her desk and asked Mr. Hillman quietly if she could speak to him alone. He didn't seem surprised. He nodded, got up without speaking and led her to the little back office and closed the door. They sat down and he folded his arms and waited.

"This is where we started," she said.

"It is," he said, and waited.

"A lot of water under the . . ." She stopped. "I sound like an idiot, don't I?"

"No," he said.

"Mr. Hillman . . ."

"I can't get you to call me John, can I?"

"I guess I'll always be a secretary at heart."

"You're a reporter now," he said.

"So many years I called men 'Mister.' Fetched their coffee. Jumped up when they called me."

"Well, you won't have to do that anymore."

"I have you to thank," she said.

He looked out the window.

"I have other things to thank you for. Leaving my . . . ordeal out of the paper."

"I guess I felt partly responsible for what happened."

"You weren't," she said.

He looked at her for a moment, quiet, pensive. His brown eyes were deep wells of both strength and sadness.

"I have one other thing to thank you for," she said. "Letting him go away with me."

"I don't see that I have any choice," he said.

"Yes, you do. I wouldn't go if you opposed it."

"Lane would."

"He'd go alone, then."

Mr. Hillman nodded. "All right," he said. "I'll accept that."

"I won't divide him from his family. That's one thing I never want you to be able to say about me."

Mr. Hillman turned his chair and gazed out the window. "I accept that, too."

"I just wish you'd trust me," she said.

"I'd rather you didn't put it that way."

"What other way is there?"

"It's the situation we don't trust. If you were a younger woman . . ."

"You think I don't wish that?"

"I'm sure you do."

She looked at him, coloring, and her eyes blazed. "And you don't?" she said.

He didn't answer immediately but sat immovable and stubborn with his arms folded and his gaze fixed somewhere beyond her.

"Wishing doesn't change things," he said.

"But you have to," she said. "For some things, at least."

"Why?" he said.

"Because . . ." Her anger had died as abruptly as it had leapt up. "Because if you don't, they never happen," she said.

"Maybe." He unfolded his arms and glanced at his watch. "I suppose we should get back to work," he said.

"Wait," she said.

He paused, wishing only for her to finish and let him get back to the newsroom, where his role was her boss and not her lover's father.

"You're sorry you hired me," she said.

"Are you telling me or asking?"

"I think you know the answer to that."

He nodded and stood up without looking at her.

"I never regret hiring a good reporter," he said.

. . .

HE GAVE them Friday off. A reluctant gift, or perhaps he just wanted to get them out of his sight, and that way stop thinking about it. And so a little after five on Thursday evening, Lane got up from his desk and crossed the newsroom and sat down for the last time in the maple chair beside John Hillman's desk. The news staff had all gone home, and father and son were alone. Claire had left an hour ago.

"You going to be okay tomorrow?" Lane said.

"Sure."

"We could still go tomorrow. Cover fire and police, then take off."

"We'll be all right," his father said.

"Dad . . . ?"

His father looked at him in the old silent and unapproachable way. "You'll miss your boat," he said.

"I wanted to thank you," Lane said.

"I'll see you on Sunday," his father said.

The hell with it, Lane thought. He stood up. "So long," he said.

"So long," his father said.

He paused in the doorway and took one last look around. His father was reading copy, hunched over with his chin against the block of his fist. *This is it,* Lane thought. *This is really it.* He went into the back shop, where Jimmy Wheeler was setting type, alone among the silent machines. A cigarette dangled from the corner of his mouth and he was humming softly as he worked.

"This was my last day, Jimmy."

Jimmy took the cigarette out of his mouth and laid it on the edge of the makeup table. "I didn't know that," he said.

"I'm leaving early next week."

"Inky hands," Jimmy warned.

"That's all right," Lane said, and they shook hands fondly.

"Give my regards to Broadway," Jimmy said.

"Detroit," Lane said.

"Well, give 'em to Detroit."

Lane took a last look at the printing press in its shallow pit. He inhaled the sweet smells of newsprint and ink. *Good-bye,* he thought, and left the cavernous room and went out into the cool, golden, almost-September evening.

. . .

SHE PICKED him up on the corner in front of Dimmock's Gulf. She was driving her mother's Mustang. The two suitcases, his and hers, were in the back seat.

"What have you got in that suitcase?" she said. "It weighs a ton."

"Books," he said.

She gave him a quick kiss, then looked over her shoulder and swung the car out into the traffic moving through the intersection on its way into town.

"So we're going to spend our honeymoon reading," she said.

"I thought we could read aloud," he said.

She smiled. "Is that what you did with your college girls?"

"No," he said.

"Liar," she said.

"I had one girl who read to me a few times."

"Dickens?"

"She didn't like Dickens. She said he was maudlin."

"She was the wrong girl, then."

"They all were," Lane said.

On the ferry they bought cans of Pabst Blue Ribbon and took them up top and stood at the railing in the salt wind. The water was steel-blue. The low, flat hills of the Elizabeth Islands were a fading jewel-green. The western sky was pink cream. They leaned against the railing and nursed their icy beers, and after a while Claire moved closer to him and took his arm. The clean sea air buffed her skin. The beer lightened her and made her happy.

"You think your father'll be okay without us tomorrow?" she said.

"Sure."

"Who'd ever have thought I'd be wondering if a newspaper editor could get along without me?"

"Anyone who knew you," Lane said.

"Who'll do fire and police?" she said.

"Stop worrying about it," he said.

"I'm not, really."

The boat moved out into the open water. The Vineyard lay in front of them, shadowy and green, with the white speck of a building here and here, a twinkling point of light. The deck was crowded but quiet except for the deep interior rumble of the engine; it was as if everyone were awestruck by the clarity of the moment, the rich dark colors of land and sea, the vivid liquid sky.

"Anyway," Claire said, "it was nice of your father."

"Yeah, I guess," Lane said.

"You guess? Is that all?"

"Are you getting high on one beer?" he said.

"I seem to be."

"He was so damn grudging about it."

"Your father loves you, Lane."

"In his way."

"There's only one way. And your wonderful mother. And all those nice, smart sisters. God, when I think about them, and think about my brothers . . ."

"Do you ever see them?"

"At Christmas. Thanksgiving, sometimes. At Christmas they get drunk and fight with their wives. At Thanksgiving they get drunk and watch football games."

"What about your nieces and nephews?"

"They're different from April, let me put it that way. They hate school, they don't read books. The girls start putting out when they're sixteen. They think April's a freak."

"April's going to have the last laugh," Lane said.

"I think so, too."

They drank their beer and watched the water slide by. They looked at the growing silhouette of the Vineyard.

"I wish I could change things for you," Lane said.

"You already have."

"The past, I mean. All the bad luck."

"We make our own luck, Lane. Good and bad."

"Not all of it," he said.

They drove off the ferry in the dark with Lane at the wheel, up into the leafy hillside village of Vineyard Haven. The road climbed gradually out of town past old weathered-shingle houses and an occasional small business with an unlit sign out front. Soon they were in the country. A full moon had risen. It laved the open fields in pewter-yellow light, and beyond them the woods stood ink-black against the soft sky. The road branched and the woods tightened in on them, overspreading the road and shutting out the bright moonlight.

They left the blacktop and drove down a dirt road, enclosed like a tunnel under the trees. After a slow mile or two—Claire had lost all sense of distance—Lane stopped the car in front of a gabled house that stood on a rise above the water.

"Be right back," he said.

She watched him go up the gentle slope to the house and knock on the door, timidly at first, then harder. An old woman answered. Claire saw her nod, and the two of them disappeared inside. Claire could hear the soft plash of the waves along the beach on the other side of the house. After a few minutes the door reopened and the old woman stood in its rectangle of light and watched Lane descend to the car.

"What took you so long?" Claire said.

"She wanted to talk. You have to jiggle the handle or the toilet'll run. She said to put a heavy rock on the lid of the trash barrel or the racoons'll get into it."

They drove another quarter-mile down the dirt road. The cottage stood on a treeless lawn surrounded on three sides by a dense scrub of wind- and salt-stunted oaks. The ocean lay perhaps a hundred yards away, beyond a low range of dunes. It was a narrow, gaunt building, its weathered shingles bleached to a pale gray. Lane carried the suitcases to the back door. Claire opened the trunk and hoisted a bag of groceries in each arm and followed him across the moon-glazed lawn. Lane unlocked the door and found the light switch.

The house smelled of mildew, sand, sea salt, and dry wood. It smelled of the good old summertime. Claire walked through its small rooms, turning on lights. Tiny kitchen, fully equipped. Bathroom not much bigger than a phone booth, but there was an outdoor shower, she'd been advised, with a view of the ocean. The sitting room was sparsely furnished. No TV, but who wanted TV? Cheap dog-eared paperback books stood in slanted rows along several built-in bookshelves.

There were two small bedrooms and a master bedroom at the top of the steep, narrow staircase. The master bedroom looked out over the water. It had a double bed, a dresser with a mirror, and an antique spinning wheel for ornamentation. It smelled of pinewood and saltwater and wool blankets, and had windows on three sides.

They unpacked and put away the groceries, then took off their shoes and walked hand in hand down the path to the beach. The sand was sugar-white. The water was still and silvered with moonlight.

"I'm going swimming," Lane said.

"Now?" she said.

He undressed unselfconsciously and without ceremony, and

strolled down to the water. He waded in above his knees without looking back, dove and felt the electric pleasure of sliding naked through water. He swam straight out, turned, treading water, and watched her strip in the moonlight. She didn't look at him, but she was comfortably aware that he was watching her. She came down to the water's edge, waded in hip-deep, paused, and scooped water in her hands and wetted her face and neck. She ran her hands back through her hair, her head back-tilted, her eyes closed. She breathed in deeply and plunged into the dark, glimmering water. Lane now swam toward her, and they met in chest-deep water. She put her arms around his neck, smiling, and swung herself up, and he caught and cradled her in his arms.

"You okay with this?" he said.

"Don't I look okay?"

She raised herself in his arms and gave him a salty kiss.

"Ever worry about sharks?" she said.

"No."

"Crabs?"

"No."

"Don't you wonder what's down there?"

"Same thing that's down there in the daytime."

"I hope you're right."

She rolled away from him, and they swam in side by side and emerged dripping in the moonlight. They picked up their clothes, and he took her hand and they walked up the path between the dunes to their lighted dollhouse of a cottage. They took an outdoor shower, watched by the wide eye of the full moon, and toweled each other dry.

"Come on," she said.

"I don't want to rush you," he said.

"It's gone now," she said. "I feel clean again."

He followed her into the house and up the stairs, and they lay down on top of the covers on the double bed. Her brown body looked varnished in the moonlight.

"I think I'd be happy just to lie here and look at you," he said.

"I don't think I'd settle for that," she said.

"I don't think I would, either," he said.

They made love gently, patiently, then fell asleep with Lane's arm around her waist. They woke and made love again, then went downstairs and drank bourbon while a sirloin steak seared on the gas stove. Lane ate his half of the steak plus a stack of Oreos and a quarter of a watermelon. They went back to bed sometime after one. They lay on their sides with their heads on the same pillow, and Lane moved his hand down her shoulder, waist, hip, leg, and stopped. He closed his eyes, and his breathing steadied, and he was asleep. Claire smiled. She cradled his head against her breast and lay awake a long time listening to him breathe, and to the fitful whispering of the ocean waves. She thought she might not be able to sleep and decided she'd be happy either way, and that was the last thing she remembered.

. . . .

THEY MADE love upon waking, drowsily and simply, and she dozed off again while Lane put on shorts and sneakers and ran the mile and a half to the paved road at the top of the hill and back. He took a swim and showered, and Claire came downstairs in shorts and a T-shirt and no underwear and fried bacon and eggs for the two of them. She was surprised at how hungry she was.

They drove to town and bought swordfish and peppermint

ice cream and island tomatoes. They walked a couple of miles along the beach and everyone watched Claire go by, men and women both. She wasn't flat-bellied and lissom anymore, but she was in her prime, at the zenith of her midlife vigor and beauty, moving across the summer tableau of sand and sea and sky in her two-piece bathing suit with the leggy grace and self-possession of a fox or a deer or a lynx. She smiled at people as she passed, and they smiled back. When she and Lane got hot, they swam and then walked on, letting the sun dry them.

They went upstairs in the middle of the afternoon and peeled off their damp bathing suits. Sunlight scoured the room at that hour. It was very warm, even with the windows open. They licked the sea salt off of each other, and made love twice, and afterward slept till cocktail time.

She dressed for dinner, chiffon and pearls and high heels, and they ate fettucini by candlelight and killed a bottle of chianti.

"Let's go swimming," she said.

"You're all dressed up," he said.

"So what?" she said.

She stood up, tipsy, and pulled off her dress and dropped it on the floor. She unhooked her bra and dropped it with a coy flourish, like a stripper. Lane got up from the table and took off his shirt. He staggered and almost tripped getting out of his jeans.

The water was as still as it had been the night before. Claire turned on him impulsively and pushed his head under, and they wrestled. She remembered that first time, how she'd initiated the roughhousing and one thing had led to another. She remembered how surprised she'd been at his boldness with her, and realized she'd been asking for it, and at some level had known she was. Tonight some madcap caprice got into her, some imp or

302

devil, and she shoveled water in his face, tried to bite his hands when he held her wrists, and threw herself on him and dunked him again. The rough contact excited her, and she thought of wrapping herself around him here in the water, but instead led him back toward the house and pulled him down on top of her in a hollow among the dunes.

In bed finally he read aloud to her from *Huckleberry Finn* and *The Great Gatsby.* When he'd finished, he slid down beside her with the bedside lamp still burning.

"I'm going to read them," Claire said.

"You never read *Huck Finn?*"

"I was supposed to read it in a lit course at Dean, but I didn't."

"Why not?"

"Why do I do a lot of things?"

"Because you've got a mind of your own," he said.

They lay awhile in the yellow lamplight.

"Lane? Was I too rough with you in the water?"

"It was fun."

"I don't know what got into me."

"Old Crow and chianti."

After another pause she said, "What other books did you bring?"

"Hemingway short stories. *The Sound and the Fury* by Faulkner."

"We'll never get to all of them," she said.

"Not this weekend, but sometime," he said.

"Want to go to sleep?" she said.

"No." He reached for the lamp.

"Leave it on," she said.

.   .   .

She chose Saturday afternoon to talk about it. They'd just made love in the warmth and hard thin light of two o'clock. Claire got up, and he watched her move to the dresser and get her cigarettes and an ashtray. She lit one and sat cross-legged on the bed with the ashtray beside her.

"I wish I hadn't cried," she said.

"You sure you want to talk about this?" he said.

"This is a good time to talk about it. It might be the only time."

"Who wouldn't have cried?" he said.

"Plenty of people. I wish I hadn't cried, and I wish I hadn't undressed."

"You had to undress or he'd have killed you."

"At least I'd have died with some honor."

"Then I'd have lost you. And April would have."

"You'd have fought back," she said.

"Did you hear me?" he said.

"I heard you," she said.

"If I had a gun in my mouth, I'd do whatever I was told."

"You wouldn't let him win."

"He didn't win," Lane said.

"He saw me cry. He saw me strip. He saw me so scared I almost wet my pants."

"Then he saw it all disappear and he shot himself."

She rubbed out her cigarette and moved the ashtray to the bedside table. "I wonder if he knows I'm sitting here beside you."

"With your clothes off," Lane said.

"Making love all weekend."

"He does know," Lane said.

304

"I doubt it."

"He knew it when he shot himself. It all came clear to him in that moment. The past *and* the future."

"You really believe that?"

"It's what happens when you die."

She smiled. "You're full of shit, you know that?"

"You'll see," he said.

She still sat with her legs crossed. A faint breeze came in through the screened windows. She could feel its warm soft breath on her back. Lane looked up into her face. He reached up and lightly ran the back of his hand down her cheek.

"I love you, Claire," he said.

"Same," she said.

. . .

SHE KEPT him awake most of that last night. As though if you loved often enough in one night you could go without for weeks or months if you had to. As though you could quell desire by overwhelming it. They made love and talked and listened to the waves and made love again, and one hour succeeded another. They fell asleep as the luminous minute hand beside the bed crept toward 4 A.M.

Then she was awake, and the sun was rising and the long day was in motion. Lane woke a few minutes later. He rolled out and ran up the dirt road on four hours' sleep, then took his swim and shower. At breakfast he told her he'd put aside some money from his earnings this summer to help pay her air fare when she visited him in Detroit. Claire sipped her coffee and looked out at the smooth, slick, slow-heaving ocean, and thought about keeping house for a weekend in a ghetto tene-ment and smiled. She thought of all the people on this pretty island who didn't have to go anywhere today, or tomorrow, or the next day, or the day after that. Some, many, would never have to say good-bye to each other. Not until they wished to, or till death did them part.

"Are you okay?" Lane said. He was wolfing down the last of the eggs and bacon, hungry to the end.

"Just tired," she said.

They washed the dishes and went to work cleaning the house, sweeping up sand, scrubbing porcelain and linoleum, bundling dirty sheets, folding blankets. Soon the place wasn't theirs anymore, and the sun's fierce light fell on clean, bare, neutral rooms where tomorrow or the next day strangers would take over, cooking breakfast, tracking sand, hanging wet bathing suits to dry, and, if they were lucky, undressing each other in the airy master bedroom. They bagged the garbage, and Lane stuffed it into the metal barrel by the back door. He remembered to put a rock on the lid.

"Let's take one more swim," he said.

"I'm so tired I'd drown," she said. "But you go ahead."

"Not alone," he said.

She sat down at the little kitchen table and wrote out a check to the landlady.

"I hate having you pay," he said.

"Hush," she said.

"I'll make it up to you."

"You already have," she said.

She got up from the table and took a last look at the dunes, with their swaying blades of beach grass, and at the restless silver-blue ocean beyond.

"Have we got everything?" she said.

"My mother says you should always look under the bed before you leave," Lane said.

"I'll meet you at the car," she said.

She crossed the sandy lawn and got into her mother's Mustang. She could hear the waves falling with a muffled turbulence along the length of the shore. Lane came out with the suitcases, and they drove up the winding dirt road to the landlady's house on its rise above the sea. Claire opened her purse and handed the check to Lane.

"Tell Mrs. Luce I never got a better bargain," she said.

Chapter Twelve

SHE STOPPED the car in front of his house, and Lane got out and dragged his suitcase out of the back seat. He leaned down at the open window and kissed her.

"We'll go back next summer," he said.

"That would be nice."

"Well, we'll do it."

She watched him open the white picket gate. He went through with his suitcase and closed it behind him. At the front door he turned and blew her a kiss.

She drove home slowly, distrustful of her alertness and reflexes. She was light-headed with fatigue, and the afternoon light was hard on her eyes, even with dark glasses. The roads were nearly empty. She drove along the shore and saw that the crowds had vanished like a dream or mirage. The summer was over; people were heading home.

The Camaro was in the garage. Claire got out of her mother's car and hauled out her suitcase, dragging it with both hands. The kitchen door opened and April came out on the porch. She stood with her hands in the pockets of her shorts, watching Claire come across the yard lugging her suitcase.

"How was it?" she said.

"We had a good time," Claire said. It sounded absurd in its simplicity and blandness. *I've never been so happy. Would anybody believe that if I said it?*

She climbed the porch steps, and April gave her a brief, tight hug that said she'd missed her but things were okay. April took the suitcase from her and held the door. Violet got up from the kitchen table.

"So," she said, "you engaged yet?"

"Hi, Ma."

"You look exhausted. You get any sleep at all?"

"None of your business," Claire said.

The kitchen table was littered with Coke cans, beer bottles, playing cards, and plastic poker chips.

"What's going on here?" Claire said.

"Grandma's teaching me to play poker. We found these chips in the upstairs closet."

"What do you want to play poker for, April?"

"Grandma took me shopping yesterday for school clothes."

Claire looked at her mother. "Did you, Ma?"

"Somebody had to do it," Violet said.

"Thanks, Ma. Really."

"We had fun, didn't we, April?"

"I'll pay you back," Claire said.

"Don't worry about it," Violet said. "This is why they have alimony."

Claire carried her suitcase into the living room. She set it down on the floor and fell into the deep embrace of the old sofa. April and Violet sat down on either side of her.

"So you had a good time," Violet said.

Claire nodded.

"I wish someone would take me to Martha's Vineyard," Violet said.

"I hope the clothes you bought April are appropriate," Claire said.

"Want to see them?" April said.

"You should talk," Violet said. "You ought to see the way she dressed in high school, April."

"I don't want to hold myself up as a model for April," Claire said.

They sat awhile without speaking. A cricket sang somewhere in the hot, still afternoon.

"Are you all right, Clairie?" her mother said.

"I don't know, Ma."

"Why don't you go take a nice nap?" her mother said.

"All right," Claire said, but didn't move. Her mother put her arm around her and pulled Claire against her.

"Is Lane coming over tonight?" April asked.

"Not tonight," Claire said.

"Why not?"

"He's got a family," Violet said. "We can't hog him every night."

"He's leaving day after tomorrow," April said.

"We're aware of that," Claire said.

"You go take a nap," her mother said. "You take a nap, and the world'll look a little better to you."

. . .

He went to bed at eight and slept till noon. He ate a can of cheese ravioli and a couple of peanut butter sandwiches and a can of fruit cocktail, then walked to the beach and sat on the jetty, on the rock, where he'd sat with Claire on their nocturnal strolls to the beach. The sky was pale, and already the smoky southwester had brewed up off the horizon. He thought about Detroit. He wondered if the neighborhood that would be his home for a year would be like the ghetto they'd visited in Baltimore. He thought of Claire. Her absence here, where they'd sat and talked and looked at the moonlight, was suddenly palpable, as if he'd discovered an article of her clothing, a high-heeled shoe or a scarf, and he fled the place and walked home in the solitude of the old rail line.

He packed before dinner, filling the largest suitcase the family possessed with every usable item of clothing and footwear he owned. There was still some room, and he added a one-volume *Complete Works of William Shakespeare,* Modern Library editions of *Absalom, Absalom!, The Sun Also Rises,* Joseph Conrad's *Victory,* and the paperback edition of *The Sound and the Fury* that he'd taken to the Vineyard. He looked for *Bleak House* and remembered that Claire still had it. The suitcase was very heavy, probably over the airline weight limit, but Lane didn't care. He didn't care what happened tomorrow at the airport.

He sat down on the bed. The girls were out, his father still at work. He could hear his mother puttering in the kitchen. He looked around. Above the mantel of the blocked-off fireplace hung a Frederic Remington print of an Indian or part-Indian in buckskin, kneeling with his long rifle cocked, while a sporadic-seeming fight went on behind him, horses huddled nervously inside a ring of men, also in buckskin, standing up and taking shots at an invisible enemy down the hill. Lane had always wondered why they fought standing up.

On the center of the mantel stood a plastic model of the *Queen Mary,* on which he'd traveled to Europe with his grandmother Schmidt when he was fifteen. There were football trophies—cheap gold-plastic statuettes of running backs in mid-stride—and pen-and-ink action drawings of the New York Giants of the Frank Gifford era. There was a framed reproduction of the front page of the *Bismarck Tribune* of July 6, 1876, carrying the first account of the Battle of the Little Bighorn.

He sat on the bed and his mind drifted to a winter night when he was thirteen or fourteen and a blizzard had struck unexpectedly, blowing in just after dark. He remembered sitting at his desk doing his homework and listening to his transistor radio. The snow whirled, eddied, in the light of the streetlamp out front. The road had vanished under a rolling sea of white. The wind shook the old windows, and the snow peppered the panes and whispered along the sides of the house. The steam radiator clanked and hissed. The room was deliciously warm. There would be no school tomorrow. Happiness had overcome him, an almost physical sensation of warmth and serenity, and as he sat here now the moment seemed very close in time, the happiness itself an indestructible or perhaps renewable commodity that would recur in other places, at other times, again and again and again.

He had two bourbons before dinner and his optimism grew.

His mother made her meatloaf, and there was ice cream pie for dessert.

"I'll send you cookies," Lizzie said.

"From college?"

"There's a kitchen in the dorm."

"Let us know as soon as you have an address," his father said.

"I'll be at the YMCA for a while," he said.

"I have the address somewhere," his mother said.

"Better write it down again," his father said.

"Who wants more salad?" his mother asked. "Heavens, I made too much."

"I'll finish it," Lane said.

"I'll have to remember to make less when you're gone, won't I?" his mother said.

Jessica and Lizzie were the first to get up from the table. Lizzie was going back to Swarthmore in a few days, and her boyfriend came to see her every night now. She jumped up when he knocked and gave Lane a kiss on the cheek.

"I'll see you in the morning," Lane told her.

"Come on, Jess," Lizzie said. They were going to drop Jessica somewhere. She got up and kissed Lane as Lizzie had.

"Night, kiddo," he said.

He sat for a few more minutes, then got up and carried his plate into the kitchen. He rinsed it and put it in the dishwasher. Meg and his parents were still at the table.

"Can I take the car, Dad?" Lane said.

The Chevy was no longer his. On his last day of work he'd parked it in the dirt lot under the trees and hung the key on a hook inside the doorway to the back shop.

"The keys are on the mantel," his father said.

"Will I see you in the morning, Meg?" Lane said.

Meg shrugged. Her eyes filled.

"Meg," he said gently. "Meggie. I'm not going to Siberia."

He went to her and took her head between his hands and kissed her forehead.

"I'll wake you in the morning and say good-bye," he said.

"I'll be up," Meg said.

"Fantastic dinner, Mom," Lane said.

"Don't stay out late, child," she said.

.   .   .

THE THREE of them were finishing supper. There was a pall in the room, not of dissension or anger, but of sadness. Lane felt it instantly. He gave Claire a kiss and sat down.

"Have some dinner," Violet said. "You like fried clams?"

"I've had plenty," Lane said.

"That never stopped you before," April said.

"You aren't sick, are you?" Violet said.

"You two leave him alone," Claire said.

"We're *joking,* Mom," April said.

Violet looked at her watch. "What do you say, April?"

April sighed. "Yeah, all right," she said.

"April and I are going to a movie," Violet said.

"What's playing?" Lane said.

"We don't know," Violet said. She picked up her purse and pulled the strap up over her shoulder. "You need anything, Clairie? Ciggies?"

Claire shook her head.

"Let's go, April," Violet said. "Chop-chop."

April pushed back her chair and stood up.

"Have fun," Claire said.

"We will, won't we, April?"

"Yeah, right," April said.

Lane and Claire watched them cross the yard together in the twilight. Violet tossed her purse in the back seat and jackknifed nimbly down inside the Mustang.

"This is nice of them," Lane said.

"It was Ma's idea," Claire said.

"Your mother's been terrific," Lane said.

"Do I have to get almost killed before she can love me?"

"Maybe she always did," Lane said.

They climbed the stairs and undressed unhurriedly and without preliminaries, like a married couple on an ordinary night. They got into bed and lay facing each other in the ghostly light of the streetlamp. Lane put his hand on her.

"I'm afraid I'm not going to be a very good lay," Claire said.

"There'll be other times," he said.

But after a while they did make love, simply and briefly, and when it was over she pressed her face to his chest and wept.

"Don't," he said. "There's no reason."

"I don't know what I'll do," she said, weeping.

"I'll write to you," he said. "I'll write to you every day."

He held her and rocked her and told her it was going to be all right, that he would write her every day and see her once a month, and she lay quiet against him, and he thought she was asleep. He lay still and took in the lovely vital smell of her and listened to her breathe. A car went by. He heard the steeple bell of St. Patrick's toll in the distance.

"What time is it?" she said.

"I thought you were asleep," he said.

"There's too little time for that," she said.

He looked at the bedside clock. "A little after eight-thirty," he said.

"We have another hour."

"What does April think we're doing right now?"

"Being together on our last night."

"In bed?"

"Probably."

"Is she okay with that?"

"She loves us, Lane."

Another quarter of an hour slipped by. Claire shifted onto her back and pulled him to her. "Don't think about me this time," she said. "Be selfish."

"You don't have to do this," he said.

"I want to," she said, "and I want you to enjoy it."

He fell asleep afterward and dreamed he was playing football in the great reverberating horseshoe of Harvard Stadium on a brilliant fall afternoon. He ran like a deer, swift and weightless, dodging tackles, breaking them. Then Claire shook him awake.

"I didn't mean to do that," he said.

"It was only ten minutes," she said.

"Ten minutes wasted," he said.

"I like watching you sleep," she said.

At ten after nine she kissed him and got up, and he lay on his side and watched her dress one more time. She stepped into her underpants, balanced gracefully on one leg. She adjusted her bra. It was as if something infinitely precious were being taken from him, not forever but for a long time, and he felt a momentary helplessness before circumstance and fate. She buttoned her blouse and pulled on her slacks and stepped into her shoes.

"Better get up, love," she said.

They went back downstairs and sat on the sofa in front of the blank TV. He turned to her and kissed her in the chaste way of lovers just getting acquainted. She smiled. He kissed her that way again. He was beginning to get excited now, but in another moment a car came around the corner and turned into the driveway. They heard the two doors slam, and the kitchen door creak open.

"We're home," Violet said in the kitchen.

April came in and threw herself into the soft chair. She hooked a leg over the arm.

"How was the movie?" Claire said.

"We didn't go," April said. "It was some dumb James Bond movie."

Violet came in with a bottle of Bud and a glass. "Your daughter's awful particular," she said. She set her beer and glass on the coffee table and sat down beside Lane.

"So what did you do all this time?" Claire asked.

"What did we do, April?" Violet said.

"We had a Dairy Queen and drove around awhile and then Grandma let me drive the car."

"Drive the car," Claire said.

"Not on the road," Violet said. "We went over to the beach parking lot."

"You're dangerous, Ma, you know that?" Claire said.

"Lane, whyn't you have a nightcap with me?" Violet said.

"All right," he said.

. . .

HE LEFT at eleven-thirty. The three of them followed him into the kitchen, and he turned at the door to say good-bye to April and Violet. April approached him with her gaze averted and her hands thrust into the pockets of her jeans. She unpocketed her hands and he embraced her, and she hugged him hard, surprising him with her wiry strength.

"I'll write to you," he said.

She nodded with her head against him, gave him a final squeeze, and stepped back with tears in her eyes.

"What about me?" Violet said. "You going to write to me?"

"Sure," he said.

She reached up and took him by the chin and looked into his eyes. Hers were pale blue, and there was a gleam in them, penetrant and sly.

"You're a good boy," she said, holding his chin. "For Clairie's sake I wish you were twenty years older. If you were thirty years older, I'd go after you myself."

"Be good, Ma," Claire said.

"Give us a hug, Lane," Violet said.

She felt small and frail in his arms. She felt breakable. She smelled of cigarettes and an unfamiliar perfume, stronger than Claire's.

"Good-bye, Violet," he said.

"Don't let those colored people walk all over you out there," she said. "White people have rights, too, remember."

"Stop it, Ma."

"Good-bye, April," Lane said.

"Good luck to you, Lane," Violet said.

Claire walked him to his car. The night was cool. They faced each other, and their eyes met, and they gazed at each other wordlessly. Lane took her in his arms one more time.

"I'll see you tomorrow bright and early," she said.

"I wish I could sleep here," he said.

"You belong at home tonight," she said.

He kissed her and got reluctantly into the car.

"Lane," she said at the window. "I've still got *Bleak House.*"

"I know," he said.

"I was wondering if I could keep it awhile."

"As long as you want."

"If you change your mind . . ."

"I want you to keep it," he said.

.   .   .

SHE WAS already at the bus station when he arrived with his parents at twenty to seven. Violet's Mustang was parked by the old train platform and Claire was pacing up and down in a powder-blue summer dress and heels, smoking a cigarette. She saw the car and stopped. Lane and his father and mother got out. Claire dropped her cigarette and stepped on it, then came toward them. Her dark glasses hung on the neckline of her dress.

"Good morning," she said.

"Good morning, Claire," Lane's mother said.

Lane kissed her briefly. His father nodded without speaking and went into the bus station to buy the ticket. Lane hauled the big suitcase out of the trunk. He carried it to the platform, and he and Claire and his mother stood under the overhang above the station door.

"Did you get any sleep?" Claire said.

"Some," Lane said.

"You can sleep on the bus," his mother said.

The green office car sat alone in the parking lot under the elms. It was wet with dew. Lane looked away from it, down the dirt and gravel road into the woods.

"Call us tonight and let us know you arrived," his mother said.

"I'll call both of you," he said.

The bus came up the avenue, turned, and came across the open blacktop with its wrinkled silver flank flashing in the sunlight beneath the tinted windows. Lane's father came out of the depot with the bus ticket, pushing his wallet down into his hip pocket. The bus made a U-turn and wheezed to a stop. The door folded back and the overweight bus driver descended stiffly. He threw open the door to the luggage compartment and disappeared into the bus station. Lane heaved his suitcase in and gave it a shove with his foot. His father handed him a leather shoulder bag. The bus driver came out and took up his position by the open bus door. There were about a dozen people waiting to get on.

"I guess this is it," Lane said.

He shook hands with his father. His mother hugged him, dousing him in the familiar and beloved fragrance of face powder, then stepped back, eyes luminous with tears. He turned to Claire, and his father took his mother's arm and led her to the car, where they stood and watched, out of hearing.

"I'll see you next month," Lane said.

"I have something for you," she said, and opened her purse and pulled out an envelope. She'd written his name, *Lane,* in her small, pretty, feminine script.

"What's this?" he said.

"Read it on the plane," she said. "Promise you won't read it till you're on the plane."

"What is it?" he said.

"Let's go, buddy," the bus driver said. Everyone else had boarded.

"Good-bye, love," Claire said, and stepped into his arms. He kissed her passionately, indifferent to the gazes of his parents, the fat bus driver, invisible faces behind the tinted glass, and began to doubt he could live without her for a week, let alone a month. She released him and stepped back with tears running down.

"Claire," he said.

"Get on the bus," she said. "Please, Lane."

"You coming, buddy?" the bus driver said.

"Go," she said. "Please."

He looked at her as he gave the man his ticket. He would never forget her eyes at that moment, yearning and lovely, nor her wet perfect cheeks in the light of the new-risen sun. The driver put the ticket stub in his palm and he tore his gaze from her and climbed up into the bus. People eyed him discreetly as he moved down the aisle. He found an empty seat near the back, across the aisle from a tough-looking man in a white pinstriped shirt rolled up above his wrists. He nodded at Lane as he sat down. Lane returned the nod, placed his shoulder bag on the seat beside him, and sank back and looked out at Claire, and at his parents, who stood back from her by their car, his mother holding his father's arm.

The driver took his seat and reached for the door handle. The door unfolded and clamped shut, and the bus growled and began to move. Lane knew that Claire couldn't see him through the tinted window. She'd put on her dark glasses. She stood with her arms folded and her hip gracefully side-swung, still as a statue and frozen that way forever in his memory.

He looked down at the envelope in his lap. It was tucked, not sealed. It was thick: a long letter. He drew it out. The sheets were triple folded, vanilla stationery with pink and gold fleurs-de-lis at the top. The bus paused at the intersection by Dimmock's, turned, and accelerated out of town, gears meshing smoothly now, the growl of the engine leveling down to a smooth guttural purr.

Dearest Lane,

How do you tell the only man you've ever loved and ever will love truly that you can't see him anymore? That is my problem as I sit here on this end-of-the-summer afternoon listening to the kids play in the field at the end of the street. You've been home for more than an hour. You've probably unpacked your weekend bag and put away your books, your Hemingway and your Faulkner and your Mark Twain. Tomorrow you'll have to pack again. (Why aren't those kids at the beach? It's HOT.) Ma is downstairs playing poker with April. Poker, do you believe it? Next thing, she'll be teaching her how to shoot craps.

As you can see, the answer is I don't know how to tell you. I'm putting it off. Procrastinating. You taught me that word, remember? From Latin, you said, and I looked it up and you were right. *Crastus* or *crastinus,* I can't remember which, which means tomorrow. Anyway I thought a letter would be the easiest way—the cowardly way, you're probably thinking—because I won't have to look at you, which would kill me, or hear all your arguments, which might talk me out of it. I'd want to be talked out of it, do you see? April and Ma will try, but I can still win an argument with April, barely, and I am not in the habit of giving in to Ma no matter what she says. But I do listen to you, Love. That's how we got here, isn't it?

Lane, the reason we can't be together is your family. I can't come between you and your family. I would rather die than do that. I would even rather lose you which is a kind of death for me. This summer I've thought a lot about family. I believe it started with poor David Kasselman dying and the way his family were—was?—in their grief, so joined in loving and missing him. Then I came to your house for dinner and saw your family and how much you mean to them, the only son. How could I come between you and them? How could I force you to choose between them and me?

And it would happen eventually, I guarantee it. Because sooner or later, and probably sooner, I would begin to hold you back. I'll soon be in my forties, remember. And with me as your partner you couldn't go everywhere you ought to go and meet whom (!) you ought to meet and take jobs you ought to take and grow the way you must grow. Because those little sweeties with the flat tummies (I could scratch their eyes out) have things to teach you, too, believe it or not, and you have things to teach them (especially now), and you have to find one that's right for you and then you can be happy for more than the few years you'd have with me.

Your parents know this, and when they saw me preventing it they would turn cool toward me, much more than now, and that would be disastrous. You'll side with me (of course you will, you're my best friend) and there will be a split, and you know what? You'll regret it in the end if not right away. You would blame me someday for dividing you from your family, and you'd be right. You might even eventually hate me for it.

Plus how could I willingly be the cause of your parents' only son having no children? No more Hillmans—do I want that on my conscience? Maybe you won't have children after all, although that would be terrible (haven't I watched you all these weeks with April?), but no one will ever say it was my fault. (No, Sweetheart, we couldn't have our own. You aren't ready, no matter what you might think, and by the time you are, how old will I be? Too old, Love.)

You see? I have covered all the bases. Plus, I'm going to start to sag soon, and the wrinkles are going to get deeper, and my hair will go gray. And you? You'll still be in good enough shape to play against Yale if they could grandfather you in. You'll want a firm young sweetie, and she will want you, and how will that be for me?

Your father quoted somebody to me who wrote or said, "I would have written you a shorter letter but I didn't have time." Was it Mark Twain? I don't remember. Anyway, it looks like I didn't have time to write a short letter. It is after four now and the kids have stopped playing in the field. It's very quiet downstairs, too. What are they up to down there? Is Ma teaching April to smoke?

When I see you tomorrow night I won't have the words to say what I feel, or will be afraid to say them, so I must do this now. You are the best friend I ever had. You taught me things no one else ever would or could. What I am is because of you, and what I will always be. No woman will ever love you more.

One other thing. I would like to keep *Bleak House*. I will

mention this to you and hope you say yes. I know you will. It is still your book and always will be, and someday, when all the pain is gone and forgotten, maybe you'll visit me in the old-age home and I'll return your book to you.

You won't try to contact me, I know. Not if you love me. Your father still has more to teach me, but I don't know how long I can stand to be here with the memory of you everywhere I look. As soon as I can I will find a job at another newspaper. Am I crazy to think so? I'll be gone before Christmas, anyway. Come home and enjoy the holidays with your wonderful family.

You are in some pain, I know, but it will pass sooner than you think. And when it does, please don't be angry, remember me fondly if you can. I will remember you lovingly all my life. We had fun, didn't we?

Love always,

Claire

The letter lay in his lap where his hands lay also, limp, as if they'd ceased to work. He let his head fall back against the seat cushion and looked out unseeing at the weary landscape, where lawns had turned brown and the trees had a drooped, spent, heavy-limbed look.

"Bad news?"

It was the man next to him, across the aisle. Lane looked at him. His face was narrow, aquiline, his eyes deep-set. His hair was brown and quite long, swept back from his high forehead.

"I was watchin' when she give it to you."

Lane came forward in his seat. "I've got to get off this bus," he said.

"A Dear John letter?"

Lane looked at him. "What?" he said.

"I say, did she give you a Dear John letter?"

"No," Lane said.

He refolded the letter. His hands shook. He stuck the letter in the envelope and zipped it into the side pocket of the leather shoulder bag.

"Where's the next stop?" he said.

"Boston."

"I've got to get off sooner than that."

"Why?"

"I've got to talk to her," Lane said.

"What for?"

He didn't answer. He got up, bringing the shoulder bag, and went to the front of the gently swaying bus, aware of the quick curious glances on either side of him. The bus driver watched him approach in the rearview mirror. Lane stood beside him and leaned over and spoke quietly.

"You stop anywhere between here and Boston?" he said.

"Whatsa matter?" the driver said.

"I want to get off."

"There's a bathroom on the bus."

"That's not it," Lane said.

"You sick?"

"No."

"I can't stop. It's against the regulations."

Lane looked out of the huge window and saw the white highway rushing at them, coming and coming, vanishing underneath and behind them, a mile a minute, the miles as final and irretrievable as the minutes themselves.

"Go sit down," the driver said. "You're not supposed to be here."

Lane looked at him, the face knobby and querulous and intent on the highway.

"I ain't going to ask you again," he said.

"All right," Lane said.

The stares now were open and clinging, and he could feel the superiority in them, the pity and distaste, and he was alone in the world as he'd never been, had never imagined being. He fell into his seat with the bag on his lap.

"Fuck her," said his companion across the aisle.

Lane looked at him. The unsmiling face had been gnawed down to the bone, and what was left was indestructible.

"Don't call her, son. Be a man."

"She doesn't want me to call her."

"That ought to settle it, then."

Lane took the bag off his lap and placed it on the seat beside him. He looked out the tinted window with eyes as blue and dry as the high September sky. His heart beat slowly and coldly, and as he watched the heartless world go by, he knew he would never forgive her.

Epilogue

SHE LEFT the office at noon and drove without turning on the radio until she'd gotten around Boston, out of the anarchy of Route 128 and through the Braintree cutoff that swings over onto Route 3, the Pilgrim's Highway. Her late husband had introduced her to classical music, and as often as not she tuned to public radio or the classical station, WCRB, but today she wanted something lighter than Mozart and Vivaldi. She pushed the seek button, found the Boston oldies station, WODS.

The traffic was light on Route 3. She drove south through the gray smog-haunted industrial outskirts of the city. There had been rain this morning and more seemed likely. The day was warm, the sky low and soggy. On the radio the peppy disc jockey, Paula Street, was taking requests over the phone. The callers gave their first names and said where they were calling from. Jimmy from South Boston. Lisa from West Roxbury. Jimmy wanted "Pretty Woman." Lisa wanted "All You Need Is Love." From the voice Claire pictured Paula Street: pretty, of course, with bright eyes and the glowing health of a tennis player or jogger. Definitely blond. The callers used her first name as if they knew her personally.

She was well clear of Boston now, eating up the miles, with low woods on either side of the highway. The trees were budding. Another spring. They came and went, didn't they? The seasons, the years. Paula the DJ repeated the request number and Claire, who had never called a radio station in her life, had never considered it, reached for her car phone. The normal rules didn't apply today. Live dangerously.

The line was busy. She pressed redial and on the fourth try got a ring. It rang and rang, like a phone in an empty house. She decided to give it twenty more rings and then give up. Paula answered the twelfth ring.

"Hi, who's this?" she said warmly. Smiling broadly: you knew it.

"Donna," Claire said, on the outside chance someone she knew was listening.

"Donna on the car phone," Paula said, and Claire wondered how she knew that. "Where you headed, Donna?"

To a funeral, honey. You want to put that on the air? "The Cape," Claire said.

"Neat," Paula said. "I hope the weather gets better for you."

"I hope so, too," Claire said, though she didn't, really. It was the right kind of day for a funeral. The day of Peter's funeral had been heartbreakingly beautiful, the apple and cherry blossoms fluttering along the greening hills.

"What can I play for you?" Paula said.

"Do you have 'For Your Love'?"

"Sure," Paula said, "by Ed Townsend. You have a great day, Donna."

She hadn't heard the song since she'd danced with Lane in his mother's fluorescent-lit kitchen. Twenty-eight years. She remembered how much she'd wanted him that night, with what fierce, uncomplicated desire. He'd come over later. April had gone out. She'd waited for him in the dark, propped up naked on her bed with one knee up and the other leg out straight. She'd heard his car turn in. He'd come pounding up the stairs.

I would do aaaaa-nee thing, foh-ho-or your love . . .

She glanced beside her. The book lay on the passenger seat next to her purse. No harm had come to it; it was unchanged from the day she'd first held it, accepting it from him as he handed it down to her, standing above her with the summer sky behind him, his gaze flicking down perhaps involuntarily to look at her in her two-piece.

It's for April, he said.

Don't I count? she said.

Foh-ho-or . . . your lu-uv . . .

Going to a funeral, honey.

And to return a book.

Maybe.

.   .   .

She was early. She parked in the lot beside the parish hall, a brownstone like the church. Down a gentle hill behind it lay a pond whose name she'd forgotten, still and black on this sunless day, with the woods growing down to its edge.

She grabbed her raincoat and got out of the car. She was wearing a navy dress and matching jacket and pearls. Navy high heels. There were four other cars in the parking lot. She wondered if one of them was Lane's. She looked at her watch. She had nearly an hour.

She locked her purse and *Bleak House* in the car, draped the raincoat over her arm and walked down the church driveway to Main Street. She walked past the village green and noticed that the ancient elms that had stood along its three sides were gone. Dutch elm disease, she guessed. She looked around at the old houses that faced the green, clapboard and shingled beauties two and three centuries old.

She was still a rapid walker. She went briskly past the green and on down the street to the intersection by Dimmock's Gulf, still Dimmock's but a Hertz agency now as well as a gas station. She walked down the avenue. Here, too, the elms had disappeared. The bookstore was an architect's office, but the Buick dealership was still here, as was the lawnmower sales and repair shop.

The newspaper office—of course—had grown to twice its former size. Amazingly, the elm tree still grew out of the sidewalk by the front door, spreading umbrellalike over the building and no larger, that Claire could see, than on the day she'd first looked at it, standing on the depot platform and wondering what work she might find in a newspaper office. The bus station hadn't changed, but the abandoned railroad line had vanished beneath the smooth asphalt ribbon of a bike path.

She spread her raincoat on the wet stone wall where the delivery boys used to sit waiting for Manny Dutra to come out and wave them over to get their papers, and where she and Lane had sat talking things over the morning after the two kids had died, one by murder, one by drowning. He'd been waiting for her here when she'd come out with her coffee. He'd lit her cigarette for her and tossed the match into the street. She sat on the wall and looked at the newspaper office and thought about going in. She knew that Lane's youngest sister Meg was running it now, but Meg wouldn't be there today. Hardly anyone would, she thought, though through the windows she could see people at their desks. Strangers, of course. The old press would be gone, and the Linotype machines and typewriters. Gone, too, would be the sharp smell of printer's ink and the softer, sweeter smells of newsprint and liquid paste.

Another time, she thought, and dropped lightly to the sidewalk, picked up her raincoat, and walked rapidly down the street toward St. Andrew's.

· · ·

THE CHURCH was packed, as she'd known it would be. She entered at the last minute and sat down in the rear pew. The family were up front, out of sight. The church was wood-fragrant. The air was close and musty. Claire looked up at the arched stained-glass windows and remembered Lane telling her how much his grandmother loved them, and how he had found them oddly depressing as a boy. I'd like to see them, Claire had said, but they'd never gotten around to it.

The minister mounted the steps to the pulpit and cleared his throat and began. "We're gathered here to celebrate the life of John Hillman," he said. She thought that was a nice way to approach it, to celebrate instead of mourn. She pictured Mr. Hillman as the minister spoke, the powerful arms folded, the gaze wistful and far away as he sat listening to her, thinking over what she was saying. *Wishing doesn't change things, he said. But you have to, she said. You have to wish.* He'd sent her a note when the *Chronicle* had promoted her to managing editor. It had been succinct but cordial, and she'd written back and said she owed her career to him. She'd written him again when Sally Hillman died, but he hadn't answered.

The service lasted a good hour. Claire didn't hear much of it. She hadn't been in a church in a long time—April, naturally, had been married on the beach by a justice of the peace—and now she thought of her own nominally Catholic childhood, her sporadic attendance at mass and confession and catechism, her indifference to it all, her haughty disregard. She remembered the phrase "impure thoughts," and how absurd it had always struck her, how naïve. Who didn't have impure thoughts, and what was wrong with them, anyway? She wondered when hers would cease to occur, and if the withering of the body brought a simultaneous shriveling of desire itself. I'll give him the book, she thought. I'll hand him *Bleak House.*

The service ended finally, and the family all stood up and there he was. There he was, and time collapsed in on itself and nothing had changed. He'd lost a good deal of his hair, and the glow of youth was gone, and the crags had steepened on his face, but these alterations affected the whole in the negligible way that a change of dress might have. With him was a girl in her twenties, tall and brown-haired and pretty, unmistakably his daughter. Claire looked for the beauty who would be his wife, but in neither of the two pews of family members was there such a person.

The congregation remained seated while the family filed out through the vestry. There was a gaggle of children and teen-agers, and Lane's three sisters and their husbands. The carved vestry door swallowed them and closed with a resounding oaken boom. The congregation rose and the shuffle and thump of footsteps filled the church. Claire slipped out ahead of every-body.

She stood by the buttress at the corner of the building and looked across the village green at the white-clapboard Con-gregational Church, the two churches facing each other like friendly august rivals happily immune to the passage of time. The funeral congregation poured out of the arched double doors of St. Andrew's and flowed slowly and quietly around the corner toward the parish hall. Claire saw Fred and Dot Purdy go by. Dot had grown very thin and Fred was gaunt, and his rust-red hair had blanched to ivory-white. Jimmy Wheeler went by with his wife; he was still muscular, but graying now, and stooped. Claire almost didn't recognize Ruth Engle, an old woman now and clearly half-blind. The walking wounded, Claire thought, and knew her own time was coming.

She waited till they'd all gone, then followed at a distance. The parking lot was full now. The last of the congregation were straggling into the parish hall. Quiet descended, disturbed only by the faint hum of cars and the wet hiss of their tires on Main Street. Claire unlocked her car. She got in and opened her purse. She unsnapped her compact and examined herself in the mirror. She freshened her lipstick, took another look at herself, and shut the compact and put it back in her purse. She picked up *Bleak House* and got out of the car.

The parish hall was loud with the buzz of conversation. Claire stood inside the door with the book in her hand and looked around the big room. Lane was on the opposite side with his daughter and sisters and their older children in a kind of receiving line. His daughter held his arm as April used to hold hers and still did sometimes, in a way both proprietary and protective, anchoring you, as love anchors.

She stood by the door, wondering what to do. Heads turned to look at her. An old man caught her eye and smiled. She looked around for the handful of people who might remember her, but none were nearby and those she could see were deep in conversation.

There was a refreshment table in the corner. She threaded her way to it. Another man met her eye, younger than the first; she gave him a brief unencouraging smile. Children crowded around the refreshment table stuffing themselves on the homemade cookies and brownies and cupcakes. Claire looked the cookies over and passed up the chocolate chip for the sake of her figure and chose two oatmeals to eat on the drive home. Keep up the old blood sugar, she thought. She wrapped the cookies in a napkin, turned, and saw that he had seen her.

He said something to his daughter. Claire stood still. The daughter nodded and let go of his arm. He wove his way toward Claire with a look almost of alarm on his face, watching her fixedly as he came, as if he were afraid she'd get away, vanish, if he took his eye off her. He moved with the old alternating bob of the shoulders, but with the difference that it was dogged now instead of cocky. She waited, waited, waited, and he stood before her as tall as she remembered him, and she knew it wouldn't be as easy as she'd thought, hoped, or perhaps had only pretended to herself it would be.

"Hello, Lane," she said.

"I wondered if you might come," he said.

"Well, he gave me the biggest chance I ever had. I was so sorry to hear."

He looked away. He had his own crow's feet now. In his blue eyes was a quiet sadness or longing that reminded her of his father.

"I have something for you," she said.

"I noticed," he said.

"You do want it back, don't you?"

He looked at her. "I don't know," he said.

"I brought it all this way."

He looked away again. They were being noticed now, stared at. Old family friends wondering who she was and why Lane had crossed the room to see her.

"I'm an editor now," Claire said, "did you know that?"

"Yes," he said. "Congratulations."

"It isn't the *Times,* but it's okay."

"The *Chronicle*'s a good paper," he said.

"Your daughter's lovely."

"Heather," he said.

"Heather Hillman. Pretty."

"It was my wife's idea. I wanted to name her after my mother."

"I'm sorry about her, too."

"You knew about it."

"I saw her obit in the *Globe*. I wrote to your father."

"But not to me."

"Did you want me to?"

Again he looked away and didn't answer. Like his father, she thought. Avoiding eye contact.

"Maybe," she said, "I'll drop the book in your car on my way out."

He looked at her. "You're leaving?"

"I've got a long drive," she said.

"I want to talk to you," he said.

"I'm not sure this is the best place."

"We'll go outside," he said.

"You can't do that."

"I'll tell Heather," he said. "Wait for me."

A fine mist had begun to sift down. She stood under the porch roof with *Bleak House* and her cookies. Lane came out, saw what the weather was doing, and took the book from her without speaking and shoved it under his jacket. Cradling it against his chest, he led her out into the mist and across the lawn toward the pond.

"Wait," she said.

He stopped, and she held on to his shoulder and stood on one leg and removed her shoe. She took off the other shoe and they went on. The grass was wet and cold through her nylons. Lane walked ahead of her.

"Will you wait for me, for Christ sake?" she said.

Again he stopped, turned, and this time he was smiling faintly.

"Doesn't your wife ever wear high heels?" she said.

"I don't have a wife," he said.

They went on together, but without touching, down the gentle slope to the edge of the pond. On the grassy bank a granite bench squatted, cut and glazed like a tombstone. They sat down, Claire with the two napkin-wrapped cookies in her lap, Lane with *Bleak House* tucked under his jacket. Claire could feel the chilly stone through her dress and the fine cool veil of mist on her face.

"Tell me how you are," Lane said.

"What do you want to know?"

"Anything."

"I'm a widow."

"I know. I'm sorry about Peter."

She looked at him. "You knew about it, then."

"When I read his obit. 'He leaves his wife, Claire O'Brien Rutledge.' Surprised the hell out of me. I wasn't even sure it was you at first."

"We weren't married long. Eight years."

"He was a good newspaperman. I know a couple guys at the *Times* who worked under him at the *Post*. I hate to say it, but he sounds like a good guy."

"He was."

"Where'd you meet him?"

"At a dinner party. I was working at the *Milford Cabinet*. Peter had come back to Boston, and my boss at the *Cabinet* invited us both to dinner. He'd known Peter in college."

"He was a lot older than you," Lane said.

"Over twenty years," Claire said.

"Ironic, huh?"

"It makes all the difference when the man's the older one."

"To whom?" Lane said.

She looked out at the pond curving back into the woods. "Society. The world."

"It does if you let it," he said.

"Don't," she said.

"All I wanted was two or three years," he said. "Just two or three. Why not, Claire? Why not two or three years?"

"Because it wouldn't have been two or three," she said. "It would have been four, five, six, and you'd never have had Heather. You walk up that hill and look at that girl and tell me you wish that."

"I don't see it that way," he said.

"You have to. I don't regret marrying Scott Malek, and you know why? Because if I hadn't married him, there'd be no April."

"There might be."

"No. A daughter, maybe, but not April."

"All right," he granted.

"Heather, her mother, your career. How much would you have given up for five years with me?"

"I'd have given up Ann gladly."

"Then you'd have given up Heather."

He sat hunched down with the book under his arm, looking out at the pond.

"Come on," she said, brightening. "Tell me about the good stuff. The Pulitzer, for instance."

"A Pulitzer isn't such a big deal."

"Like hell it isn't."

"You've done all right, too," he said.

"I'm not going to win any Pulitzers," she said.

"You might."

A car started at the top of the hill. Somebody leaving the reception. Lane turned and looked, but the parking lot was out of sight over the brow of the hill.

"You should go back," Claire said. "People'll miss you."

"I don't want to go back. How's April?"

"The same. She can still be a pain in the ass."

"I'd like to see April," he said.

"She'd love that."

"I liked her books," Lane said.

"She overdoes the feminism, if you ask me."

"A little," Lane said.

"But she can write."

"Hell, yes."

"Did she get along with Peter?"

Claire shrugged. "Not really. He was older, Lane. It was different."

The mist had wetted their faces. It clung in tiny droplets in their hair.

"What happened in your marriage?" Claire said.

He smiled drily. "She decided she didn't want to be married to me anymore. She said it wasn't working."

"Foolish girl," Claire said.

"I asked her to give it another shot, but the truth was, I didn't care. I wouldn't have cared if she'd stayed, and I didn't care when she left."

"That must be why she left."

"I suppose," he said.

They sat awhile in not uncomfortable silence. The trees dripped steadily.

"You look good," Lane said.

"For an old lady."

"You're not an old lady," he said. "Not with legs like that."

She smiled.

"It's the truth," he said.

"So what about *Bleak House?*"

"I don't know," he said. "I haven't made up my mind."

"It's time you do. I've got to head home."

"Why don't you come meet Heather?" he said.

"Maybe another time," she said.

"There won't be another time," he said.

"There might be," she said.

"And who decides that?" he said.

"No one *decides* it," she said.

"You do. You decide it."

"Maybe."

"And what if you decide wrong?"

She looked down into her lap. "I don't know," she said.

"Why don't you let me decide this time?" he said.

She looked beside her for her purse and, had it been there, would have opened it unthinkingly and rummaged for the cigarettes she hadn't smoked for twenty years.

"Lane," she said, "I'm sixty-five years old."

"I know how old you are," he said.

And as he took her hand to raise her to her feet and walk with her up the wet green hill and on into his life, she thought, Why not? Today. Tomorrow. Why not?